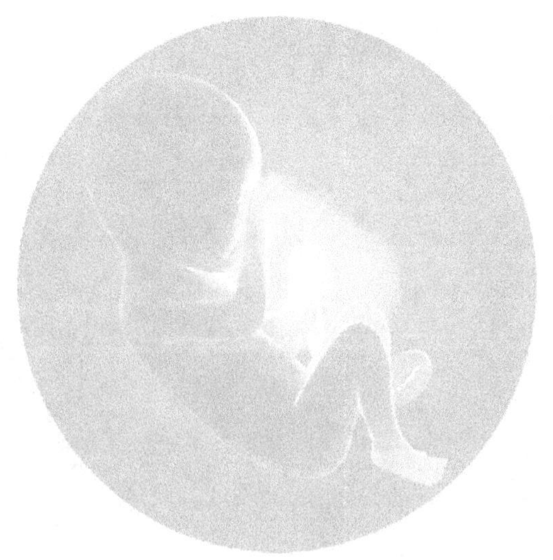

DONATION

Karen A. Wyle

Published 2022 in the United States of America
Oblique Angles Press
ISBN 978-1-955696-02-9

Cover design by Kelly A. Martin of KAM Design

Dedication photo by Judith Squier
Author photo by Holy Smoke Photography

Dedication

To my mother.

Prologue: The Beginning

Soon

The patient sat on the examining table, but not alone. As soon as the obstetrician had let her sit up, her husband sat down beside her and put his arm around her shoulders, his stare defying any objection.

The obstetrician called up the information he needed on his tablet and said to them, "It's too early to know whether this spotting means trouble. As we discussed, your risk of miscarriage is somewhat elevated, even though your lupus is under control. I'll start you on a drug that may help. But there's also some good news I want to give you, something very new that you may not have heard of or thought about."

The patient lowered her chin and looked the doctor in the eye. "This would not be a good time to talk to me about adopting."

The obstetrician put up his hands. "No, nothing like that! I wanted to tell you about a new procedure, new equipment . . ." He wasn't sure what to call it. "The federal government has approved a trial of a new type of incubator. It's really an artificial uterine environment. It can accept a fetus the age of yours, or even younger — even embryos."

The husband put a protective hand over the patient's abdomen. "You want to take the baby out and put it in some sort of *tank?*" The doctor's hope that the man would be a calming influence receded into the distance.

"Hush, hon." The patient patted her husband's leg. "Are you suggesting we do this right away?"

"Not today. But if your spotting increases, or if it's still happening a week from now, I'll recommend it. Depending on the circumstances, we may be able to do an outpatient procedure. If this is something you'd consider, I'd better start on the red tape immediately." And if the administrator in charge weren't a medical school classmate he'd helped study for his boards, it might be impossible to get her enrolled in time. But there was no need to mention that.

The husband seemed about to object again; the wife went from patting his leg to applying pressure, and he subsided. "Where would this incubator be for the rest of —" She stopped, tearing up for the first time. "I can't call it the rest of the pregnancy, can I?"

The obstetrician suppressed the urge to shift about on his stool. "As I said, this option was just recently approved. I believe the nearest hospital with a prenatal ward taking part in this trial is at Central Health."

The patient blinked tears away; they were immediately replaced by new ones. "That's two hours from here."

The husband looked thoughtful, a welcome change. "We could probably stay with my sister. I can work anywhere, and you could commute."

The doctor cut in. "By all means make some contingency plans. But that's all they are, so far. Let's see what happens."

Three days later, the patient arrived at the local hospital by ambulance. After a four-hour wait in ER, at the end of which the receptionist was on the verge of calling security to handle the husband, she was examined, her chart reviewed, and the obstetrician consulted. Another ambulance ride, this time to Central Health, and another wait, during which the husband was too exhausted to make trouble.

The patient was finally prepped and taken to surgery; and an hour and a half later, the surgeon came out to the waiting room. As the husband jerked upright in his chair, crumpled coffee cups falling from his lap to the floor, she gave him her most reassuring smile and told him, "Your little boy is safe and sound. Your wife is in recovery, down that hallway. You can go see her. And then, when she's up to it, you can both go see where the baby will be spending the next six months."

It took the husband two tries to get to his feet before he walked, walked faster, ran down the hall.

The surgeon fell into a chair and said to the obstetrician, who had arrived a few minutes before, "And now you can tell me what I've just taken part in. And whether anyone is likely to ask me to do it again."

The obstetrician, almost bubbling over with a blend of relief and enthusiasm, did everything but show brochures. The new incubator design would maintain an artificial uterine environment for an embryo or fetus. Its features allowed for recreation of all the sensory stimuli available in the womb itself, even reproducing the mother's likely routine shifts in position, and provided a significantly greater ability to monitor the occupant's condition. At the appropriate time and in a safe environment, the incubator would be opened, and the newborn — or rather, newly delivered — infant would move on to whatever awaited it.

When he'd wound down, he added, as an afterthought: "I just hope the regulatory bureaucracy doesn't hold up this technology for years. I'd hate to see more babies lost that could be saved."

His hopes were, after a fashion, realized. Though not for a reason he had foreseen.

* * * * *

The company's Vice President for New Technology, the company's patent attorney, and the company's chief lobbyist gathered around the conference room table to share sandwiches and frustration. The lobbyist had the latest news. "Anyone else want a beer before I fill you in?"

After beers all round, the lobbyist took a swig and said briskly, "I've finally found out what the holdup was. To be blunt about it, they've been delaying in order to soften you up for what they have in mind. They know that the driving force behind this technology was to save pregnancies that were headed for disaster. But they have another goal in mind. And there's no way we're getting the patent, or full approval, unless we go along with it."

The patent attorney shook his head in a slow, weary way, as if reminded of a familiar sorrow, and chewed away at his ham and Swiss. The VP just gritted her teeth and gestured for him to continue.

"First, there'd be a new federal bureau in charge of new clinics. They're the only ones who'd be using the incubators. No one else."

The VP drummed her fingers on the table. "Is this part of the latest plan to bring all medical practice under a federal umbrella?"

The lobbyist started to shake her head and then stopped. "That may actually be a secondary purpose. But there's another reason, more topical and political." She traded her beer for her soy loaf on rye, looked around to ensure the attention of his audience, and went on. "There are quite a few people, in Congress as well as in various departments, who see the incubators as providing the ideal solution to the problem of abortion. It's still a highly contentious issue, with so many genuine hardship stories. You offer a way out. A woman no longer has to choose between terminating a pregnancy and carrying the baby to term. She can exercise her reproductive freedom by simply having the embryo or fetus removed. Once women have that option, it's much easier for states or Congress to prohibit abortion and make it stick."

The VP hit the table with her fist, almost spilling the two beer bottles not gripped in anyone's hand. She grimaced an apology, regained control, and asked, "What about using the incubators to ensure that high-risk pregnancies make it to full term? Does that just — not happen?"

The lobbyist shrugged. "The clinics might be available for that purpose as well. If we cooperate, we might be able to push things in that direction. After all, the larger the role of the clinics, the greater the power accruing to the new bureau. But for now, using them for donation – that's what they're calling it – of unwanted 'preborns' has priority."

"And then? What happens to the babies?"

The lobbyist considered confessing to ignorance on that point, and chose to wing it instead. "Adoption would be the obvious way to go. Placing babies for adoption hasn't been a federal function in the past, but it would be if things go this route."

They had not hired her to share her wilder speculations. But if every unwanted child became, in essence, a ward of the State, it struck her as likely that the choice of adoptive parents would acquire a political dimension. Sooner or later, some influential functionary would ask whether this new bureau should meekly hand over all those future citizens to be raised, willy-nilly, by those merely willing and able to care for them.

Chapter 1

ten years later

Toni Greene

Toni Greene uncurled herself enough to check the time. How much longer she could stay in her room, in the embrace of her giant stuffed panda, before she would have to put on shoes and leave? She could not afford to be late, not when every hour meant the embryo – not a fetus, not quiet yet — grew larger. At least she was nowhere near the time for quickening. It was bad enough that she had, a few times, caught herself talking to it, almost as if it were a companion. To feel its movement would add an unbearable reality to that idea.

Five minutes before she needed to get ready.

She looked at her choices of footwear, the faded dark blue tennis shoes leaning against the legs of the flamingo and the combat boots nestled in the lap of the boa constrictor. Combat boots better suited the occasion. She would be confronting officialdom, not to mention the doubts that might ambush her, and would need any psychological boost available.

At least she no longer had a roommate. No need for explanations, no opposition to worry about, no consolation to put up with.

She slumped deeper into the fuzzy embrace of the

panda. If she were going to have the baby, they could cuddle there together on mornings like this, cozy together . . . . No more of that! She had to think practically. For every moment like that, how many more would be poisoned with anxiety or even terror? The few commissions she was finding barely paid the rent. No, to be honest, they didn't even cover that, not without the frequent infusions of support from her parents. And any other job she could get would mean someone else taking care of the baby, and then what would be the point? And how could she be anyone's mother? Whatever transformation that required, she had not gone through it and couldn't imagine it.

Instead, the baby would have its own bedroom, and toys of its own. And a mother, a real one who knew how to be one. Probably a father as well, or maybe a second mother, or one of each. While Toni moved at least a little further toward self-sufficiency.

Maybe she'd actually find someone to share her life with, someone loving and kind and reliable and *not* a self-centered jerk who'd drop her with no notice, and not even wonder if he'd left the beginning of a child behind.

No more time for stalling. Toni forced herself to roll off the panda, grab the combat boots, and pull them on. Then she got off the floor and walked heavy-footed through the kitchen, grabbing a banana and one of her mother's brownies on the way. Not enough time for oatmeal. She could cook up a big bowl of it when she got home.

It would be warm enough later, but this early, she'd be chilly in shirtsleeves. Grabbing her well-patched denim jacket off the hook next to the door and shrugging into it, almost dropping the brownie, she managed to get out the door on time, second thoughts pushed aside. She crammed the brownie into her mouth on the way to the subway. She could eat the banana before the subway reached downtown.

Whatever she had expected, this wasn't it. Toni started to relax as she stepped through the doors and smelled something almost like fresh air. The light had the quality of sunlight; the walls were painted in light pastel colors. The small waiting room just inside the door had flowering plants, or maybe very good artificial ones, in the window sills. And the young male receptionist had blue hair. She might try that color when she got tired of pink.

She had thought they would take her right away to wherever the procedure would be performed, but instead the receptionist called over another young man to give her a tour. Not that the facility was all that large, as it turned out: a short wide corridor with large abstract photographs, streaks and blobs of fuzzy colored light; a larger waiting room with upholstered armchairs, and tablets for anyone who hadn't brought one; more of the roomy and well-lighted corridors; and finally, up an elevator to a large room full of incubators. They were smooth cylinders with rounded edges, more than twice as long as a typical full-grown baby, and about two-thirds as high as they were long. She'd expected metal, but they looked more like plastic, their colors like the colors of the walls except a little richer. Each one had a couple of hoses attached, and a control panel with lights twinkling like overactive fireflies. Toni bit her lip and asked, "What if the power goes out?"

"Each incubator has a fully charged backup battery that can last for days, and we have three generators, all inspected weekly. Nothing's going to happen to these little darlings. They're safer than any of us, or any child a woman is carrying around. And by the way, we don't just leave them sitting in one position all the time. The inner chamber is programmed to reproduce all sorts of movements a fetus would experience . . . otherwise."

Toni had never thought about the details of reproducing a uterine environment. Was it comforting or chilling to think of a machine mimicking the movements she would have made, carrying the developing fetus through the day, lying down with it at night? Both, maybe.

Her guide opened the door to the room so she could hear the music playing inside. "Classical guitar right now, but we play all sorts of instrumental music, and some choral, and some pop. Nothing jangly or loud — we alternate soothing and upbeat." He closed the door again and turned toward her. "Ready to get this done?"

There must be something else to see first. "What about the delivery rooms, and wherever the parents — the adoptive parents — get the babies?"

"I'm sorry, but that isn't part of the tour. I'll take you to the procedure room, then, shall I?"

She bit her trembling lower lip and nodded.

It smelled different here, more like what she had expected — almost aggressively clean.

The nurse who came in and gave her a gown — cloth, not paper, with crude flower shapes on it — also told her to take off her phone patch, for no obvious reason. If it could withstand wood dust, saw vibrations, and sweat, it should be close enough to indestructible. But maybe it interfered with the equipment somehow. She peeled off the patch and felt even more naked. She pulled the gown over her head.

The nurse might have thought she needed reassurance, or she might make the same speech to everyone who came in. "You came here in plenty of time — the incision will be quite small. And it shouldn't hurt a bit. Later on, you will have some soreness, but we'll provide you with medication for it. We won't even have to put you out. We just spray your back, there —" She pointed near Toni's spine. "— and you'll start to feel very relaxed and comfortable." She pointed next to a monitor nearby. "You can watch, but most of our visitors choose to watch the ceiling instead. The controller's right there." The ceiling had a large screen, currently showing a series of nature photos. Some included animals, but none, Toni noticed, showed puppies or kittens or cubs.

"You already know that today's services are free, right? And if you want one of the latest birth control implants, that's free as well."

Toni ground her teeth before she answered, "The shot I got doesn't always work — I found that out. These implants are more foolproof?"

"Just about 100 percent. And if you get the shot also, I don't know of anyone who's conceived after both. And you can get the implant removed any time — though you'd have to pay a doctor for that — and get medicine to counteract the shot for good measure."

And that was apparently all there was to it. The nurse handed her a tablet. "You'll need to put your thumbprint at the bottom of the screen before the doctor gets started. The technicalities, you know." She slid out the door, leaving Toni to make her way through the stilted and confusing language. She would be giving up any "parental rights," whatever those were. That made sense. She was giving up being a parent — letting someone else, better able to do the job, raise her baby.

Her baby, except that by the time it was a baby, it would no longer be hers.

Maybe this was why they had people change into gowns. So they wouldn't yield to any last-minute urge to run out the door.

The nurse came back in, one hand out to receive the tablet, a hypno-spray in the other. No going back now.

In another hour, Toni was dressed in her own comfortable clothes and her boots, phone back on her wrist, and out the door, instructions on how much to limit her physical activity saved on her own tablet for reading later. The street, its noises and crowds, came as something of a shock after the soothing colors and controlled sounds of the clinic. Almost like being born . . . .

She hadn't yet started to show. Nothing about her would look different to the old man on the subway, to the young man in charge of the robot street sweeper, to the squabbling neighbors in the yard next door. And she felt perfectly healthy. In a few more hours, she'd feel at least a little sore, but for now the anesthetic protected her even from that.

She opened her front door and stood in the doorway for a moment. The day yawned before her. Her only commissions were not due for several weeks — just as well, with the need to avoid stretching high or hauling heavy weight. And the pieces were massive enough that she was working on them in her studio downtown. All she had in the house were the drawings and studies the clients had approved, with nothing left to be done to them.

She could make that oatmeal. Or some hot tomato soup, and grilled cheese. Comfort food. Because damn it, she did need comforting. Hormones at work, probably. No point in fighting them. She may as well feed them instead.

Soup drunk, sandwich reduced to crumbs, she trudged without enthusiasm to the sink. If she had a cat, the cat might want to lick up the remnants. . . . Oh, too obvious. Now, suddenly, she thought of having something to care for, something soft and needy? She would put aside any such thoughts for a month, at least.

She could call her mother, or even go visit. But that would mean telling Mom what she'd done. The donation. "Donation." Such a benign, bloodless word.

At least Toni had already told her mother about the pregnancy. If she had to face revealing both the pregnancy and the conclusion of it in one conversation, she might prefer to find a port, change her name, and take a slow boat to China. Or wherever boats went to. Not that changing one's name would be effective these days, with all the ways of tracking people and tracking them down.

If she'd expected advice when she confided in her mother, she should have known better. Mom had just listened, and consoled, and expressed confidence that Toni would find a solution. Come to think of it, she hadn't said it would be a good solution, let alone the best. If anything, though, she would probably consider Toni's decision inevitable. How could Toni, living on her own for the first time, so fiercely eager to try that independence despite shaky finances, manage motherhood? And there had been no chance Mom would have wanted to raise the child herself. As a mother, she had been thorough and conscientious and affectionate, but there was no missing her relief at finally bringing both children to adulthood. And if she'd been willing, surely she would have said so.

At least Mom wasn't one to haul out old lectures and repeat them. Toni couldn't have stood to listen to another round of Mom-about-Finn. "If you're going to have casual lovers, they may as well be men or women you could imagine staying with. Learn what'll work for you longterm by practicing. Why waste your time with a man who'd never measure up?" Toni hadn't wanted to argue about whether Finn might measure up better than Mom figured. Two points to Mom . . . .

Maybe she'd call tomorrow. Now, the soreness was kicking in. She would take a hot bath, and then a nap. She hadn't slept well last night. She was tired enough to sleep, surely. Then she could go out for something spicy and exotic, as long as it was cheap.

And then on to the studio! She could imagine herself already there, breathing its special odor of clay and sawdust, a smell that meant work and inspiration, the smell of her future. She could work all night, if she wanted, as long as she didn't lift or shove too much weight around. She owed diligence to her clients, and no one had any greater claim on her. Not now.

She got home from the studio at two in the morning, had a late night snack of avocado dip and vegetable sticks, followed it up with another brownie, and fell into bed, fully expecting to sleep until noon. So when she awoke at seven, still exhausted, she was furious at her traitor of a body, or brain, or whatever had double-crossed her.

Where her father lived, she could have gone outside, walked half a mile, and shouted curses at the top of her lungs. A great stress reliever, and no one close enough to mind or care. At her mother's, there was a time she could have gone out back and cussed at the chickens, as long as she didn't use a volume or tone that would put them off laying. But Mom had had to get rid of the chickens the year before, when the county decided they made too much noise. Never mind revving motorcycles, leaf blowers . . . .

Here, there were only the stuffed animals. She jumped out of bed, stalked over to the grizzly bear, and pounded its belly, then stuck her face in it and yelled muffled yells until the anger wore down enough for her to feel silly instead. Shoving herself to her feet, she blew an apology kiss at the bear and sat back down on the bed.

Yelling and pounding a stuffed animal hadn't been enough when she found out she was pregnant. If she'd been at her father's and could have walked into the woods, cursing Finn's thoughtlessness and the sadistic workings of fate, would it have helped her arrive at a better frame of mind for making decisions?

Not that she could see a better decision she might have made.

But now, finally, exhaustion turned friendly, pulling her back down toward the warm embrace of her bed. She fell sideways against the mattress, pulled the nearest edge of blanket over herself, and went back to sleep.

When she woke again, early afternoon sun warming her pillow, she looked around disoriented. Dreams did that to her sometimes. It could take her several minutes to disentangle the dream's reality from her own.

What had she dreamed? She had been talking to someone. And she had been amused, and relaxed, and happy.

Then she remembered, and the smile froze on her face.

She had still been pregnant, farther along than before, and the baby had been moving, wriggling around, poking her with an elbow or a knee or maybe a foot. And she had been talking to it, saying something like, Hey, watch with the gymnastics already! Plenty of time for that later! And as if teasing her, it had seemed to flip entirely over. How had she managed to, literally, dream up so peculiar a sensation?

Some dreams seemed so normal, however strange, until you woke up and thought about them and shivered from the creepiness. This was one of . . . . no, it wasn't.

It should have been creepy to dream of something living inside her and shoving at her and pushing her belly out of shape. She wanted it to chill her, now that she was awake. But the dream had been, still was, so . . . sweet.

Toni found herself humming a tune, something old and seldom heard. They might have been playing it at the clinic, in the waiting room. What was it? She fumbled with her phone and sang the tune wordlessly at it, clicking for an identification. The phone answered her immediately, along with a helpful translation.

"Je Regrette Rien. French title, meaning I Regret Nothing, more commonly known as No Regrets."

If only she were sure that was true.

Chapter 2

Toni

Toni would visit Mom, rather than call. It was easier to fake calm by phone, though she wouldn't bet on fooling Mom any — but a phone couldn't give you a hug. And neither could her stuffed animals, at least not enough of one.

She sent a short message. *Could I come see you today?*

The "bing" of the reply came almost at once. *Lovely! Come any time.*

Toni inspected herself in the mirror. No obvious stains, eyes barely pink. She'd do. Coming over now.

It was obvious where Toni had acquired her love of comfort food. Mom greeted her first with the longed-for hug, and then with a tall, steaming mug of cocoa — a year-round treat in their family — and a plate of freshly baked oatmeal cookies. With chocolate chips. YUM.

Mom put the plate on the table in the breakfast nook and sat in her chair, too big for her but made comfortable by plenty of cushions. Toni took the seat cushion out of the other chair, leaned it against the wall, and sat on the floor, warming her hands on her mug and then warming her face with her hands. Mom smiled with nostalgia for a habit Toni had had as long as she could remember.

Mom did the talking at first, updating Toni on her garden and garden pests while Toni drank half the mugful of cocoa and ate a cookie. When Toni sat back and sighed in satisfied greed, her mother finally asked, "How are you doing, sweetheart?"

Toni picked up another cookie, took a smaller bite than before, and tried to smile. "Kind of shaky."

Mom studied her face. "I can think of a few different reasons for that. Want to tell me which it is?"

Toni took a deep breath, as shaky as the rest of her. "I had that procedure. The donation. I'm not —" It was hard to say, as hard as it had been to confess the pregnancy in the first place. "I'm not pregnant any more."

Mom reached out to take her hand and squeeze it. "Are you in any pain? Do you have medication for it?"

That was Mom, always practical. "I'm fine. They gave me pills. Just don't ask me to transplant any trees."

Mom sipped her own cocoa, then got up to fetch the pot and refill Toni's mug. She patted Toni's shoulder, sat down again, and said, "So you have your life back. Now what can you do to make it more satisfying?"

Toni tried to remember the visions that had filled her mind as she contemplated her options so recently. "I can bid on bigger projects. By the time I get any, if I do, I'll be up to managing them, physically. And in between, I can do more traveling. I still haven't been to Thailand, and you know I've always wanted to."

Her mother arched an eyebrow. "And?"

Toni huffed in frustration. "Meeting someone isn't something I can just *arrange*. And I am *not* going to try any of those match sites. Not even if you pay for them."

Mom nodded vigorously. "No danger of that. I learned my lesson. If I'd met your father in some more natural way, maybe at a gardening club or a professional conference, things might have worked out better."

A chance to change the subject! "Didn't you just get back from a conference? Was it interesting? Did you learn anything?"

Mom's mouth twitched in a way that said *I know what you're up to*, but she answered. "More than I expected. I got some great questions from the audience when I gave my own presentation, and the updates I attended about the new federal rules will keep me from making embarrassing blunders in my latest case."

Toni looked down in an attempt to hide her blush. She tended to forget just how well respected Mom had become in the legal profession, and that she was more likely to give presentations than attend them. At least she'd done some of each, this time.

Mom's gaze went unfocused as she pondered something or other. Toni finished her cookie, contemplated another, held off for the moment, and finally asked, "What are you thinking about?"

Mom shook her head. "Just something that occurred to me. I might go into it later, if it seems pertinent. But for now, tell me about how your sculptures are coming along. Show me pictures!"

Toni called up the photos on her phone, peeling it off and handing it over so she could sink back into the chair with another cookie. She tried to think of nothing but cookies and cocoa and her mother's eager interest, and almost succeeded.

The clinic had sent more material after Toni left, and Toni had been putting off reading it. But it was time.

The message seemed to be intended to reassure mothers like her — donors — who might be coping with regrets. It talked up the adoption process, the care with which adoptive parents were screened and the paragons of virtue that got picked. It reeked of bureaucratic happy talk. Toni moved to toss her tablet into the grizzly's lap, then reconsidered and opened the search program. "Adoption of donated fetuses."

More detail, here, though the usual mishmash of sources. Most of them agreed on a few points. People applied for adoption in general, not for particular fetuses. The Bureau gave the applicants a preliminary review and then, if they passed, kept their names on file, to be considered when fetuses became available. Applicants were immediately disqualified for felony convictions within twenty years, misdemeanor convictions within ten years, psychiatric hospitalization within ten years, ongoing medical problems requiring more than fifteen doctor visits per year or involving a prognosis of death or certain kinds of disability within five years, donation of an embryo or fetus within ten years —

Toni dropped the tablet on the bed and got up to pace. It made sense, in a way. It wouldn't be fair to the child if someone adopted it out of guilt. Guilt might not last — the day to day frustrations and burdens of parenthood might wear through it all too soon.

She picked up the tablet again, too tense to sit, and read standing up.

The point at which adoptive parents were assigned a pre-born child depended on the embryo's or fetus's stage of development at donation. There was speculation about what might happen if somehow, no parent had been approved by the date of delivery — but nothing even rising to the level of rumor. Apparently this had not been an actual problem.

Next topic. Some adoptions were "open," with the donor getting various updates and sometimes playing a part in the child's life, but it was up to the adoptive parents whether to go that route. The department didn't do anything to encourage it, though it provided a way for the parents to contact donors if they chose.

Toni left the tablet on her bed and headed for the kitchen. Time to finally make that big pot of oatmeal. There was nothing wrong with oatmeal for lunch. And maybe cocoa to go with it.

Stirring the oatmeal, she imagined adoptive parents getting the hoped-for message, turning to each other, clutching each other in joy . . . . Were any of her friends likely to want families soon? And if so, would they have any interest in adoption as a way to do it?

She stirred harder, splashing a little oatmeal out of the pot. What a stupid idea. Even if she found someone, the odds that they'd get her baby were less than tiny. Some couple or triad, on the list for months, might already be visiting it, talking to it, singing to it or reading it stories.

She turned the heat down on the stove and picked up her tablet again. Had the information from the clinic said whether the baby was, would be, a boy or a girl?

No, not even that. She could have asked. They might have told her. Now she'd never know.

She clenched her teeth on her lower lip and went back to the stove. Hot, filling oatmeal couldn't come too soon.

Six days after the procedure, Toni headed in to see her doctor, as per the clinic's instructions. She had explained why when she made the appointment. And she was probably imagining things when she thought the receptionist gave her a longer look than usual at the check-in window. There was no stigma about donating. It was, in fact, a socially useful and public-spirited thing to do.

All true. Even if it felt like rationalizing.

Her doctor did various sorts of imaging and then examined her by touch. "Tender there?"

Ouch. "A little."

"That's only natural. It took me a few weeks before all the surface soreness went away. Though of course I had to be careful for longer about lifting heavy objects." The doctor peeled off her gloves and studied the images on her monitor. "All looking fine."

Toni stared at the doctor. "You donated?"

The doctor bit her lip and then released it. "No. My apologies, that was careless of me. I should have said, it took that long after my C-section. Which took place when the baby was only six months along, so the incision wasn't as large as for many, though much larger than yours."

She hadn't known how much she wanted the reassurance of another woman, someone respected and successful, having made the same choice until it was dangled in front of her and snatched away. She gritted her teeth and breathed through her nose until she was sure she wouldn't cry.

The question popped into her head and out her mouth. "What would happen if someone had a fetus implanted?"

The doctor's head jerked around. She got up from the monitor, came over to Toni, and took her hand. "Your uterus has already reverted to its pre-pregnancy condition. It would take months of preparatory hormone treatment before you could possibly have a fetus transplanted into you, and it would be significantly more risky. Not that any doctor would be allowed to perform such a transplant."

Months. Her own baby would be too big to fit, by then. Unless there was some way to stretch the uterus in advance. And no one would consider helping her do anything of the kind.

She'd made her choice. There was no taking it back. She could only move on. But move on in what direction?

Chapter 3

Poloma

Poloma Clark relished days like this one. Whatever the demands on her, she almost always made time two or three times a month to put aside managerial duties and do the work that felt more important, helping distraught women and their future offspring and society all at the same time. She dropped her briefcase on the reception desk, smiled at the security guard, made sure the Open sign was illuminated, and went back to the desk to extract her tablet. One of her cousins, a software maven, had sent her a new puzzle program for her last birthday; she could work on it between arrivals, and perhaps get past the "expert" level.

Almost immediately, a girl and an older woman — from the resemblance, probably her mother — came through the door and approached the desk, the girl tugging the mother along. Interesting family dynamic there. The girl bounced a little as she walked, full of energy, fit and muscular — probably active in sports, in pursuit of a championship or medal. The mother might have wanted the girl to keep the child, but realized there was no way to force the issue, not with social services and the courts ready to support the girl's decision. Poloma greeted them, invited them to sit, reassured them, took down the necessary information, and summarized what would happen next.

As she had expected, the girl had no questions except

"How long will it take?" and "Can I do whatever I want to afterwards?" The mother looked as if she had questions aplenty, but no hope of liking the answers. She opened her mouth a couple of times, once looking at Poloma and once at the girl, but closed it again, her face sagging further into sadness.

When she was sure no more questions were forthcoming, Poloma summoned a guide. The daughter looked the young man up and down, and followed him with that same spring in her step, already looking forward to the freedom she was about to regain. The mother trudged after.

There was a lull after the two of them vanished inside. Poloma opened her puzzle, racing her previous record. She was almost annoyed for a moment when the door slid open again, but she shook off the inappropriate feeling, paused the program, and turned toward the newcomer with a smile. Young, a few years out of the nest; medium to tall; short pink hair that used to be blonde, a light pink Poloma could not have attempted without bleaching her hair first; lean, if not so thin as Poloma. Boots so bulky they must be some kind of ironic statement. Loosely fitting clothes in various colors of faded denim — not Poloma's style, but an aesthetically agreeable effect. And smart. Smart showed, in the eyes and even the posture. Overall, potentially simpatico. It would feel especially good to help someone like this, help her preserve and pursue what was probably an interesting life.

Poloma was already welcoming the woman while she sized her up. She was prepared for the woman's first words to be a little different, original. She listened with a sense of pleasant anticipation.

"I'm not — I don't need a tour."

Was she a repeat client? Poloma would not let herself frown. There might have been some good reason for the woman not to accept an implant. Though two unplanned pregnancies, even without an implant, suggested carelessness. It would be a shame if this woman was careless.

"I was here nine days ago."

She couldn't possibly be pregnant again that soon. Not carelessness, then, good.

"I was wondering whether I could see it. The — baby."

One of those. Not what Poloma had taken this shift for. But it would be a useful exercise, and would help her train receptionists in dealing with these awkward situations. And at least the woman cared. That smug teenager would never reappear with such a request. "I'm sorry. We've found that any further contact isn't helpful in the donor's adjustment process."

The woman stood up straighter and lifted her head a little. She probably didn't like the bland social-worker language. Understandable. If they ever got to know each other, maybe she could give Poloma some ideas on a less cookie-cutter response. But their getting to know each other was looking less likely.

Some reassurance was indicated. "I assure you the embryo —" A guess, but if the pregnancy had been far enough along for "fetus" to be accurate, the woman would probably show more signs of the pregnancy. " — is doing just fine, developing every bit as well as before the procedure." With some reluctance — Poloma thought this policy ill-advised — she added, "And if you look at the literature we sent you, you'll see that when the baby is delivered, you'll receive a thank-you note from all of us here." At least the actual date wouldn't be included for donors to obsess over.

Would the woman give up and go home? No, she wouldn't. If anything, she would probe further. Yes, there she went: "Do adoptive parents get to visit, before the baby is, is . . ."

"Once applicants for adoption go through an extensive process and are approved, they're allowed to visit before the delivery, most often once a week. The incubators are mobile and can be taken to visiting rooms, so the parents can talk to the fetus more freely. A microphone system lets their voices pass through to the fetus much as a biological mother's and even other family members' voices would if the fetus were still in utero."

Poloma's fondness for detail had led her into a misstep. The woman winced at the words "biological mother," or the reference to hearing a mother's voice, or both. Poloma softened her tone. "I'm sorry. What I was going to say is that only approved adoptive parents have visiting privileges. It's better not to raise anyone's hopes prematurely. Or to confuse the fetus with extraneous voices."

The woman flinched again at "extraneous." Poloma's sure touch with clients had somehow gone missing this morning. What else could go wrong?

"What if I, if I wanted to adopt my own baby?"

To think she had felt an initial interest in, even kinship with, this troublesome client! Poloma's disappointment had a sharp edge almost like betrayal. "Such an application would not be considered."

Not that she actually *knew* as much. But she couldn't imagine any such thing being permitted.

The woman, thank goodness, was finally in retreat. "That's what I thought. I saw something in the paperwork . . . but it was about adopting any baby. I thought it, it might be different if . . . I'm sorry. I've had trouble sleeping, and I keep thinking instead." She dropped her eyes, light brown lashes obscuring the green, and said again, "I'm sorry."

Back on familiar ground, and what a relief that was. "Such symptoms aren't uncommon. You should have been provided with instructions about what to expect, and some sample medication." Poloma rummaged in her desk drawer. "I may have some additional samples here . . . ."

The woman stepped back, hands up as if fending off the offer. "No, they gave me all that. I just forgot about it. Thank you." And she turned and walked slowly out the door.

Poloma blew out accumulated tension in a long whistling breath. "Well. Life on the front lines." She shook her head and settled back in her chair.

She made a hash of the puzzle.

Poloma was on her way to lunch, still unsettled, when the tableau at the reception desk caught her ear and her eye. A new hire, more girl than woman but stylish and sure of herself, sat behind the desk. The woman across from her made for quite a contrast, positively unkempt from her dirty tangled hair to her too-tight, fraying sweater to her too-small spangled pumps. The girl at the desk was not effectively hiding – or not trying to hide — her contempt.

Poloma skidded to a halt and approached the desk, smiling at the woman with practiced ease before telling the girl, "I'll take over here. Please wait for me in my office."

The girl, obviously not in the habit of concealing her feelings, shoved her chair back sharply and stalked off in a huff. Probably hungry. Poloma certainly was. But treating a client properly took precedence. She sat down and smiled again. "Have you already been thanked for coming in today? I hope so."

The woman looked bewildered and gave no answer beyond a twitch of her shoulder, possibly meant as a shrug.

Poloma glanced at the screen to see how far the girl had gotten. She completed the intake interview in her most soothing tones, taking her time, waiting for the guide to arrive before thanking the woman again and heading back up to her office.

The new hire was waiting, fidgeting in a chair. Instead of sitting behind her desk, Poloma took the other visitor chair and pulled it to face the girl. She began by asking, "Have you been through the new hire orientation?"

The girl rolled her eyes, with some excuse given that the orientation was mandatory. Poloma ignored it and went on. "Do you remember the demonstration of how to treat incoming clients? And the role play exercises?"

The girl's affirmative response was as close to surly as she could have gotten away with. Poloma held tight to her patience. It was crucial to make this young woman understand. And she knew the story most likely to get through her resistance.

"I can understand how the woman with whom you were dealing this morning might have rubbed you the wrong way. I'll admit she had the same effect on me." Reluctantly, Poloma decided the occasion called for revealing personal information. "In fact, she reminded me of a couple of my least favorite neighbors, from where I lived as a child and adolescent."

The girl sat up abruptly, almost as if Poloma had stuck her with a pin.

"When I was relatively new here, I had a client come in who was even younger than I was, and several months into her pregnancy. She sat in the chair cracking her gum and checking her nails, paying me no attention. It irritated me. I wanted to get to her somehow, to make her treat me seriously. I started asking her questions about how she came to be pregnant."

The girl's eyes went wide.

"Yes, it was against the rules, then as much as now. But her attitude had gotten under my skin, and I didn't much care if I made her uncomfortable. Naturally, she was embarrassed. She didn't want to answer me." It was hard to tell this story. It never got easier. "And then I said that if she was ashamed to talk about it, she should have been ashamed to do it."

The girl's jaw dropped a little.

"She burst into tears and ran out of the building. By the time I could get out from behind the desk and follow her, she was lost in the crowd."

The girl was breathing a little faster now, caught in the suspense of the story. "Did you find her? Did she come back?"

Poloma swallowed the sour taste in her mouth. "I never found her, and she didn't come back. But I did see her again — or rather, a picture of her, on the news. She had been arrested for getting an abortion. The clinics hadn't been open that long, then, and abortion had been legal here until a year or so before this happened. Abortionists weren't as hard to find."

She had accomplished her goal. The girl stared at her, upper lip quivering a little, on the verge of tears.

"I expected to be fired. I certainly deserved to be fired. But they let me stay on, after some more training. And I have tried my best, ever since, to make up for that day, that tragedy. To make sure that every woman who comes through that door is thanked for coming to us, and for giving her baby a future."

A wave of faintness ran through her. Her blood sugar must be low, and reliving that day, not to mention the other memories she had shared, took its toll as well. She sighed and stood up. Maybe she could still establish some rapport with this girl, and be of help to her in the days to come. "I'm going to get some lunch. Could I buy lunch for you? I'll sign off on your getting back a little late."

The girl eyed the door as if wondering whether acceptance were the price of escape. She gulped and nodded.

Poloma used her knowledge of the neighborhood to choose a cafe where the girl would feel at ease. Over her sandwich and the girl's fusion plate, she managed to move the conversation to lighter topics, drawing the girl out, getting her to chatter about her pastimes and pursuits. By the time they finished, the tension had eased. Maybe she should leave things there. But there was an angle she still wanted this young woman to appreciate.

"When you were talking to that client, what did you think you might be able to achieve, with the approach you took?"

The girl stiffened a little at this return to the topic, but Poloma stayed relaxed, with an expression of earnest interest. The girl hung her head and spoke into her lap. "I guess I wasn't really thinking. I wasn't trying to do anything in particular."

"It isn't as likely, nowadays, that a client you discouraged would be able to find an abortionist. And attitudes have changed enough that she's less likely to try. Women know that donating an embryo or fetus is free, easy to arrange, physically painless, and — if we do our jobs properly — free from any unnecessary difficulties. But there is another problematic option.

"If you make a woman feel uncomfortable, feel belittled or judged, she can still turn around and leave. Instead of seeking an abortion, she can decide to keep the fetus and carry it to term. And that outcome, while nowhere near as dreadful, may be far from desirable."

The girl was nodding in agreement. At least their new hire orientation managed to get this message across. But just in case, Poloma spelled it out. "A woman with an unplanned pregnancy, and lacking the personal and situational resources to deal with one, is not likely to offer a child as good a life as our carefully selected adoptive parents. And we want to give these children the best possible life."

The next evening, Poloma went out for drinks.

Her coworkers, especially the young ones, were often surprised that she liked beer. It was fun to watch their double-takes when she invited them to the pub around the corner for an after-work brew or two.

And it felt good to unwind. It used to embarrass her that unwinding got so much easier if she had something to drink; but after some quiet analysis, she'd decided that assisted relaxation was better than none. It wasn't as if she needed to steer her car home. If she ever learned how to laugh at silly jokes, or dance in public places, without that aid, so much the better.

Todd, the more senior of the day shift guides, came along. Poloma knew better than to make anything of it, or of his bits of flirtation. Todd flirted with anyone he liked, male or female, young or old, but it had never progressed to anything more personal. It had taken her a while to realize as much, and to put aside the faint hopes his behavior had prompted. But she had never been sure she herself was interested; and by now, she enjoyed his habit for what it was, and practiced responding to it in case someone new and interesting ever approached her. Now Todd brought four frothing pitchers of ale, two in each large hand, and set them on the table with admirably little spillage. She smiled and brushed her hair back in what she vaguely recalled to be a coquettish gesture.

He winked and turned toward the screen above the bar, which was showing a darts match. As Todd offered amateur critiques of the contestants' form, more people arrived from the office, a nurse and an adoption counselor. They ordered drinks, tipping extra to have them brought to the table, and found chairs to drag over.

The two of them had been talking to each other as they approached the table, the counselor saying something about a parent crying. Todd put out an arm like the gate on a toll booth. "Share it with the class, please!"

The counselor laughed, shoved Todd's arm upward, and obliged. "I was just saying we had a newly approved parent who started crying. That happens often enough, but it turned out she was crying because she wouldn't be able to carry the fetus herself. Her husband looked embarrassed and said she'd been going on about it for weeks. She just glared at him and wailed about how she was afraid she wouldn't *bond* with it properly."

The new maintenance tech looked more sympathetic than the counselor. "What did you tell her?"

"Well of course, I told her it would be all right. And that incubators had so many advantages that a few years down the road, most mothers would probably use them for their own babies, and she'd be right in step."

The nurse jumped in. "Just think of all the risks of an in vivo pregnancy! It's not just that the woman could get caught in a fire or some other disaster. You've got preeclampsia, low amniotic fluid, placenta previa —"

"And what about —"

Poloma stood up. "If all of you will stop with the parade of horribles, I'll buy the next round. Deal?"

Her proposal was adopted by acclamation. Poloma collected the orders and made her way through the crowd to place them. As she dodged and tapped shoulders and apologized, the debate she had interrupted played on in her head. She could, actually, see the attraction of carrying a child inside her. It would feel like nothing else in the world. (Well, except that fetal movement was reported to resemble gas bubbles.) But any responsible mother should weigh the alternatives dispassionately, for the fetus's sake and her own.

As she headed back to the table, she could hear that those seated there had failed to keep up their end of the bargain. She could only hope that the actual arrival of beer would provide a sufficient change of subject. If not, she could probably persuade Todd to assist.

Chapter 4

Toni

Toni and Andy had gone through her childhood as The Denim Twins. Andy was two years older, but their shared fondness for overalls and jeans, their physical resemblance, and their almost identical full names might have given rise to the nickname even if they had not spent every possible moment together. In fact, Mom had sometimes referred to them as the Conjoined Denim Twins, though not where anyone outside the family might hear and be offended.

Andy had never made a point of being the leader. That had been Toni's doing, following, copying, sticking close. But Andy didn't mind the role. Even when he hit puberty and started being interested in girls, he'd been savvy enough to realize that the girls he wanted to attract would appreciate kindness toward and tolerance of a little sister. Toni tried to repay him by not whining, and by picking up on clues that he needed a little privacy for a change.

But as Toni herself went through the teenage years, the image of a little sis tagging along began to clash with what she wanted to become: fearless and independent, a pathfinder, self-assured. She pulled back. She might have pulled back pretty suddenly. Andy had been understanding, and maybe a little relieved — but maybe, also, a little hurt.

All of which had made it seem impossible to go to him and say the equivalent of "Hi! Sorry I froze you out after a lifetime of closeness. By the way, I need some closeness now. I'm pregnant and don't know what to do."

What would he have said to her? What courage might he have given her? It was too late to know. But she could use some courage now, or whatever else he might have to offer.

Andy welcomed her with a smile and a hug, if not the bear hug she would have gotten years ago. He knew her well enough, still, to know something was wrong, and to give her time to come out with it. When he put a plate of cookies on the coffee table, she saw with a pang that they were chocolate chip with peanut butter chips added, a simple recipe they used to make together at the slightest excuse or none.

Toni let herself stall long enough to finish one cookie before she looked out the window, took a deep breath, and blurted out the news. She heard an indrawn breath and made herself turn back toward Andy. He was staring at her, eyes wide. That pushed Toni over the edge. Tears ran down her face; she wiped them on her sleeve.

Andy shoved up from his chair, sat next to her on the couch, and pulled her into a hug. She put her head on his shoulder and bawled.

A few damp and snotty minutes later, she gave him a squeeze and pulled loose, searching for a tissue. Andy reached out a long arm to grab the box and bring it to her. She took a tissue, nodded her thanks, and blew. When she had stuffed a fairly disgusting tissue in her pocket, she felt able to continue. "I wish I'd told you."

Andy sighed. "So do I. Wow. A niece or nephew. Do you know which?"

She gulped and forced herself to answer. "No."

Andy ran his fingers along his knees like a pianist playing a trill, the way he did when he was thinking. "I don't know what I would have said. But I wouldn't have tried to tell you what to do."

"I know." Though maybe telling him would have helped her think more deeply about what she wanted, and why.

Andy glanced toward his large paper wall calendar, the sheet above the dates a complicated — fractal? — and wildly colorful pattern. "How long ago did you donate?"

She could have told him exactly how many days. "About two weeks. And I was maybe seven weeks along."

"Did Mom know?"

It was still hard to talk without her voice trembling. "I told her I was pregnant. I didn't tell her I donated the — the baby until afterward. And I didn't tell Dad about any of it." That, at least, she wouldn't need to explain. Dad had kept at a friendly distance since Andy had hit the teenage years.

Andy offered the plate of cookies, but Toni shook her head. Andy patted her hand and then got up and went into the kitchen, returning with two tall glasses of milk. "This'll help you get your medicine down." He grinned his quick grin and handed her one glass. She managed to smile back, took the glass, picked up a cookie after all, and dunked it in the milk.

Andy sat next to her again, picked up another cookie, dipped it deep in his glass, swished it around, and took it out, dripping. He licked his lips dramatically and crammed the cookie into his mouth. "Mmmm." And then, casually: "Is there anything else you feel like telling me — about being pregnant, about the donation, any of it?"

Why else, come to think of it, had she come here? She drank half of what remained of her milk, put down the glass, and started. "I didn't realize it at first . . . ."

She made it through her own growing dismay, the positive pregnancy test, her collapse into crying, her night curled up between the stuffed panda and the giant stuffed leopard cub, her panicky call to Mom, and the sleepless night when she made her decision. That seemed like enough, at least for now.

Andy listened to it all. He put his arm around her shoulder halfway through, and pulled her back down to lean against him as she finished. They sat that way, cozy, listening to the background noises of the apartment, for a few minutes. Then she pulled herself up and gestured toward the kitchen. "Ready to switch from milk to something hot? I'll fix it, whatever you like."

"I'll go with you. Hot milk for me. You?"

"Coffee, for once. I think I need to get back in gear."

Mugs in hand, they returned to the living room and the couch. Andy looked briefly lost for words before he asked, "What's going on in your studio lately? What are you working on?"

Toni held the coffee mug against her cheek, borrowing its warmth, then moved on to sipping the hot drink. "I'm finishing up some pieces. These." She called up the pictures on her phone. He made a face, as usual, at the sight of the patch — he used a pocket phone, claiming phone patches made him itch. But he made the right appreciative noises as she scrolled through the pictures. As she finished, she pondered how little she had planned after these pieces went to the clients. "I guess I haven't been doing much to move forward." In more ways than one.

Why was that? Why was she feeling so stuck? Was it some sort of natural process at work, a sort of grieving? Or was it something else?

Andy sat sipping his milk, not rushing her, just being there. She'd almost forgotten the way he did that. Mom would have been antsy by now, nudging her to verbalize what was going through her head, even if it wasn't verbal yet.

The company, the closeness, the coffee, or all three — something did the trick. Suddenly she knew what to do, or at least, to try.

She drained her cup and stood up. "Andy, you've been wonderful. I'm sorry I've been such a lousy sister, such a lousy Twin. I'm over that now. I'll be around, if you'll have me. But now, I have to go talk to Mom."

Toni was too keyed up for cookies or cocoa. Mom did a double-take at her refusal. Then she got a twinkle in her eye, waved Toni to an armchair so comfy she would almost have to relax, and dug into the pantry for a bottle that proved to be sherry.

Toni had to laugh. "All right, but give me one of the *small* glasses!"

Mom chuckled and handed her a glass that would hold about four thimblefuls, pouring the sherry almost to its brim. Mom's own glass was around twice the size, but she filled it only about halfway. She settled into the matching armchair, took a sip, rolled it around in her mouth, and swallowed it with a satisfied sigh before asking, "So what's shaking the earth where you stand, this afternoon?"

Toni took a tiny sip of the sherry and put it down again. "This isn't the answer to that question, but I thought you'd want to know that I went to see Andy."

Mom did a subtle double-take and then beamed. "I'm so glad. The family hasn't been the same with the Denim Twins hardly talking to each other."

"Which was my fault." Just another of her short-sighted, wrongheaded decisions.

Mom tilted her head and mock-frowned. "Hey, no beating up on my daughter! . . . So back to my question. What's on your mind?"

Now that she was here, her idea seemed hopeless, pointless. She'd already been told as much. Mom looked at her and put aside her playful manner. "Honey, what is it? Just talk." She smiled just a little. "Say whatever you practiced saying in the car, no matter how it sounds now that you're here."

Toni picked up her sherry and chugged it. "What if I wanted to get my baby back? Adopt it, or whatever else they'd call it?"

Mom sat back, nodding her head and body like a sage on a mountaintop. "I wondered whether that was it. Can you tell me how you came to the point of asking? What's happened, or changed, since you made your original decision?"

Toni pulled her legs up and wrapped her arms around them. "Nothing has really happened, and nothing has really changed. Except me, I guess. I've changed. I keep dreaming about the baby. About still being pregnant, or about holding her — I have this feeling it's a girl — after she's born." She laughed again, shakily this time. "I even dreamed about changing her diaper. And it was such a mess! It went *every*where. But when she was changed, I kissed her forehead." She was crying now. "I kissed her. And then I woke up, and she was gone. Gone from inside me, gone from my life. And it hurt. It *hurts*."

Mom sighed. "I'm sorry, sweetheart. I'd hoped this wouldn't happen. There's no way to know, really, whether it will. It used to be worse, though, before the incubators.

Some women would have those regrets after an abortion. You know how keen the loss is that you're feeling. Imagine if it came with guilt, as well."

Toni flinched. "But — it does. Not the guilt of having, having *ended* the baby. But the guilt of giving it up. Of giving up on it. Abandoning it to strangers."

Mom gazed at her, searching her face. "Even loving strangers, presumably better prepared to care for a child? Not that I wouldn't help, one way and another – and I imagine your father would too, once someone tells him what's going on – but the Bureau doesn't approve adoptive parents unless they're in a significantly better position than you are. And those parents would give thanks every day for the gift you gave them."

Toni gritted her teeth. "Now you're making me feel guilty for feeling guilty! For having second thoughts. Thanks a bunch." Though at least she'd stopped crying.

"I just want to know you've thought things through." She didn't add *this time*, but she might just as well have.

Toni slumped in her chair. "I don't guess I have, not completely. But . . . I could manage. Somehow. I could get an actual job, something reliable. Even if it was a job I couldn't do from home, or bring the baby to, I'd see her before and after work, every day. She'd still be my daughter."

Mom reached out and grasped her hand. "Of course. And you could handle it. I'm sorry about the cross-examination. It's second nature, I suppose."

Toni relaxed and dredged up a smile. "It's all right. And what you said about adoptive parents, it's true. But . . . It can't be wrong for me to want my own baby. I didn't owe it to anyone to get pregnant and give the baby away. Not even to people who can't get pregnant themselves."

Mom gave a decisive nod. "That's quite true." Then she

added, a deliberate weight to her words, "But if you're going to take action, or try to, there are reasons to do it quickly."

Toni gasped. Somehow, even though she was here asking for help, she hadn't really believed it possible. "Is there action to take? Is there anything I could do?"

Mom had a look that many a client must have seen over the years, confident, a little smug. "As a matter of fact, after the last time you came by, I did a little research on the subject."

Some of the load Toni had carried into the house rolled off and disappeared. It was just fine for her mother to read her like a book if she took what she saw that seriously. "What did you find out?"

Mom reached over to the side table where she'd left her tablet and scrolled through what must have been notes. "I don't want you to think what I found is straightforward, or makes everything simple."

Toni tried not to look as impatient as she felt. From Mom's glance, she didn't pull it off too well. "And what you did find?"

"Mostly, I was confirming what I remembered reading at one time or another. Some of it has to do with rights that people have had for hundreds of years, in our legal system and the British system it's based on. The right to raise your own child as you see fit is one of those rights. Then there's the question of adoption and how it affects those parental rights. Ready for a bit of legal jargon?"

Maybe she should ask for more sherry after all. But then she wouldn't remember what Mom told her. "Go ahead."

"Let's see, how to sum this up without distorting it too much . . . . British law, and as a result, American law are partly based on a whole lot of general principles. Those principles and some of the pickier rules that arise from them are called the common law. And where a statute — a written rule that legislators, elected officials, vote into being — doesn't have some root in the common law, and either contradicts it or somehow limits it, that statute gets interpreted pretty narrowly, to leave as much of the common law in place as possible. With me so far?"

Toni wished she had a cheat sheet in front of her. "Ah . . . more or less?"

"The point is, the common law didn't recognize adoption in any formal way. Adoption is 'a creature of statute,' not arising from common law and potentially inconsistent with some aspects of it. So adoption laws are 'strictly construed,' read narrowly. Which leads us to some details about how adoption laws used to work, and how the more recent laws about donating fetuses work."

Toni wordlessly held out her glass. Mom chuckled and took it, refilling it in the kitchen and coming back to hand it to Toni. "Believe it or not, this sort of stuff is meat and drink to us lawyer types."

"To me, it's just drink. All right, go on."

"Even before prenatal incubators and fetus donations, adoptions often got started before a baby was born. Sometime during the pregnancy, a mother decided to give the baby up, and some intermediary or other, often a government agency, matched her up with adoptive parents. Different states at different times cluttered the process with different procedures and red tape, but one of the recurring themes was that the mother had at least some chance to change her mind. Usually, she could change her mind even after the baby was born, for up to several days or longer."

Toni found herself breathing fast. "That doesn't match up with what the woman at the clinic told me."

"What she told you was based on how the regulations implementing the donation statute are written. Congress passed the statute, but some department or agency wrote the regulations. And wrote them to diverge quite a bit from the way state adoption statutes, and any state regs, have typically been written. The key question is whether that's a difference that could be legally challenged — that is, challenged with any reasonable chance of success. Though that's leaving out some aspects of the problem." Mom leaned forward and studied Toni's face. "So now we should talk about whether you're just playing with this idea, or seriously thinking about it, or determined to do it."

Leave it to Mom to get real. "Give me a minute. I came here not knowing if there was anything worth thinking *about*."

Mom held up a hand. "I'm not saying there is, necessarily. Trying to change the social paradigm is an involved and tricky business. And it's especially tricky when you're working against time."

Toni closed her eyes and fought back something like queasiness. "Because we'd be getting closer and closer to delivery, you mean."

Mom gave her the glance she must give students who'd missed a layer of a problem. "Not only that. They won't wait until delivery to assign the fetus to adoptive parents."

When had Toni's throat gone dry? "That's right. They told me the parents get to go into a room with the incubator and talk to the fetus. To make it more like the fetus hearing the biological mother and all." It was hard to get the words out. "They might be in a room, right now, talking to my baby. Telling her that they're Mommy and Daddy."

"And believing that they're Mommy and Daddy. If you can act before that happens, you'll spare two or more good people a lot of pain." Mom looked grave, then thoughtful. "If and when you decide to challenge this rule, I propose that's where we start — asking for the adoption process to be put on hold."

Toni gripped her hands together. "We?"

"Of course, we. Do you think I'd let someone else in on this groundbreaking action? It's all mine." Then, quiet, serious: "So it's time to decide, honey. Do you want to move on, the way you planned? Or do you want to fight?"

Chapter 5

Poloma read through the day's stack of inspection reports on applicants and assigned them to the appropriate folders. Once finished, she allowed herself the reward of going through the files for the latest approved parents, checking for any special requests that could reasonably and ethically be granted. Parents who wished to approximate their own intellectual levels, to the extent predictable from the biological parents' histories, could be accommodated. Parents with special expertise in some art or sport could, if feasible, be given a child likely to have the skill those parents were equipped to nurture. Parents seeking children who would look very much like them would find their request politely refused. Such requests could perpetuate a stigma against adoption, or at least the drawing of distinctions between adopted and biological children. Among other undesirable effects, that could undermine the goal of encouraging donations.

She forwarded the suitable requests to those in charge of the fetal database, and sat back, satisfied, almost euphoric. Every one of these good, responsible, caring people would — not soon, but eventually — attain their heart's desire. If Poloma had dreamed, as a child, that she could find a job where she bestowed such blessings, she would have expected it to come with wings and a wand. Maybe she should rename this folder the Good Fairy folder.

She read through the parent summaries one more time, heaved a sigh of contentment, and returned to less pleasant, but still necessary tasks. Incoming messages: meeting reminder, training reminder, budget update, and an invitation from Todd to go with him and half a dozen others to the race track. Only Todd would come up with such a plan! She would have to be amply paid for twice as many years before she could even consider gambling. And horses reminded her of the riding lessons her family could never afford. She sent back her thanks and regrets.

An eyes-only message from the Director?

A *lawsuit*?

A donor with regrets. That sounded familiar, though Poloma couldn't quite remember why. A few donors had tried that over the years, and gotten nowhere. But the Director seemed to be taking this one seriously. Apparently a high-powered lawyer was involved.

The donor was asking the court to enjoin — prohibit — any further work on the fetus's adoption. But the court hadn't yet granted that request. If the Bureau could match the fetus with just the right parents while it still had the chance, that fact might prove useful as the battle continued. The Director had attached the fetus's profile. Which approved parents would be best for (Poloma checked) this little girl? If there really was a danger that the court would interfere – unlikely as that seemed – which applicants would help the court see the importance of letting the adoption proceed?

Despite the circumstances, Poloma could not help but find the task intriguing. Usually, once applicants made it through the screening process, they awaited their turn and were in due course assigned a fetus with little further individual attention – only an update examination to make sure they had not become less desirable parents in the interim. Which meant no detailed procedure existed to guide, or circumscribe, Poloma as she made her choice.

The two dads who looked so much alike and sang in the same choir? Charming, sympathetic . . . but perhaps not having universal appeal. No single parents. Not too old, not too young . . . and not too high on the list. She would need the chosen parents to cooperate as the litigation dragged from one stage to the next. Applicants already near the point of receiving assignment would have little incentive to endure unexpected difficulties. Applicants unhappily resigned to waiting years for their child, suddenly offered an alternative, would be more willing to accept the uncertainties that came with it.

Maybe these two. She paused and reread their file. Adam Brown and Grace Allen, ages 33 and 31 respectively. Married, but not before a prudent period of cohabitation. Co-founders of a charity that contacted aging art collectors and sweet-talked them into auctioning off valuable art works for the benefit of children's hospitals. No arrests, no bankruptcies, no controversial public writings or posts. No children. They'd tried for several years to conceive, which showed they weren't taking the easy way out, but not for so long as to suggest they considered adoption a drastic last resort. No special requests as to which fetus, so not ungratefully picky. Highly intelligent, but no indication of psychiatric or psychological treatment, so not too high-strung to cope with what would be an unusually stressful adoption process. Sang in a community chorus. Good-looking, which would ease their way in various respects, to the benefit of their child.

Poloma checked the file data on the donor. She was apparently blonde, though with dyed hair, and had green eyes. Adam's dark brown hair and golden-brown skin had nothing in common with that coloring, but Grace was blonde, and her gray eyes were not far from green.

Poloma attached the profile to an urgent message, asking for the Director's approval to make contact.

She could have asked the Director to answer one additional question: whether to tell these prospective parents she was ushering them into an obstacle course. But the Director might say no. And if she kept the couple in initial ignorance, Poloma could foresee too many ways that decision could backfire. No, if she had chosen the right people, they would be able to cope with that news, and would be grateful to her for her candor.

Director's approval — check. Carefully worded email, calculated neither to be ignored as a bureaucratic process update nor to raise the couple's hopes too soon — check. Appointment made — check, for that very afternoon.

Two hours later, Poloma inspected herself in the restroom mirror, picking off a stray dog or cat hair — whose pet shed so much that its hair made its way to strangers? She returned to her office and paced around the small space. Mercifully soon, her phone buzzed. "They've arrived."

"Please bring them right up."

The couple's entrance gave Poloma a surge of pride. Walking close together, his hand on the small of her back as if providing support, but her posture straight and strong as if not needing it. Obvious chemistry. Too much, perhaps? Would it make people envious? No, too much second-guessing could rule out every possibility. "Welcome. Please sit down. We have a lot to talk about."

An hour and a quarter later, Poloma sat at her desk with her head in her hands, totally drained. Even people as intelligent as Adam and Grace took time to absorb news like this. Time and repetition. She had not fully factored in how accustomed the couple had become, in their successful professional lives, to knowing what to expect.

And then, Poloma's grasp of the upcoming legal procedures was not equal to the incisive questions they asked once they recovered from their shock. She had had to bring in someone from Legal, and to try and make productive use of the time spent waiting for the somewhat supercilious lawyer to arrive. And once the lawyer answered their initial questions, arranged for future contact, and left, she had desperately wanted to reestablish their initial rapport. She could only hope she had succeeded.

At least she could be certain of one crucial point. This man and woman would make excellent parents. Far better than a confused, inconsistent, self-centered donor willing to throw people into turmoil and risk a child's well-being and security.

* * * * *

Adam

Adam and Grace stepped out of the clinic and stopped at the same instant. Adam, at least, felt a sort of stunned relief at the warmth of the June day, the sweet scent of the gardenia bushes on both sides of the door, and even the sound of passing cars. The feel and odor of office air had half stifled him without his realizing it. Though to be fair, it might not have bothered him in less intense circumstances.

After a couple of minutes, they made their way to their car, and Adam silently gave thanks to car designers past and present that he didn't have to drive. The suspense of the summons to the clinic, with its careful avoidance of actual news; the tangle of good news and bad, hope and delay, which the efficient Ms. Clark had presented to them; the need to decide, at once, whether they should accept the mixed blessing of jumping ahead in line and coping with litigation, or wait who knew how long for another chance — all of it had left him more shaken than he wanted to show. But Grace knew, of course, and as soon as they climbed into the back seat, he laid his head on her shoulder, gripped her tight around the waist, and buried his face in her hair.

Such beautiful hair, all the colors from gold to ivory. If their daughter's hair was entirely different, maybe they could change it to match. But no, they should cherish their daughter just as she was, even to the color of her hair.

Once they made it through to the day when they could bring her home . . . .

Grace had been rock-steady in the office and when they first got into the car, but his mood was affecting hers, or she was yielding to her own. Her body trembled in his grasp. He pulled his head up and stroked her cheek. "Are you all right, love?"

She leaned back against the seat and blew out a deep breath. "I'm all right, darling. It's just a lot to take in and process."

Neither said anything more until the car turned into their neighborhood. Grace stirred, turning to face him. "Ms. Clark says they've dealt with this sort of problem before, and that she's confident the donor won't get anywhere with her lawsuit. I wonder if that's true. And whether she knows enough for us to trust her prediction."

Adam rarely wished he had spent more time studying law, but it might have helped him feel less at sea. He said, hesitant, "We could talk to a lawyer about it. One we hire. But that might complicate things." And if they were to talk to anyone about it, he would rather . . . "I wish we could talk to the donor. Try to find a way to make her feel better about us."

Grace pulled her arms closer to her sides. "Ms. Clark and the Bureau lawyer both said that would be a bad idea. That it'd be too easy for us to say something she could use against us later. And that it would encourage her to try to manipulate us. . . . I wonder what she's like."

So did Adam. "If we go through with this . . . ." And they would. He was almost sure of it. He and Grace would talk, and think, and talk some more, but how could they bear to return to the long limbo of the waiting list? "I guess we'll see her in court, if this actually goes to trial. She'd probably take the stand. That'd show us a lot about her."

"I wonder why she donated in the first place, and why she changed her mind."

So did Adam. "Ms. Clark — Poloma — seemed to think she was unstable."

Grace gave a ghost of a smile. "I have the feeling Poloma thinks most people are unstable. I wouldn't want her sizing me up." A pause. "Silly of me. I guess Poloma sized me up already."

Adam squeezed her to his side. "Sized you up and found you impressive. I don't think we skated through on my credentials."

Grace squeezed back. "She knows we'd be terrific parents. And we will be."

The car pulled up in the driveway, opened the garage, drove in. "Just a little longer, sweetheart. A few months.

Maybe less time than if —" Too late, he snapped his mouth shut.

Grace had opened the door, but she turned back, forgiveness in her face. "It's all right. We can talk about pregnancy. We can't do it, but we can talk about it. It doesn't hurt any more."

He knew she lied. But he would let her lie, and follow her indoors, and make it up to her with all the warmth of his body and all the fire in his soul.

Interlude – Mary and Jack

Jack Connor sat dozing on the couch, the way he often did after Sunday dinner. Mary usually sat next to him reading one of her detective stories, or embroidering a dishcloth or the collar of a blouse.

Today, she was embroidering. And as he surfaced from his nap, he noticed she was humming under her breath. She only hummed like that when she was excited about something and trying not to show it.

He sat up and reached for her hand, needle and all. "What is it, Mary mine?"

She turned toward him, fighting back a smile, and said in a suspiciously offhand manner, "It's about time for my next shot. You know, the shot to make sure I don't get pregnant."

She waited for him to say something, and he thought about out-waiting her to tease her, but instead he took the straightforward path. "You don't usually mention it. You just go and get it."

"Well, I'm mentioning it today. Because I'm thinking I won't just go and get it. I'm thinking I just won't."

What was she saying?

"I'm thinking I won't get it at all."

There came the smile, bright as sunrise. "We've done it, Jack. I went through all the numbers this afternoon. With the raise you got and the extra work we've been getting, and what we've saved, we can finally afford to have a baby." The smile dimmed. "Of course, it can take the women in my family forever to get pregnant, and things could change in the meantime. But— " She squared her shoulders. " – that'll just mean more time to prepare."

A little late, Jack realized he'd squeezed Mary's hand right where the embroidery needle stuck up. He let go, wiped his finger on his pants, and took her hand again more carefully. "I won't ask if you're sure, because you know your numbers, and you wouldn't have told me otherwise. But are you ready for this? For everything about it?"

Mary put her free hand on his arm. "Are you? We both have to be ready. You can bet I'll need you for even more things than we expect, more than we can guess at."

Jack pulled her onto his lap and buried his face in her hair. She always said it didn't bother her if he cried, but he still didn't like her to see it. He hoped she could hear him, muffled as his voice was, as he promised, "I'll be there. Whatever you need, whenever you need it. I'll be there."

Chapter 6

Judge Alexandra Rayner (Alex)

Alex Rayner sat back in her rocking chair, luxuriously comfortable in her long bathrobe, quilted slippers on her feet – she'd finally found slippers neither too short nor too wide! — and contemplated the opening motions in what promised to be a most interesting case. Interesting, and in unfamiliar territory: federal judges like herself were rarely drawn into family law disputes. Only the fact that the clinics were established under the aegis of the federal government had brought this matter to her court.

There was, of course, the threshold question: should she recuse herself because of the abortion all those years ago? She thought not. She had made that choice in a very different world, a world with different options and different consequences. That history did not predispose her to take any particular view of the present controversy.

So. The plaintiff – represented by her mother, Valerie Greene, which should guarantee plenty of twists and turns and perhaps fireworks — wanted the adoption process frozen. Problematic, at least if continued for long, given Alex's inability to freeze fetal development to match.

The plaintiff also wanted an order giving her access to the incubator, so she could talk to the fetus. Meanwhile, the clinic, should Alex decline to dismiss the case immediately, wanted carte blanche for the chosen adoptive parents to do the same, pointing out that for them to do so was normally routine. (And just when had those parents been chosen? Not that it mattered for her purposes.) She would ask for affidavits from experts about the importance to and effect on the fetus of hearing voices that could eventually be familiar and familial. And what about other voices? Did the nurses, or technicians, or whatever they were called talk to the incubators? How much? Were human voices in general more important than particular voices? Did even the experts know? Well, whether or not they knew, they'd try to sound as if they did.

Hmmm . . . That would be a possible solution. Indeed, uniquely rational. If the affidavits supported the claim that human voices, or the voices of family members, played an important developmental role, then the parties — plaintiff and individual defendants — could supply the same. Separately, and taking turns.

She could wish to be a fly — a temporary and sentient fly — on the wall when these competing would-be parents had their visits. What would they want the fetus to hear? What would they be unable to keep themselves from saying? Such knowledge would be helpful indeed, if her job was to play Solomon and send the baby where it would be best nurtured and loved. But she had no such mandate, and thank God for that.

Though come to think of it, Solomon had been asked to determine, not the best mother, but the true one. Maybe not so far, after all, from her own more legalistic duty.

And this degree of woolgathering meant it was time she went to bed. But first, she would send herself a note as a reminder. If she did order access to the fetus, she had better make sure the clinic did not take advantage of the logistics to record or listen in.

* * * * *

Toni

Toni's mother was sitting on her front steps eating a double-decker ice cream cone when Toni showed up. Toni sat next to her and made a show of staring at the ice cream. Mom chuckled. "I'll get you some in a minute. And by the way, someone should call your father. Would you rather do that, or shall I?"

Toni thought about what that call would be like, and said, "First tell me the latest, and then I'll decide."

"Good enough. I have good news and not-that-bad news. Which do you want first?" Mom seemed fairly pleased with herself, which was reassuring. It suggested they'd pulled something off, done better than Mom may have feared.

"Is there a logical order to these pieces of news? If there is, please go with that."

"Right. The good news first: the judge has ordered the clinic to give you visiting time with the fetus, so you can talk to her."

Toni did a double-take. "Her?" Mom nodded, releasing the grin she must have been holding back. Toni stuck the side of her hand in her mouth and bit down, one of the best ways she'd found to hold back tears. When she could speak, she asked, "When?"

"I already called and set up the first appointment, tentatively of course. Are you free tomorrow afternoon?"

She had a meeting with a gallery. She would reschedule it. "Sure!"

"Good! That means you'll get to go first."

That sounded a little more ominous. "Are we getting to the not-so-bad news now?"

"Yes. You and the adoptive parents — well, that's part one of the news, and the least good, if you will. The Bureau got as far as picking parents for your child before the preliminary injunction kicked in. And they get their own turn. That's part two."

Toni swallowed the bile that welled up in her throat. "And we won't know what they say to her."

Mom started to smile and visibly checked the impulse. "Honey, I don't think it'll matter to the baby. And anyway, neither the Bureau nor the chosen parents will be able to hear what you say, either. That's part of the order — no listening and no recording. If the Bureau tries to cheat, well, I know this judge. She'll cut them into tiny, quivering, wiser pieces."

She stood up and held the screen door open for Toni. "Now come on in and celebrate with at least two scoops."

Toni started toward the door and then stopped, turning to say, "And afterward, I'll call Dad myself."

The receptionist looked out of his depth when Toni announced herself and her errand. He punched one of the many buttons on his big phone and told someone, "She's here."

Saying nothing to Toni, he waved her toward a chair and retreated into an inner office, soon to be replaced by the black-haired woman Toni had met on her last visit. That had been a strange encounter, the woman shifting from sympathetic to wary to hostile. She had settled on hostility now, glaring at Toni. "I remember you."

Toni kept her chin up and her back straight. There was no point in echoing the statement. And if this woman didn't get out of her way, she was going to storm the barricades and find her baby. That intention might have shown on her face; the woman snorted, probably (or so Toni hoped) in frustration, and started walking toward the back. Toni followed her, almost confident that no one would stop her.

They had not shown Toni the visiting rooms on that first tour. Predictably, those rooms were close to the room full of incubators. Just as predictable, if unnecessary, was the way the walls and ceiling suggested a nursery, kites and butterflies and cartoonish animals on the walls and a mobile with the same sort of images cut out and rotating. And the fresh-air scent she remembered from the first waiting room had been piped in here as well.

The incubator was already waiting, a lovely rose color. (Did the clinic put girls in pink incubators and boys in blue? How old-fashioned that would be.) The hostile woman walked in first as if establishing some sort of claim, so Toni walked around her, straight to the incubator, and put her hands on its smooth surface. Despite what must be plenty of insulation, it was warm — a detail probably aimed at visitors, like the decor. And, she had to admit, an effective touch. The warmth was soothing, and somehow disguised that she was touching a piece of machinery.

Toni heard a door open and close behind her. The woman must have given up any attempt at discouragement or interference. Toni was alone in the room. Alone, except for her baby. Her daughter.

Who didn't even know she was here, not yet.

"Hello, in there."

What did the sounds mean to the fetus? It, she, had no notion of language. No notion either of other people, or the idea of people, or her own humanity. She must feel utterly alone. But no, the incubator simulated the sounds the fetus had known before. Did those uncomprehended sensations provide comfort?'

Toni spied something that looked like a microphone and moved closer to it.

"You're not alone. I'm waiting for you, right out here. And so are your grandma and grandpa, and your uncle. Your uncle's terrific — one of my best friends." Or had been, and would now be again, or so she hoped. "Grandpa's pretty cool too. And your grandma, well, I can't describe her. You'll just have to meet her for yourself." And if that happened, it would be because her mother had pulled off something like a miracle.

"There's a whole world waiting for you. Full of people, and so much more. Are your eyes open? If they are, there isn't much to see in there." Had light filtered in, before, enough to give the amniotic fluid different colors? Did the incubator do the same? "But as soon as you come out, you'll get to see all sorts of colors. And faces! You'll learn about faces." She gulped. "I hope so much that one of the first faces you see will be mine."

She couldn't think of anything else to say, not with her chest and throat so tight. She just stood there, stroking the warm sides of the exterior, until the door opened. Toni turned, slow and reluctant, knowing what it meant. It was a technician, this time, or so the lab coat suggested. "It's time to go."

He might not even know who she was. He might think she was adopting the fetus, and visiting without her partner for some unimportant reason. She mustered a smile as if nothing out of the ordinary was happening, and no suspense to cope with beyond waiting for a scheduled delivery.

She made it out of the building without seeing the angry woman or any other obstacle. She held herself together until she was safely in her car. She had thought she would cry, then; but instead, she remembered the warmth of the incubator that held her child, and lay back, closing her eyes, almost at peace.

Chapter 7

Poloma

That woman was in a visiting room right now, talking to the fetus she'd donated as if that decision was one she could casually reverse.

As if everything the Bureau was dedicated to doing for that fetus was unnecessary, even obstructive.

Fuming, Poloma jabbed at the numbers on her phone. There were times, though few, when she was glad the Bureau used such antiquated equipment — times when pushing actual buttons felt better than simply instructing an up-to-date device. And her annoyance might have distorted her voice enough to cause problems. She made herself calm down before Adam answered on the third ring.

"We've had a visiting slot open up tomorrow morning." She had opened it herself, displacing the most complaisant and least busy of the other parents. "Can you come at 9:30? Oh, good. Excellent. See you then."

And if the court hadn't thought to specify the length of either side's visits, so much the better.

* * * * *

Adam

Grace was squeezing Adam's hand so tight it hurt. He

ignored it; if she was that keyed up, she needed the reassurance more than he needed complete comfort. It wouldn't last long.

Poloma showed them into the small, cheerful room. "You can have an hour. Someone will come and let you know when it's over." She smiled, as warmly as her restrained personality would probably allow, and closed the door behind her.

Grace released his hand and walked slowly, almost shuffling, up to the incubator. She laid her hands and then her cheek against the smooth surface. "Oh, Adam, come here! It's warm."

He joined her, putting his right hand over hers. His hand was enough larger that he could feel the plastic beneath. Warm, yes, and somehow not as hard as he had expected. Was that a faint vibration he felt?

He stepped back a bit, standing behind Grace, and put both arms around Grace's waist. They had told him about the microphone, but how loud did he need to speak? Probably no louder than if Grace had been able to carry the baby. "Hi, sweetheart. It's Daddy. I'm here with Mommy. We both came to see you. But we can't wait to really see you, out here in the world."

Grace chimed in. "We want to see you, and hold you. We want to hear your voice, and feel your wiggles! And to show you, oh, everything. I wish you could see this room. It's so pretty, the colors and the pictures and all."

Adam gave Grace a kiss on the cheek. "Not as pretty as your mama. You'll see her soon."

Grace turned her head back toward him, whispering, "Can we sing her something?"

"Of course we can! What should we sing?"

"How about 'Ah! Perdona al primo'?" They both loved

its harmonies so much that he had written transcriptions for both parts, the 'breeches role' reset for baritone, the other soprano role for Grace's warm contralto.

Grace spun around and kissed him before facing the incubator again and leaning back into his arms. He tapped the time out on her forearm and began.

When she had joined him, and they had sung the aria to its conclusion, she sighed in satisfaction, then laughed. "The only thing wrong with singing is that afterward, it's such an anticlimax to speak. What else should we say?"

"Why don't we keep singing, instead?"

They made it through two more arias and three folk songs before they ran out of favorites. From music to verse, then. Adam told his phone to find Wordsworth's "Composed Upon Westminster Bridge." He showed it to Grace; her eyes lit up, and she recited it, the lilt in her voice recalling the music they had made. When she finished, looking notably satisfied, he chuckled and pondered what poem might challenge her. To preserve, briefly, an element of surprise, he searched his phone silently and showed her Gerard Manley Hopkins' "The Windhover." She laughed and sailed into it.

From that peak, they moved on to more child-level selections. He was in the middle of reciting A. A. Milne's "Wind on the Hill" when a technician knocked softly and came in, looking at them with barely disguised curiosity before saying, "It's time. But you can schedule your next visit at the desk as you leave."

* * * * *

Toni

The technician who had shown Toni out the last time was now the one to usher her in. And as he unlocked the door to the visit room, he whispered, like some sort of conspirator, "The others — the couple — they sang to the baby." Then he whisked himself away.

Toni stood in the room, clenching her teeth. So they'd been here. And they sang? So now it was her turn? Would the Bureau end up arguing that singing somehow made that couple better parents?

But no, damn it, she would do this her way. Sing her own song metaphorically, rather than literally.

She went up to the incubator and stroked it, long loving strokes from end to end. "You can't feel this, baby, but I wish you could. And I hope so very much that when you're out of there, I'll be able to hold you." She could imagine the weight in her arms, so vividly it almost eclipsed the plastic reality of the incubator.

"We'll sit in the rocking chair I made in my very first shop class, in middle school. It has a bird carved into the back, and feathers along the arms. I made it big, so I wouldn't grow out of it. I'll hold you, and rock you, and —" Well, all right then. "And I'll sing to you. Like this."

Except she couldn't think of anything to sing. But then a memory arose from somewhere in the past, some forgotten moment of childhood, a memory that came with the motion of a rocking chair, forward and back. A rhythm that matched that motion, and in a minor key whose poignancy she had missed at the time.

Rockabye, don't you cry, Go to sleepy little baby . . . .

She could imagine the fetus settling down, going from squirming to sleepy. "If only I could see her!"

"Well . . . ."

She had not realized she had spoken aloud, or that the

technician had quietly opened the door. Now he slipped inside and closed it, just as quietly. "We don't usually tell people about this. But the med techs like to be able to do visual exams along with all the scans. Since you asked —" He actually winked before he sidled around to the control panel and tapped in a sequence.

In a rectangle at one end of the incubator, the rosy color cleared away like fog, leaving the plastic as clear as glass. Toni pressed her face to it.

The movement of the fluid distorted what she could see, and it would have been startling enough without that. So tiny! So thin! And purple! *That* was her baby?

She made an effort to slow her breathing, to look as if nothing has unsettled her. It wasn't her baby, not yet. It was her fetus. If she still carried it inside her, she would have seen only black and white pictures, fuzzy around the edges. Mothers had not evolved for such sights. She had no instincts for handling it.

The technician looked flustered at her reaction, much as she fought to conceal it. He must be used to what a fetus this age looked like. To him, it was on the way to being a baby. She must think of it the same way. She managed to produce a smile and say, "Thank you. It was very kind of you." But she gasped a little in relief as the incubator went fully opaque again.

If she could recapture the mood she had achieved before — "Could I stay a little longer?"

The tech gave her a jerky little nod. "You've got five more minutes."

She turned back to the incubator as she heard him leave, going to the end farthest from the control panel and putting her arms around the incubator as far as they would go. "I love you, now and always. And I'll see you when it's time."

And she would do whatever she could, whatever her mother told her to do, whatever would let her keep that promise.

Interlude – Mary and Jack

Jack had so little time for lunch that he and Mary rarely tried to get in touch then. But as he was wolfing down his sandwich, his phone chimed Mary's tone. Her message read *That time of month. Are you working late?* She knew that if he had to work late, he would stumble home exhausted.

Afraid so.

No answer for almost a minute, and he had to get back to work. But as he stood up, the phone chimed again. *It's all right. We can wait.*

He'd have liked to tell her that no matter how tired he was, just being around her would revive him enough so they could make love. A dozen years ago, that would have been true. He risked being late to send his reply. *I'm sorry, love. I'll plan better next month. And maybe it'll happen anyway.*

Chapter 8

Poloma

It was not how she had pictured obtaining a promotion. Poloma's prior involvement with the case, with the donor and the parents, made her a proper choice to be the Bureau's designated representative in court, and her title needed to reflect the seriousness with which the Bureau took the matter. As for the increase in salary that would normally go with the title, that, she had been told, would take some time to process. Would it take as long as required for her to prove herself? If it came even then.

She would need to hold herself available for court hearings, which would usually be scheduled well in advance but might pop up at shorter notice. That meant no shifts at the reception desk for the duration. She could live quite happily with that restriction. She hadn't scheduled herself for many such shifts lately, and when she had, she had found herself unusually jumpy.

The first order of business was to learn more about what went on in courtrooms — and in this judge's courtroom in particular. She had hoped to see something similar to their case, some sort of adoption matter, but it turned out those weren't open to the public. So she just picked a hearing held as soon as possible, two days hence.

Summer had arrived, and the afternoon was almost humid enough to weigh her down as she walked the three blocks to the federal courthouse. She should have paid more attention to the weather — she would arrive looking more wilted than appropriate for the venue. The courthouse, however, was chilly enough to cool her, if not to erase the traces of perspiration. She slipped in the back of the courtroom and sat behind the scattered spectators, hoping everyone there would be more interested in the proceedings than in one bystander.

It did not take long to size up the judge. Poloma had, for years, thought of herself as grown, but now she wanted to be this judge when she grew up — so dedicated, so sure of herself, so thoroughly in control. Their case, these parents, the fetus thriving in the incubator, were all in good hands.

But she had better make sure their lawyer knew what he was facing. She took him out for a beer to clue him in. It proved unnecessary. "Oh, yes, I know Judge Rayner. Didn't you know I used to be three inches taller? She cut me down to size."

* * * * *

Toni

Mom had tried telling Toni not to be nervous. Now she was just telling her that being nervous was normal — and making her more nervous with a flood of instructions. "Just listen closely to anything the judge tells you. If she wants you to answer a question, and you're not completely sure what the answer is, ask for the opportunity to confer with me. Keep answers short. And don't lose your temper at *anyone*, not until we're out of the courtroom and on our way home."

The conference was set for early afternoon, soon enough after the lunch recess that things should be running on time — though according to Mom, this judge would keep things moving in any event. Mom made sure they arrived early, which left them cooling their heels in the hallway, trying not to visibly eavesdrop on the people standing around near other courtrooms. When the door to their courtroom opened and two small clusters of people filed out, Mom gave her a hug, then gripped her shoulders and looked in her eyes. "It'll be fine. This is just a preliminary conference. We'll be done in maybe half an hour. Up for an ice cream sundae afterward?"

Toni managed a smile. "Do you have to ask?" Hopefully her stomach would settle down by then.

She hadn't known whether she would recognize anyone from the clinic. But as soon as they entered, she saw the tall woman with the long black hair, the one who had told her an adoption was out of the question. They would see about that.

The woman was sitting, spine stiff, at a table on the left side of the room, next to a man whose bland suit and tie could just as well have been a sign reading "lawyer." A man and a woman sat on the lawyer's other side: a good deal older than Toni, well dressed in an unobtrusive way, and holding hands. Toni swallowed a sudden flood of saliva. These must be the would-be parents of her baby.

Mom steered her to a chair at the similar table on the right side of the room and sat her down. They would be looking up at the judge, assuming that elevated platform with the big desk and well-upholstered chair was where the judge would be. There was another upholstered chair next to that desk, for witnesses according to Mom's briefing. But no one was likely to testify today.

No sooner had she sat down than Mom goosed her to

stand up. The judge had appeared through a door at the back of the courtroom. Everyone stood and waited for the judge to take her seat. Then they all sat down again, and the judge looked slowly around the room, her gray eyes seeming to reach out and probe each one of them for weak spots. The judge stopped at Mom. "Counselor."

Mom stood up, her posture very straight, though somehow relaxed at the same time. "Your Honor."

"The plaintiff is your daughter, I believe." She paused for any contradiction, then went on. "I can imagine the economic and personal factors that may have gone into your daughter's choice of representation. You know, I trust, that I will expect you to be at your best and most professional at all times throughout this litigation."

Mom nodded in a way that suggested a bow. "Of course, Your Honor."

The gaze flipped over to Toni, pinning her in her chair. "Ms. Greene. Do you understand that despite your counsel's unquestioned expertise and experience, it is possible that her personal involvement in this matter may impair her efficiency?"

Mom had said she could ask to confer, but this didn't seem a good time to do so. "I don't think that will happen, Your Honor."

The judge twitched a thin eyebrow. "I want to see a waiver — thoroughly worded — on this issue filed by the end of the day."

"Yes, Your Honor." Mom sat down again.

The judge aimed her scrutiny at the other table. "Mr. Smythe. I assume the lady on your right is here representing the Bureau of Reproductive Safety. I have a surmise as to the identity of your other clients, but please inform me nevertheless."

The lawyer stood up. "Your Honor, may I introduce Adam Brown and Grace Allen, adoptive parents of the fetus in question."

There went the eyebrow again. "A somewhat premature description, under the circumstances." Out of the corner of her eye, Toni saw the man, Mr. Brown, wince, and the woman press down on his hand with her own. "And you are here representing them as well?"

The lawyer shifted his weight from foot to foot. "I am, Your Honor."

The judge turned slightly and addressed the couple. "Mr. Brown, Ms. Allen, there is a potential difficulty. To be specific, a potential conflict of interest. The time could conceivably come when, due to developments in this case, the Bureau of Reproductive Safety will determine that you have become a liability, that their own interests as a party make it expedient to vacate their previous designation of you as parents." She paused as the couple stiffened, looked at each other, and looked back at the judge. "That possibility, remote or not as it may be, makes it problematic for the same counsel to represent you all. I suggest you seriously consider retaining your own attorney." She turned back to the lawyer. "And if for any reason they do not, I want a waiver from them as well. And it had better be airtight." The judge sat back in her chair. "I would normally ask, at this time, where the parties stand on settlement and what settlement discussions have taken place. But I will wait for any issues of representation to be resolved before pursuing that question." She stopped abruptly, leaned forward again, and looked at the couple, one of whom had apparently made some movement that alerted her. "Yes, Ms. Allen?"

The woman looked a little startled to be addressed. "It's

just that, Your Honor, we'd understood that we weren't supposed to talk to the — the other side. The plaintiff."

The judge glowered at the lawyer, Mr. Smythe, if so piercing a look could be called a glower. Then she looked back at the woman, the intimidating expression gone as if it had never been. "This is a useful example of why you should have your own lawyer, to advise you as to your own interests and options." She settled into the chair again. "Do either of you have any other matters to raise before we adjourn?"

Toni and her mother waited until they had found a secluded table at the ice cream parlor before saying anything of substance. Once the waiter had brought their sundaes, Mom took a spoonful, raised it in a toast, and said, "Here's to surviving your first day in court!"

Toni had already stuffed a spoonful in her mouth; she swallowed it and took another to return the gesture. Once she had gulped down that mouthful as well, she let her spoon rest on the bowl and asked, "Should we talk about settlement? Whatever that means?"

Mom pursed her lips, considering. "Let's wait until we get home, if that's all right. I don't want anything distracting us from our ice cream, especially to the point where it ends up melting. Should we go back to your house or mine to talk?"

Mom's turf or her own? In which house did she actually feel more at ease? Maybe it should be her own, but it wasn't, at least not today. Or not unless she could curl up with her stuffed animals, which might not be exactly appropriate for the coming discussion. "Yours."

Hot apple-cinnamon tea, then, replacing ice cream, and Mom's kitchen table. Mom started out by answering the question Toni had already asked. "What settlement means, in this context, would probably be either an open adoption or some sort of shared parenting scheme. Open adoption is contemplated in the statute, so court approval would be easy, and the Bureau might not put up much of a fight — but it would leave Adam and Grace as the parents, with you having certain rights to access and/or information. We would negotiate those details, and the court would approve the agreement we reached. If problems developed later, either party could go into court seeking a modification of that order — and I would expect the legal parents to have more options, as far as modification goes, than you would."

Toni closed her eyes and imagined herself back in the visiting room, telling the baby that she had given up being her mother. "I'm not ready to settle for that. Not yet. If things go badly with the case, then I might."

"Understandable. But you need to realize that in that event, our leverage would decrease. Possibly to the point where no settlement is feasible."

This was a weirdly double experience, seeing her mother in action as a lawyer and appreciating her competence, while feeling all the confusion and anxiety of her position as a client. "Tell me about the other possibility. The shared parenting."

"The Bureau's going to do whatever they can to spike that one, for fear of setting a precedent." At Toni's wrinkled brow, she clarified. "They won't want to establish, for the future, that donors can expect or even hope to retain or regain any sort of parental rights."

Toni put her mug down with a thump, sloshing her tea. "Which is something I do want established. For the future, for future mothers as confused and conflicted as I was."

Mom took that in, sipping her tea. "We'll have to tread carefully about making that agenda known. There's a fine line, with this judge at least, between standing on principle and using the current controversy in a quasi-political way." Sip, pause, sip. "What will concern me, in addition, is the question of balance of power and how it may increase the chance of further litigation. It's all too common, in any family law dispute involving children, for the family to spend their time and resources in court until the children become legal adults. None of us wants that — " She made a wry face. " — except, possibly, whatever lawyer the couple end up hiring for themselves."

Toni put down her mug and buried her face in her hands. "What a nightmare."

She heard her mother rise from her chair and then felt a warm hand on her arm. "There are things we can do, things I can help you do, to make that less likely." Mom sat down again. "The threshold question is, are you open to a shared parenting agreement, if we can craft the details so that you'll only end up back in court under limited and compelling circumstances? Or are you determined to get back to where you started, as if the donation hadn't happened?"

Toni drained the last of the tea and held the still-warm mug against her cheek for the comfort of it before setting it down. "But it did happen. And now we have those people — Adam and Grace — caught up in it." She paused to think. "Is there something like the open adoption, but flipped around? Where I'm the parent, but I allow Adam and Grace whatever you called it, 'access and information'?"

Mom tilted her head. "An interesting proposition. We can float it and see what happens. And now let's put all this aside for a while. You're exhausted."

Toni looked at Mom. She wasn't saying so, but the lines

in her face and the slight slump in her shoulders said she was tired too. "Yes, let's. In fact — would it be all right if I took a nap before I went home?"

"Of course. Your old room is piled high with miscellaneous junk, but the couch is comfy. And I still have at least one stuffed animal you left behind that I can bring you."

Toni stood and started for the couch, but hesitated in the kitchen doorway. "Never mind the stuffed animal. The couch will be enough. And thank you. Thank you for everything." She bit her lip and hurried out of the room.

Chapter 9

Adam's and Grace's next visit wasn't until the day after tomorrow. But on his way back from inspecting the site of their next art auction, he noticed that he was only two blocks away from the clinic. Maybe there'd been a cancellation, and one of the visiting rooms would be free. No harm in checking.

He instructed the car to park in the lot and was about to head inside when he saw a young woman coming out the front door. She was in shadow, and he couldn't see her well, but she was on the tall side. Instead of leaving the building and heading elsewhere, she paused just outside the exit, leaning against the building, her arms crossed and hugged into her chest in a posture that suggested pain. Was she a donor, fresh from donating? If so, it was sad to see her so alone.

The girl straightened up and walked slowly away from the building, into the sunshine. Now he could see that she wore dark green denim overalls and a deep purple tee shirt. She would make an interesting subject for the artist whose work they would be selling next week — the man liked juxtaposing blocks of color in semi-abstract portraits.

And then he caught sight of her hair, and he knew.

He had been coward enough, in the courtroom, not to look squarely at the donor. But he could hardly have missed that hair. And Poloma had told them, her voice sharp with disapproval, that the court had given the donor visiting time. She must have had that visit, just before. And she was walking his way.

Adam leaned away from his car window, not wanting to be seen, but he could still see her. Her expression flickered between sadness and intensity. She looked intelligent, and determined, and young.

If that was indeed the donor, as seemed almost a certainty, then Adam's daughter, if all went as he hoped, might someday look much like her. And Adam would not want to see that sadness on his daughter's face; and he would want to stand with her as she faced whatever stood in her way.

He waited until the girl had turned the corner, out of sight, and then sent the car toward home. He would wait for their scheduled visit, when the girl would not be there.

Grace had known, when he got home, that something troubled him. She had also seen, almost as quickly, that he didn't want to talk about it. Years ago, when they were first getting used to closeness, she would have questioned him, the tension in her voice showing that any secrets he appeared to keep left her feeling excluded and insecure. But while she might still prefer that he confide all his concerns, she had learned that he might not be ready until he'd had days or even weeks to ponder them.

Now, two days since he had seen the donor outside the clinic, they had their own visit to think of. Adam pulled his focus back to the present, this room and incubator, this little girl waiting within, this wife waiting with him. Grace was laughing at him, in a loving sort of way. "You brought her pictures of her room. Even though she can't see anything except fluid movement and light and maybe the color of the inside of the incubator."

Adam tried for a knowing, mysterious expression. "That's all *you* know about it." She reached out to tickle him; he evaded her. "I can describe the room to her. The pictures will help me do that."

Grace relaxed her fingers, to show that the threat of tickling was past, and came close enough to kiss his shoulder. "Why not? It's no sillier than anything else we say to her. What matters is that she hears our voices, and hears the love in them."

They had arrived early and been allowed to wait in the visiting room. Now the tech came in, wheeling the incubator, with something of the air of a proud papa. "Here you go!" He beamed at them and left.

Grace reached for a photo. "We'll both do it, all right?" He nodded, and she carried the photo over to the incubator, her voice taking on the soft lilt she used to speak to the baby, and which she might not even know she used. "You have a cozy room waiting for you. It has a window seat in a bay window, with lacy white curtains tied back with lilac colored bows. And the walls are a pale violet."

Adam stepped up beside her. "A carpenter carved your crib for us." A sudden memory intruded: the biological mother worked in wood. He put the thought aside and went on. "The way it's made, we can make it bigger as you grow, until you're big enough for a bed instead. And there's a mobile over it, like the one in this room, except instead of animals, it's made of flowers, blue and green and purple and yellow ones."

Grace's turn. "There's a rocking chair, with nice deep cushions, for me to sit and rock you. And another chair, a little one, for you to sit in when you've learned how. And until then, there's a toy doggie with soft brown fur sitting in the chair, just waiting to love you."

Hardly that. But rather than say anything to contradict her, he could talk about those who actually were waiting. "You're going to have two grandmas and one grandpa. And two aunts and one uncle. They don't all live close by, but you'll meet all of them sooner or later." Not that he and Grace planned to tell them about the baby until the risk of losing her to the donor had passed.

Grace picked up the theme. " And one cousin to start with, and maybe more to come."

"And . . . and maybe, later . . . ." He didn't know how to say it, or why he wanted to. "You might meet someone else who loves you, if the time is ever right."

Grace swiveled to face him, eyes narrowed. He looked back at her, hardly breathing, waiting. And then she sighed, took his hand, and turned back toward the incubator. "I'll be your mother. But I'm not the one who gave you life. And that woman loves you too. Maybe, some day, she'll be able to tell you so." Grace shook her head in quiet frustration. "If all us grownups can learn to play nicely together."

Then her mood shifted again, and she turned aside, clenching her fists, muttering, "And if she stops trying to take you away from me before I can even hold you."

Adam moved close behind her and enveloped her in his arms. "I'm sorry, love. I didn't mean to spoil the visit."

Grace leaned her head back against him, breathing deeply, calming herself down. Then she stood up and extricated herself, turning to smile at him. "Then I won't let it be spoiled. We still have a few minutes. Let's sing to her again."

By the next week, the Bureau surrendered to the inevitable and accepted that Adam and Grace needed their own lawyer. The Bureau's lawyer even sent them a list of possibilities. Somewhat overwhelmed by their number and by his own ignorance of what lawyers actually did, Adam relied largely on gut feel to suggest one they should try first. Her photo, and her soothing voice on the website, just made him feel better, less lost. Grace did not have quite the same reaction, but offered no other preference, and was willing to test his visceral response in an interview.

The lawyer's office wallpaper, while abstract, somehow suggested flowers, and quiet music played in the waiting room, where they were not made to wait long. Her presence in person was motherly, or even grandmotherly. She welcomed them, sat them in comfortable chairs, offered them a choice of hot beverages, and looked through the file, taking her time, occasionally going back to a previous portion. Finally, she looked up at them and said, "If you would prefer to reach a settlement, we should be a good fit. Is that in fact your preference?"

Adam let Grace be their spokesperson. She took a deep breath and leaned forward, hands clasped in her lap. "We would love to reach a resolution without any of us spending more time in court. We are willing to include Ms. Greene in our lives, and our daughter's life, to some extent. We don't want to and don't need to shut her out. But . . ." She paused to take a deep breath. "We won't give up being our daughter's parents. That responsibility, that authority, that autonomy, are not negotiable."

The lawyer nodded, the soft wrinkles in her face deepening with a reassuring smile. "That's an understandable and reasonable position. I'll see what I can do. I hope we can come to an agreement with Ms. Greene on that basis. And if we can't, I will have someone else to recommend who could handle the alternatives very well indeed."

They spent only three days in suspense before the lawyer called them. She waited for Grace to fetch Adam before telling them, "I'm sorry. The plaintiff's sticking point is the mirror of yours. I got the impression she wasn't altogether immovable, but at this stage, the answer is no, unless you've changed your mind about your own position."
Adam glanced at Grace in case she had some last-minute surprise for him, then looked back at the screen. "No, we haven't. So now what?"
Again, that reassuring smile. "Now I send you to the colleague I mentioned when we met. Hammond Voxsmith. You'll find him interesting, I trust. I find him fascinating. He's the smartest chameleon you'll ever meet."

Mr. Voxsmith's website had little personal touch, but listed an impressive array of educational and professional attainments. Mention of the first lawyer's recommendation helped them get an appointment within a week. The waiting room offered current magazines covering legal and historical topics, but nothing topical or political. Grace found an article about preservation of antiques and dived into it; Adam, seeing nothing else engrossing to read, indulged in an old habit of mentally painting the office around him. His mind was much more adept at brush strokes and blending of colors than his hands would ever be.
When the receptionist showed them into the lawyer's office, they saw tastefully framed diplomas and certificates on two of the walls. Mr. Voxsmith stood, came out from behind his desk, shook hands firmly with both of them, and then sat at his desk again, waving them toward straight-

backed cleanly designed chairs. He had two computer monitors, neither of which Adam could see from his seat. After a brief greeting, the lawyer gestured in a direction precisely bisecting a line between the two of them and said, "Please tell me what you think this case is about."

The question gave Adam pause. He could answer it only in the most simplistic terms. Embarrassed, he did so. "About our being parents. Adopting the little girl we've been told we can adopt."

To his surprise, the lawyer bestowed on him an approving smile. "That's quite right. It's not about some amorphous, never-defined constitutional right. It's not about what statutes used to exist. It's not about whether Congress or the administrators acted wisely. It's not about some unforeseen danger posed to an innocent child by applying the statute or the regulations. And it's not a tug of war. It's about following a perfectly clear statute the legislature had every right to pass, as well as the unremarkable regulations implementing it — a statute and regulations that just as clearly apply to you two, the biological mother, and your daughter."

Grace let out a little sob, due either to the reference to their daughter or to some release of tension. Adam reached out to cover her hand with his and press it, then let go and wondered what, if anything, to say next. What occurred to him might seem random, but he was curious, and it might even be significant. "Why did the lawyer who referred us call you a chameleon?"

Mr. Voxsmith laughed. "She did, did she? Well, it's true enough, not just of me but of many trial lawyers. We're hams, most of us — actors on a special sort of stage." He abruptly stood up, his chin raised, fists resting on his thighs, almost glaring. "I can be highly indignant." He loosened his hands and laid his left hand lightly on his right wrist, his head tilted to one side, his face softened. "I can be sympathetic, a good listener." He pushed his head a little forward, hunched his shoulders, furrowed his brow, moved his eyes as if not quite able to focus. "Or a simple, befuddled fellow, needing a witness to explain things to me." Finally he stood upright again, his eyes keen, his shoulders relaxed. "Or second among equals, discussing with Her Honor subjects of mutual and absorbing interest, edifying those around us." He chuckled again and sat back down. "So, a chameleon, if less reactive and more premeditated."

Grace was sitting forward in her chair, face alight. "Fascinating!" Adam pushed aside a moment of jealousy. If such quicksilver variation appealed to her on any fundamental level, she would never have chosen Adam, consistent to his bones. It was just Grace appreciating what people had to offer, the way she always did.

The lawyer leaned back in his chair, its springs creaking. He must like the noise; surely he could afford a quieter chair if he chose. "And now let's get to work. Tell me all about the adoption process, from your first inquiries to the moment you were told you'd been chosen as parents. I'll go through it all with the proverbial fine-tooth comb, looking for anything especially good for us and anything the opposition might try to use." His smile came complete with a twinkle in the eye. "And feel free to interrupt and correct each other."

* * * * *

Judge Rayner (Alex)

Alex read the plaintiff's and defendants' latest submissions with mild irritation, but no surprise. None of the claimants to the role of parent was willing to step back into a lesser status. And the Bureau, of course, was even more energetically and indignantly digging in its metaphorical heels.

What she would do, if she possibly could, was to stay clear of weighing the personal merits of the donor and the assigned adoptive parents. Future federal judges would unanimously curse her name if she saddled them with such a task. No, this case would be determined on the basis of legal principles, as applied to those facts not disputed.

What a trivially simple endeavor! Alex snorted. Competing principles, with centuries of not always consistent precedents behind each. Well, she wouldn't want this job to be easy, would she? Easy would be dull.

Chapter 10

Toni awoke with a gasp and found herself sitting up in bed. What dream had set her heart to racing?

It took only a moment to remember. She had found herself at the clinic. In a room meant to be the visiting room, except somehow it looked more like an office, with a desk and chair on one side and the incubator on the other, the decals faded almost into gray and the mobile missing. Only the incubator itself had been the right color.

And the woman from the Bureau, the one who'd come to court, had stood bending over the incubator, whispering, her face twisted in anger.

Should she call Mom? Was there a way to keep the woman out, away from her baby?

She was probably being silly. The woman might be hostile to Toni, but it was much less likely she'd mean the baby any harm. And she could hardly poison the baby against Toni, even if she would have liked to.

Toni shook her head fiercely, but the dream refused to vanish. Maybe coffee would do the trick. Or tea, or cocoa.

Or maybe . . . .

* * * * *

Poloma

Poloma had barely had time to sort through the morning's first messages when the phone chimed for her attention. She grimaced, glared at the phone, and pressed the button, only to freeze when she saw the image of the caller. Pink hair, green eyes, narrow face. All that had changed from their first meeting was the determined expression, but she had already seen that in the courtroom.

"Please don't hang up."

Poloma paused, her finger hovering above the button. "You shouldn't be calling here."

The girl's shoulders went straighter. "It's allowed. Whether our lawyers like it or not. And . . . there's no reason we have to see each other as enemies."

"How would you know how I see you?" The term "enemy" gave the girl too much credit. Nuisance, annoyance, obstruction, time sink, harbinger of trouble to come . . . not so very far from enemy, at that.

The girl stuck out her lip in a childishly stubborn manner. Then her mouth relaxed, and she looked intently at the screen as if trying to look into Poloma's eyes. "I'm going to guess that you took this job because you wanted to help children, to find them good parents, and to help people who wanted to be parents achieve their dreams. Didn't you?"

She could hardly contradict that assertion. And it was true, though it hardly took great insight to see it. "Yes, I did. And part of that means —" She had no particular wish either to escalate or to extend this conversation. Verbs like "rescue" and "save" and "protect" might not be optimal. "I wanted to ensure that children were raised by responsible, mature, prepared parents. I take pride in that." And she cared passionately about that mission.

There came the lip again. "Are you so sure that a donor

couldn't be that kind of parent? Doesn't it take some kind of responsibility to make the decision to donate in the first place? And after all, nobody dragged me there."

Poloma's mind flashed back to the sports-mad teenager she had assisted the same day she first encountered Toni Greene. She had appeared to drag her mother, not the other way round, but no one would label her responsible or mature.

The girl began to look desperate at her failure to sway Poloma's opinion. "When we met, you only knew one thing about me — that I'd given up my baby — and you talked to me for less than five minutes. How can you be so sure you know all about me, or enough to write me off as a mother? Is that the way to make decisions about who can have a baby?"

Poloma felt herself flinch and hoped the girl hadn't seen it. She knew her job should not involve snap judgments. She had trained herself to read through an entire file, let herself assimilate it, then read it again — for prospective parents. She had never had to ask herself whether donors merited the same treatment.

And there was this girl, demanding it. "What do you want from me?"

The girl slumped a little, looking even younger. "Maybe . . . one less enemy."

There was a short silence before the girl spoke again. "What's your name?"

It would be making too much of the request to refuse it. "Poloma Clark."

"I'm Toni Greene. But I guess you knew that."

Another silence, in which Poloma looked for the best way to bring this startling conversation to an end. But the girl startled her once more by asking, "Would you like to go out for a drink, later?"

Drinks were for friends, or friendly acquaintances at least. "No." But by itself, that was perhaps too ungracious a response. If this girl wanted more from her, she could come onto Poloma's own turf. "You may come here again, if you wish. I can give you a little time this afternoon. After 3." On the other hand, if she waited that long, the impending meeting would distract her and make her inefficient. "Or after 1."

In making this uncharacteristic and impulsive bargain, Poloma had not fully considered the logistical difficulties. By now, many Bureau personnel knew a donor was suing and might know what that donor looked like. Poloma had not sought permission to meet with the woman, either from management or from the Bureau's lawyer. It would be safest to keep Toni from coming inside. She would leave as if going to a late lunch, linger across the street within sight of the entrance, and head the girl off. Then she could take her somewhere and send her on her way as soon as possible.

Trying to ignore her hunger, she scanned all passersby for pink hair — and almost missed the tall young figure in denim clothes, a hoodie completely hiding not only hair but much of the face. She had to dash across the street to catch up and confirm it was Toni thus semi-disguised. Toni started a bit at being approached in a hurry, then relaxed and gave Poloma a small, conspiratorial smile. "I thought it might be better if I came and went, um, quietly."

Poloma did not smile back, but gave the girl her due. "Good thinking." Though they had better go inside after all, out of the heat, before anyone wondered why the girl was wearing an outer layer. Poloma led Toni to the service elevator and thence to her office, glancing around furtively and already regretting her choice of meeting place. She expected her wary hostility toward the girl to revive as soon as they made it inside, but she only felt awkward and lost for words. It was hard to remember that this was the young woman making so much trouble. She suddenly recalled having rather liked Toni at first glance, before learning why she had come.

Poloma sat down at her desk, an act that, she now realized, usually gave her a sense of security, a bulwark against the disturbing or unexpected. She was irritated but not surprised to find, this time, that it failed to have that effect. She waved Toni toward one of the visitor chairs and said, "Here we are, as you requested. Though I don't see how your being here changes anything that's happened, or that is happening."

Toni took a deep breath, then got a concentrating expression as if remembering something rehearsed. "Is there anything you want to know about me that you don't know already?"

She may as well ask, even if the question that came to her had more than a hint of accusation. "How much thought did you give your decision to donate?"

Toni tossed her head, the gesture conveying defiant admission. "Not enough." She dropped her head again, looking into her lap. "I panicked. I let all my insecurities gang up on me." The hands in her lap clenched. "And all the ads for the clinic, all the 'give your child the best' and 'serve your future and your child's' and the rest, made it seem — not so much an easy decision, but a decision that should be easy."

Poloma narrowed her eyes. "If the ads push women to

donate who aren't really ready, why don't we see more donors coming back with regrets, the way you did?"

Toni lifted an eyebrow in a way that reminded Poloma of someone — the mother, she realized, Toni's attorney. "You work with one clinic in one city. Would you know if that was happening elsewhere?"

"Do you know it is happening?"

Toni's mouth twitched halfway to a smile. "Look here." She showed Poloma her phone, on which she had called up the site for some kind of support group whose banner said in bold script, *Donors Are Mothers.*

Poloma glanced at it. "I'll look at this later. But you must know there are groups online for every conceivable cause or notion. It doesn't prove anything." As soon as she said it, she wished she could recall the claim. She could hardly know what something proved before she had examined it.

Toni seemed to sense that it was time to back off. She actually moved her chair backward a couple of inches, and when she spoke again, her tone was quiet, almost hushed, and her statement unexpected. "I had a dream last night. A nightmare. You were in it. That's part of why I wanted to see you.

Poloma had often enough needed to try her hand at amateur psychological counseling, but never with some vision of herself as a symptom. "What happened in this dream, to make it a nightmare? What part did I play?"

Toni was picking her way just as awkwardly and carefully. "Have you ever talked to one of the fetuses? Through the incubator microphone?"

"No, of course not." She had never thought of doing so. It would have been improper — or so she assumed. She had never let her thoughts stray in that direction enough to look up the relevant regulations. "Is that what I did in your dream?"

Toni bit her lip and nodded. "I couldn't actually hear what you said. But I knew, the way you know things in dreams, that you were somehow turning her against me." The girl paused for a deep, somewhat shaky breath. "I know, when I'm awake, that it couldn't work that way. But . . . I guess I wanted to talk to you, to see you, so I could figure out whether that's something you'd do if you could." Another pause, and a quirky, somehow appealing smile. "And I feel better, now. I still see you as – an opponent. But if I try to imagine you as a villain whispering poison to my baby, it doesn't come naturally any more. So thank you."

Poloma had never, to her recollection, been thanked for such an ambiguous benefit, nor one she had done so little to deliver. But she responded as the occasion required, and took the necessary precautions to usher her visitor out of the building without attracting notice.

Hours later, when she normally left the building for the day, Poloma found herself instead heading for one of the two principal incubator rooms. Even after doing something so prosaic as checking in which room, and where in the room, the Greene/Brown/Allen incubator was located, she felt as if she were now the one dreaming. What was she doing walking into this room, with no parents in tow, about to visit a baby that wasn't hers?

The music this evening was a cheery instrumental version of a popular tune Poloma vaguely recognized as a few years old. She resisted the temptation to let it determine the rhythm of her steps as she walked up to the incubator. Admiring its deep rose color, she reached out and, for the first time since her orientation years ago, touched the warm, slightly vibrating surface of one of the devices that gave purpose to her daily life. To think that inside, quietly developing, was a tiny human being, unaware of the conflicting and passionate claims made on her, floating peaceful and protected.

It was time to go. After all, she had no business here. But the shadow of Toni Greene's dream hung over her, almost as if she could hear the whispering of some malign version of herself. She spoke to dispel it.

"We'll keep you safe, little baby. We'll care for you, and keep you from any harm, until the moment you leave your little warm ocean and join us in our world. That's what we're here for. It's what we do. It's what I do." She found herself beaming fondly at the incubator and what it contained. "You'll be healthy, and whole, and beautiful. And you'll have parents who love you."

But which ones? Would they be the two whom Poloma had so carefully selected? Or the young woman who had just reached out to her, and who had bewildered her from the beginning?

Would the baby be safe with Toni Greene? Safe, and happy?

It would be more comfortable to be sure the answer was "No."

Chapter 11

Judge Rayner (Alex)

Alex sat in her chambers, studying her flow chart of the Greene litigation and where it was headed.

Different cases required different approaches to the process known, aptly enough, as discovery, in which the parties were allowed to investigate each other. In any case involving competing claims to parenthood, one could expect the parties to dredge up every personal detail of each other's lives. And the plaintiff, in particular, would want every closely held secret of the Bureau's operations. The approach the judge hoped to take to this case, focusing on undisputed facts and finding the right legal rules to apply to them, might make such a comprehensive discovery process unnecessary.

Except that when one or more of the parties appealed her decision, as seemed well-nigh inevitable, the reviewing court might rule that her approach had been inappropriate. It might say she should have played Solomon after all, exercising her discretion to decide who was truthful and which facts were most important. It would be irresponsible to let the parties get to that point, months or years from now, without the factual ammunition they would need in that horrific contest.

But she would, by God, ride herd on the attorneys and make sure the process dragged on no longer than absolutely necessary.

* * * * *

Poloma

Poloma had known very little about lawsuits before she found herself entangled in one. The notion that a donor, or the donor's lawyer, could go rifling through all manner of files, that the Bureau would have to fight for every remaining shred of confidentiality, was a shock she found hard to absorb. She had not realized the comfort she drew from being part of an institutional fortress until it came under siege.

And now she had the job of going through massive numbers of files, and then recommending which ones would be worth a pitched battle to prevent their disclosure. And nowhere near enough time to do it.

On the bright side, she would doubtless fill some gaps in her knowledge of the Bureau's history and policies.

Eight days later, she came upon a memo dated almost two years ago, reviewing some trend lines and positing where they might lead.

It appeared, for several years, as if the advances in fertility treatments had plateaued. However, in the last several months, breakthroughs have occurred that disprove that hypothesis. While future trends are to some extent unpredictable, the historical tendencies of subsidiary technologies following upon more fundamental discoveries suggest that the numbers of couples unable to conceive and applying to adopt infants as a result will decline. As a corollary, it is likely that within the next several years, if nothing occurs to reduce the number of donations,

donations will begin to exceed a shrinking number of available adoptive parents.

The possibility had never crossed her mind.

Would she be obsolete?

What would happen to the children donated?

She read on.

Several proposals follow to address this predicted trend. . . .

Now that she thought of it, she vaguely recalled some feel-good news item a while back about new fertility treatments. One of these proposals might be well into development by this time.

The first, increased interstate and even international coordination in the search for adoptive parents, was unremarkable and sensible, if not likely to solve the shortage problem entirely. It could be combined with the second, an initiative to provide adolescents, and parents who considered their families complete, with free contraception. If the idea of reducing the number of new souls brought into the word gave her pause, well, that was probably some remnant of romantic mysticism she would have to put aside.

For some reason, the language of the memo shifted into denser bureaucratese for the third proposal. She skimmed through, looking for substance.

. . . Initially, the facilities would provide infant and toddler care, with staff hired pursuant to applicable regulations. . . . Should the situation prove stable, teachers will be hired pursuant to . . . .

Facilities, to care for donated infants should no adoptive parents be available. But what "stable situation" were they talking about, leading to the need to hire teachers rather than caregivers? Was this a description of federal orphanages? Boarding schools?

For how many children?

It wasn't, necessarily, that radical an idea. In some ways, it was only an extension of several familiar and longstanding institutions. But it made a chilling contrast to the image with which she had so often warmed herself, of parents laying their new baby in a crib for the first time and beaming or crying with happiness.

Finally came what she might call a sub-proposal, in that it was apparently dependent on the adoption of the third. She glanced at it, saw that it had something to do with how children would be selected to go to these facilities, and found that her considerable endurance was at an end. She had enough to go on. The real issue was what had happened with these proposals since the memo was written and distributed. If any of the proposals remained under consideration, it would bear directly on whether this memo had to be disclosed.

She made the call. But when she started describing the memo, her supervisor cut her off. "Oh, that! That never went anywhere. The memo's projections were flawed. So we don't have to turn it over." The woman paused, and when she went on, she spoke more abruptly. "In fact, go ahead and delete it. Use the permanent delete program. Any more questions?"

No, no more questions. She murmured the appropriate words, hung up, brought up the program she'd been instructed to use. But something stirred in the back of her mind, some instinct informed by years of experience.

Yes, she would delete the memo, with the software that was supposed to defy all but the most high-tech restoration techniques.

But first, she would make a copy for herself. Just in case her superiors later disavowed those instructions, or some other need arose.

* * * * *

Toni

Toni climbed Mom's front steps with an orange and a yellow leaf in her hand, and snatched up a reddish-purple one at the top before the wind could blow it away. She might get hold of some fabric that matched and make patches for her newer overalls. They could use some added character.

For now, she had less cheering things to look forward to.

Toni had heard of depositions, some time or other. All she knew, really, was that they happened in lawsuits and weren't the same as trials. Now Mom sat her down and explained. A deposition involved testimony taken under oath or affirmation, usually not in a courtroom, and provided the parties not just answers to questions but leads on where to pry next. Not all the answers could be used at trial, but some could, and she shouldn't try to guess which ones. Mom could object to questions, but not to as many types of questions as she could in a trial. And that was just the beginning.

"The opposition's goal, in a deposition, will be to get you to rattle on and reveal information, or lose your temper, or both. More generally, to gather ammunition you didn't intend to provide." Mom got her professorial expression, a way of peering at Toni that suggested invisible spectacles. "So what should your strategy be?"

"Name, rank, and serial number?"

Mom smiled. "Alas, that would be considered unreasonable. But you've got the right idea. Answer questions in as few words as possible. Suppress all expression and body language. Pretend you're a somewhat old-fashioned robot."

Toni sat up straight in her chair, pulled her elbows down, and tried to look at nothing.

"That's close, but you're crossing your eyes. Next and most important point, though I've already implied it: volunteer *nothing*. I'm going to sit close enough to step on your foot if you need reminding. I mean that quite literally.

"And if you aren't sure of the answer, say so and then stop. If you don't understand the question, say so and then stop."

"Do I say it like a robot?"

Mom didn't smile this time. "You can be a smart-ass now, but don't be a smart-ass then. That's just another way of saying too much."

Toni rolled her eyes, then regretted it. "Understood."

Mom was ticking off items on her fingers. "If you're starting to feel overwhelmed or confused, or you need to use the bathroom, or you're about to lose your temper, say you need a break. Don't ask, just declare. If they resist, I'll handle it. You can sit there like — like a deactivated robot until they acquiesce."

"So that'd be a good time for me to ask you any questions — how I'm doing, or what something meant, or how I should answer if they ask some followup question."

She'd been sure enough of Mom's answer that it startled her to see Mom frown. "*Not* a good idea. When you go back in, their lawyer can ask you about what was said."

"But I thought — isn't anything we say to each other privileged?"

"Usually. But in mid deposition, they're allowed to check for witness coaching during breaks."

Toni tried to think of what else she needed to ask. Oh,

yes. "Do I have to answer all the questions?"

"Most of them. Even if I object, you might have to answer. There are a couple of circumstances where you shouldn't — if I've objected that they're asking about privileged information, like what I've said to you some other time or what you've said to me, or they're prying into something the judge has said is off limits. If that happens, I'll tell you not to answer."

That sounded good. "You can tell me not to answer, and I won't have to?"

Mom shook her head, her mouth twisted a little sideways. "Not exactly. The other lawyer can call the judge and ask for a ruling. And if I didn't have a solid basis for telling you not to answer, she'll skewer me. So I'm going to be very careful about giving you that instruction."

Toni closed her eyes. "This is making my head spin."

"Better now than later. Why don't we both have something hot to drink, and then we'll do some practicing."

One cup of tea and two chocolate wafers later, Toni sat at Mom's kitchen table, Mom sitting opposite, and tried not to hyperventilate. "Ready."

Mom grabbed a blazer from a nearby chair, shrugged it on, leaned forward, and became The Inquisitor. "Ms. Greene, when you first came to the clinic operated by the Bureau of Reproductive Safety, you were given this form, were you not?" She shoved a paper printout under Toni's nose and then yanked it away again.

Toni opened her mouth to protest, then remembered. Robots don't protest. "I'm not sure." (Robots might not use contractions, either, but there was no point going overboard.)

"Why aren't you sure? Weren't you paying attention?"

Robots wouldn't breathe, either, but evenly spaced breaths, neither shallow nor deep, would suffice. "I couldn't read it when you showed it to me."

Mom gave a theatrical sigh and shoved it back to her. "Please read it, then."

Toni bent her head and scanned the dense verbiage.

"Well?"

What exactly had Mom, or rather The Inquisitor, said? "Could you repeat the question?"

Mom relaxed her posture and spoke as herself. "They'd probably have the court reporter read it back. Like this." She donned a deadpan expression and droned in a monotone, "Ms. Greene when you first came to the clinic you were given this form were you not?"

Toni bit back a smile. It wasn't fair of Mom to be funny. Though that might also be good practice for minimizing her reactions. The moment of lightness faded away as she remembered that day at the clinic. "This looks something like the form I was given."

Mom semi-sneered. "Take your time. Or didn't you pay enough attention then to know whether this is the same form?"

Toni suspected Mom was going overboard, but that was fine. If the lawyer deposing her was truly an asshole, she'd be prepared. "I was upset enough that day that I can't remember all the details."

Mom paused. "Hon, were you letting yourself feel very upset? Do you think you seemed upset? Because they may have testimony from the people you dealt with, and if you didn't act upset, those witnesses could undercut your credibility."

This was an advantage most people wouldn't have — a lawyer who knew them well enough to ask that kind of question. (Unless Mom thought of every possibility with every client.) Because Mom was right. She'd been trying to stay calm, to convince herself that she was doing the right and mature and reasonable thing, doing what would be better for the baby and herself and some lucky parents out there.

Her face must have admitted as such. Mom looked her in the eye and said, "A deposition is no time to get creative, or to try to show someone up. Stick to the truth, keep it short, volunteer nothing. Let's try that again." She repeated her court reporter impression, which went oddly with the snarky wording of the question, and waited expectantly.

"I'm not sure whether this is the same form."

Mom smiled in approval before resuming her adversarial expression. "Do you remember clinic personnel explaining to you that the decision to donate could not be revoked?"

True and short left little alternative. "Yes."

"Did you understand what they were telling you?"

Under the circumstances, she couldn't ask what Mom, or the lawyer she was playing, meant by understanding. Therefore: "I'm not sure."

Mom tilted her head a bit and pursed her lips. Toni suspected there would be questions about that answer, later. Meanwhile, Mom pressed on. "*Why* did you decide to donate?"

True and short. "I thought it would be best for the baby."

Mom paused again, frowning slightly. "Time out. Just you and me, now. Why did you think it would be best for the baby?"

Nonplussed, Toni tried to re-inhabit the days during which she had struggled with the decision. "I had no

experience with babies . . . . My income was unpredictable .
. . . I was sort of in shock, really. I felt young and confused
and — and alone, even though I should have known you and
Andy — and even Dad, probably — would have been there
for me." She took a shaky breath. "For us. I don't know why
I didn't realize that."

"Okay. Think back over everything you just told me,
except the Dad part. Take a minute. And then we'll try that
question again."

Toni leaned back in the chair with her eyes closed and
did her best to remember what she'd said. When she thought
she had it, she opened her eyes, and said, "All right, I'm
ready."

Mom turned the intimidating posture and expression
back on. "Ms. Greene, why did you decide to donate?"

"I was scared, confused, sort of in shock. I wasn't in
good enough shape to realize what resources I had."

Mom broke character again. "Much better!"

And then they went on.

* * * * *

Adam

Adam had made it this far in life without ending up in
court, or having to prepare for the same. That happy state of
affairs was about to change. Grace seemed to be taking the
matter calmly; Adam did his best to lecture himself into a
similar frame of mind.

When they had served their time in the waiting room
and a receptionist admitted them to Mr. Voxsmith's office,
the lawyer immediately led them to a conference room
whose furnishings struck Adam as unusual. The table was

smooth, polished wood, an elegant oval, but the chairs were straight-backed wood with no arms and less than ample seats. Mr. Voxsmith waited until they had seated themselves, rather gingerly in Adam's case, before he explained. "The plaintiff's lawyer may decide to make you uncomfortable. I didn't want it to take you by surprise, and you can practice ignoring it."

Adam practiced ignoring the chair while the lawyer ran through some basic instructions. Common sense, mostly: don't volunteer information; don't answer unless you know the answer of your own knowledge; don't guess what a question means; don't lose your temper; tell the truth. As to that last, Mr. Voxsmith elaborated. "If you try to color the facts, let alone outright lie, then you have to remember what you said. That's hard when you're nervous, and lawyers are very good at making people nervous. And unless you're habitual liars, lying is emotionally exhausting, especially if you have to do it over and over. And if you get caught — well, to use the precise legal phrase, you're toast.

"Let's move on from physical discomfort to other sorts. I'm going to start with some personal questions. I'll point at whichever of you should answer — we'll save time by skipping the Mr. This and Ms. That. Ready? Here we go."

The lawyer pointed at Grace. "How long did you try to conceive naturally before giving up?" Then he looked not at Grace but at Adam, assessing his reaction. Adam had shifted in his chair and clenched one fist. The lawyer lifted an eloquent eyebrow; Adam forced himself to sit still with hands open on his lap.

Meanwhile Grace had started answering the question. "We tried for four years. But really, we've never stopped trying."

Mr. Voxsmith, to Adam's astonishment, took a kazoo

out of his pocket and blew on it twice. "This is my buzzer. When you hear it, you know you screwed up somehow. Ms. Allen, you made two mistakes. You contradicted yourself, and you gave the enemy some ammunition. You wouldn't necessarily find that out until the trial, when you're on the stand and opposing counsel brings up that statement in cross-examination, asking why you're insisting on seizing this poor woman's baby if you haven't given up on your efforts to conceive."

Grace gulped and said, "What should I have said, then?"

The lawyer wagged his finger. "No, no. I can't tell you what to say. That's coaching the witness." He turned toward Adam. "Mr. Brown, do you have any suggestions?"

Adam thought for a moment. "She could say that we tried for four years before deciding it just wasn't going to happen. That's true, even though we can't help hoping a little bit anyway."

The lawyer did not reply; apparently, the absence of a kazoo blast was sufficient approval. He pointed at Adam next. "Describe the methods you used in your attempt to conceive naturally."

Adam couldn't help staring. "Can they really ask me that?"

"They might. That or something else equally obnoxious. Partly in the hope of throwing you off balance. So — give."

Adam gritted his teeth, then had to relax his jaw to answer. "Once we decided we needed help, we used two positions recommended by our fertility specialist."

The finger stayed pointed at Adam. "Did you get a second opinion?"

"Ah — no." As Adam opened his mouth to say more, out came the kazoo again. BLAT!

"Don't guess at a followup question and then try to answer it." Now it was Grace's turn again. "What percentage of your annual income did you spend on your effort to conceive during those four years?"

Grace was good with numbers, both remembering them and calculating them. "Approximately fifteen percent." How should Adam answer the same question? "I don't know," probably. Except now he did — he trusted Grace. But no, he wasn't supposed to answer out of anything but firsthand knowledge.

Still Grace's turn. "And what is that annual income?"

Adam blinked at Grace's answer. Were they really doing that well?

Back to Adam. "Did you consider spending more?"

Had they? "I don't remember."

No kazoo. Good. Here came the next question, for Grace. And a gleam in the lawyer's eye suggested it would be the nastiest one yet. "When you applied to adopt, did you anticipate that you would be depriving an unwilling mother of her baby?"

Grace's eyes went wide in distress. The lawyer blew a short, somehow softer note on the kazoo. "Of course you didn't, and there's no need to hesitate. You can just say a businesslike 'no.' Remember the plaintiff, the donor, was willing. She's not claiming anyone ambushed her and drugged her. She came in of her own accord, signed the papers voluntarily, lay on a table in a procedure room instead of jumping up and running out."

He looked back and forth between the two of them. "Getting tired? Well, we've only just started. So the night before the real thing, get plenty of rest. Eat hearty, if you can, the morning of the deposition, but nothing that'll upset your stomach. And wear comfortable clothes. We want you focused, not distracted. Focused, but as close to relaxed as possible. If there are activities that help you relax, plan on doing them the night before or even that morning."

Adam started to fight the smile that came, and then decided not to bother. He turned to Grace and winked. "I think we can manage that."

A smile lit her face, and she winked back. The lawyer waited ten whole seconds before interrupting them, kazoo at the ready. "Back to work."

Interlude – Mary and Jack

Jack was changing into his street clothes when the foreman ran up and said, "Hey, hold on. I need you to work the evening shift. You can use the overtime, right?"

The hell of it was, they could. Mary had done a terrific job of calculating and predicting, but there would always be some expense even Mary hadn't thought of, something you only needed once you had kids.

But they'd never have kids if he kept working overtime on the best nights for making them. "I'm sorry, I can't. Not tonight."

The foreman frowned. "I was sure you would. I don't have enough people without you."

"I can find someone else. Collect a favor." He had plenty of favors due him, one way and another.

Of course the foreman had another objection. "I can count on you to do what you say you will, and do it right. That's why you got that raise."

Jack took a deep breath, more for courage than to stay calm. "My wife has to be able to count on me too. And I told her I'd be home tonight."

The foreman didn't quite sneer, which let Jack pretend the man hadn't come close to it. "Well, you make sure you find someone else to help out. And then you can go home to the wife, just like she told you to."

There was no point in answering back. Or in wondering whether the man would hold a grudge. If he did, it wasn't likely he'd do much about it. He couldn't afford to lose as good a worker as Jack. With luck, he'd forget all about it in a week or so, and Jack would make a point of working late the next chance he got.

He finished changing and scurried around to find someone else to work the shift. When he'd managed it, he left, half running, before anything else could go wrong. By the time he'd got halfway to the subway, he was able to put the whole mess out of his mind, mostly, and think instead about what Mary might be wearing – or not wearing — to welcome him home.

Chapter 12

Poloma

With Poloma's promotion had come the suggestion that she routinely monitor the front desk. She had had the necessary software for some time, but the idea had never appealed to her. For a new hire's first few weeks, yes – though if an interaction was proving problematic, there was little she could do, remotely, to correct it. But done as a matter of course, it suggested a certain disrespect of the Bureau's employees. (Was someone higher up the ladder even now monitoring her keystrokes?)

It was also impractical. She could do her own work, or she could pay attention to the images and sounds coming from the lobby. She could hardly do both with optimal attention.

She had gone so far as to write up a memorandum raising these concerns. But she could think of none of her superiors who would have given it any consideration, except as evidence that Poloma had not proved equal to her new position. So she kept the volume from the front desk at a level where any anomalous conversation would get her attention. It did so now. The receptionist was arguing with someone, in a tone that suggested he was rather enjoying himself.

She now wished she had been paying attention earlier. Rather than attempt to reconstruct what she had missed, she buzzed down and asked what difficulty the visitor had posed. The man replied, now sullen at being interrupted, "That woman is here for her visit, the one who's suing us, and she brought some guy with her. I was just telling them he couldn't go in with her."

Poloma frowned. "Some guy? Did she say who he was? Or can you tell anything from their interaction that might provide an indication?"

The man's gaze shifted to the visitors and then back to her. "Well . . . they look kind of alike. And they dress alike."

Poloma went on high alert. The Bureau's interrogatories had asked about family, and the answers revealed the existence of a brother. The rival claimants' family structures could, she had been told, end up playing a role in the litigation. Banning this brother might conceivably boomerang. "Let him go in with her."

The man's face went stubborn. "But —"

"Pick up your handset, please, for what else I have to say." When he had done so, she added, "And make sure someone observes both of them on their way to and from the visiting room. Unobtrusively. Have that person write up notes and send them to me."

The man relaxed and smirked. "Okay, that makes sense. Will do."

Poloma closed the connection and turned her chair away from the screen, leaning back and looking at her framed print of Escher's *Waterfall*. She had made a practical, a defensible, decision, and one at least arguably within her authority. If, coincidentally, she gave the donor some gratification, there was no need to let that trouble her.

What would it be like to have a sibling? Was there as much comfort in it as she sometimes supposed?

She shook her head, a jerky motion as if shaking off flies, and returned to her backlog of work.

The buzz of her phone, ten minutes later, failed to surprise her. Taking time only for one short sigh she picked up the call from the Deputy Director. He was not quite scowling, but his frown conveyed suspicion. "You didn't think it necessary to consult me before approving access by a member of the plaintiff's family?"

Poloma tried to strike the proper balance between indignation and subservience. "If I'd known you wished to be troubled, sir, I certainly would have contacted you. But an opportunity for some unscheduled and informal discovery seemed to me to be worth taking."

The look the DD gave her suggested he was not entirely convinced. Which Poloma would have found offensive, if not for her own sneaking sense that she had acted, at least in part, from other motives.

* * * * *

Toni

When they got to the door, Andy stood aside and made way for Toni with a grin and a grand flourish of his hand. "After you, milady!"

She laughed out loud at grin and gesture both. Could she ever have laughed before, in this room, faced with the evidence of what might be her worst mistake? But she had never before come here, or come to the clinic at all, with someone by her side, let alone one of her closest lifelong allies. She could feel the difference in her posture: back straight, head held high, gaze ready to challenge. Andy looked her up and down as she marched in, and exclaimed, "That's my sis!"

She reached back, grabbed his hand, and pulled him in right after her, until she stood about two feet from the incubator. "Come on! I'll introduce you. Sweetheart, this here's your uncle Andy. He's my twin, except not really. We'll explain it all to you. We'll try to explain everything you ever want to know."

Andy stepped up to the incubator slowly, hands outstretched, as if he might find himself coming up against a force field. When he reached it, he laid his hands on it the way Toni had done on her first visit. "It's warm!"

"Yup. For visitors' benefit, I'd guess, not hers."

"It's a nice touch anyway. And it fits the color. Do you know how many colors they come in?"

Toni raised an eyebrow. "They haven't exactly encouraged me to ask questions."

"And the microphone's where?"

Toni pointed. Andy ahem'd and started talking, in a higher tone and with a sing-song she'd never heard from him. It must be his version of baby talk. "Hey there, little niece. I came with your mama to see you. Well, to say hello, anyway, and to see this cool ride they've given you." Toni snorted a little laugh; Andy threw a grin over his shoulder at her and then turned back toward the incubator, the grin fading from his face. "I really hope I get to meet you, and as soon as you show up. Your mama's fighting for you, sweetheart. She's really something. You'd better appreciate her when you come out." He turned toward Toni. "I wish I could give her something. But I guess she's got everything she needs, for now."

Toni remembered her second visit. "Actually, there is something. You could sing to her."

Andy's eyes lit with humor. "What, incubator karaoke? Where's my screen and music track?"

"We don't need no stinkin' music track. Remember the a capella number we used to do for talent shows?"

Andy blew out a breath. "I guess. It's only been, what, ten years?" He moved into the old position, standing behind her, hands on her shoulders. "Wait a minute. I'm supposed to be able to see over your head. You went and got taller. No fair!"

"Stop whining and come stand next to me." Toni tugged on Andy's arm to bring him around. Arm in arm, they faced the incubator. Andy tapped his feet to set the beat, and they launched into "Do It Again, Like You Used to Do."

They let the last note fade and stayed linked together, Andy's arm warm in hers. Then Andy gently pulled loose and approached the incubator again. "Hey, has anyone told you yet what your mama looks like? Well, to start with, she has pink hair, a lot lighter than that ride of yours, but almost as pretty . . . ."

* * * * *

Adam

Adam and Grace had been visiting for about fifteen minutes. Grace had brought a seasonably appropriate picture book about autumn, illustrated by an artist friend, and they were taking turns reading the text and describing the pictures when a technician came in. They ignored the woman at first, used as they were to people in uniform coming in and out for never-explained purposes; but he stopped near Grace's elbow and peered at Adam. "Sorry to trouble you, but I just wanted to make sure — is this the father?"

Adam let go of the book and stood up. He wasn't sure why — or rather, he hated to acknowledge that he was engaging in something like a dominance contest. But he had been lost in a unique blend of contentment and anticipation, reading with Grace as they would do so often once the baby came home with them, and the interruption made for a jarring transition. He forced himself to speak in a calm, friendly tone, even while noting that he was about three inches taller than the technician. "I'm the father. Why do you ask?"

The other man looked away and then back at him. "I — it's just that we had an unexpected, uh, situation with the other visitor. The mother —" He took a step backward. "That is, the donor came in with her brother, and the DD — the Deputy Director — wasn't pleased about it afterward."

* * * * *

Poloma

Poloma had come to work with a headache and an uneasy stomach. She had mostly managed to ignore both, submerging herself in her work and substituting some crackers and ginger ale for lunch. As if in compensation, her day had been blessedly free from interruptions, but now, with only half an hour to go, her phone loudly demanded her attention, making her head throb and her stomach lurch. She spared a few seconds to curse before answering. The screen showed her special adoptive parents, Adam and Grace. Adam looked uncharacteristically ruffled; Grace was harder to read until she spoke, her voice tight. "We've heard about an incident that we'd like to discuss with you. May we come up?"

Poloma did her best to project a calm and soothing manner much at odds with her newly intensified physical discomfort. "I'll have someone come and escort you."

Grace would, given the opportunity, take charge of what was shaping up to be a confrontation. Poloma headed her off by asking Adam, "Would you tell me what happened, and what about it upset you?"

Adam's face was flushed beneath the brown, though whether from anger or embarrassment was less clear. "One of the technicians questioned me about who I was. Because of the . . . blowback from the donor bringing her brother to her visit."

Grace broke in with, "That was a brief misunderstanding, soon dealt with. But we're concerned about the potential expansion of these visits, and what effect it may have on the baby."

Adam glanced over at Grace as if he hadn't expected that supposedly shared concern. Grace avoided meeting his eyes.

Poloma waved toward the chairs the couple hadn't yet sat in, and sat down herself. "I'm sorry you were taken by surprise. But as far as the effect on the —" Should she say "fetus," as she normally would, or echo Grace's language? "—the baby, hearing more voices will echo the natural environment better. That's why we don't discourage the technicians from speaking when they tend the incubators, though naturally they don't do so during parental visits."

Adam looked at Grace again, then back at Poloma. "I'm wondering more about whether additional visitors, visitors somehow connected to the donor, may start developing an attachment to the baby." He cleared his throat and added, quietly enough that Poloma had to strain to hear the words, "There's going to be enough heartbreak involved here without increasing the number of people who end up suffering it."

Grace started to nod, then stopped. Slowly, as if surprised to be speaking, she said, "I suppose it's up to those people, to decide whether they want to take that risk." And then, with a quick transition to something like her earlier fierceness: "But the donor and her lawyer may try to bootstrap their way from exposing family members to that risk, to the equities tipping more in her and her family's direction."

Poloma managed to suppress a sigh. "I will, in future, keep such possibilities in mind."

Chapter 13

Toni would have liked to bring some wood, a small chunk she could hand-carve, but she knew without asking that wood shavings would have violated the clinic's regulations and given them an excuse to cut off her visits. So she brought a piece she had just finished, a lioness in mid-stride, and tried to describe it to her hidden daughter. "The wood is a dark gold, like honey, and catches the light in almost the same way. It's smooth to the touch, almost as smooth as the fluid you're floating in. But different. Solid. You've never felt anything solid, have you?" She paused and smacked the side of her head. "But of course you have. You'll have felt your own arms and legs. Well, wood is harder than that. Hard like your knuckles, but with nothing softer in the way."

What would her daughter say, if she could reply? "What's honey? Oh, how silly of me! But I called you that because you're such a sweet baby, or you will be, and honey is sweet. And sweet is a sort of taste, one most people like, and even lots of animals. Which humans are too. Which you are. Oh, there's so much you don't know yet! And I can't wait to show you, and teach you. And to see what you love most, of all the new things you're going to find once you come out and join me."

She heard a sniffle behind her and jerked around to see

a woman in uniform — she couldn't remember which uniforms meant what — standing in the doorway. The woman froze. "I'm so sorry! I didn't mean to listen. I was coming to tell you it's almost time to go, and then I couldn't help but hear. That was beautiful." She sniffed again and smiled tearily. "You're going to be such a good mother."

The woman didn't know, then, who Toni was, and what the Bureau thought about what sort of mother Toni was bound to be. It hit her harder than she'd have thought, to have someone here, anyone, think better of her. She bit her lip and then, seeing the other woman start fidgeting nervously, managed to smile in return. "Thank you very much. I hope so."

Heading down the corridor, too few minutes later, Toni played the conversation back in her mind and tried to resist the superstitious urge to see it as some sort of omen. She had to stay clearheaded. Practical. Like Mom. Maybe she should tell Mom about what had happened. Maybe they could even call the woman as a witness . . . .

She was preoccupied enough to overshoot the elevator, realizing it only when she came to an unfamiliar turn in the corridor. As she stopped, about to turn around, she heard an irritated voice coming from the open door just ahead of her. "Well, you'll just have to humor him. We don't have so many approved parents that we can discourage any with backtalk."

Toni's hands slowly clenched into fists. So they had a shortage of people ready to adopt? And yet they'd insisted on assigning Adam and Grace, not to any of the other babies waiting to be born, but to her own?

The caller must have spoken again, because the same voice, now amused, said, "Wouldn't that be gratifying! But even when the residences are ready, there'll be a transition period. Parents already in the system will probably be processed as agreed. Can you imagine the headaches otherwise?" Then a pause, followed by, "As if we don't have enough litigation on our hands! But you might be right."

Toni stumbled backward, then turned around and almost ran for the elevator. When she made it to the ground floor, she walked steadily out of the clinic, across the street, down another street, until she reached a sandwich shop she knew, bound to be empty for another couple of hours before the heading-home rush.

Should she call Mom? But what did she really know? She should have listened longer, tried to learn more.

Instead of calling Mom, she called Poloma.

Toni hadn't really expected the woman would consent to talk, let alone to meet. But here they sat, sharing a cheese and avocado sandwich on wheat bread. Toni slathered her half with brown mustard, ignoring Poloma's twitch of distaste, and poured herself more ice tea from the shared pitcher. She would have thought her stomach would be in knots, but instead she craved food, as if needing to fuel up for future battles.

Apparently, what Toni overheard sounded like a reference to some proposal Poloma had read about. But she'd been told (or so she said) that it was never pursued. Now Poloma was talking more to herself than to Toni, trying to explain this away.

"The idea grew out of some statistics — not even statistics, projections — that proved inaccurate. I would have been notified if the Bureau were changing orientation in such a way. Indeed, I would have noticed if the pool of prospective adoptive parents had shrunk to any significant extent. Whatever this person was talking about —" The stream of words cut off abruptly. Poloma looked up, seeming as startled as if she had been suddenly transported to this spot and found herself mysteriously holding a sandwich. She put it down and drank down half her glass of tea.

Toni swallowed her last bite and washed it down. "That's the question. What else he could have been talking about."

Poloma looked down at her sandwich and back up again, not quite at Toni. "I must admit I can't come up with an alternative explanation. It's possible the proposal I saw has . . . mutated into rumor and gossip." A faint trace of a smile flitted across her face, followed by something more ironic and sadder. "And it's at least as possible that if there are such rumors, I would be considered a less than satisfactory person with whom to discuss them."

How far could Toni push? She might not have another chance, now when Poloma had been knocked at least a little off balance, and before she'd had time to talk herself into ignoring the matter. "Is there any way you could check?" Give her an acceptable reason . . . . "To make sure these rumors get stopped, if there's nothing to them."

Poloma looked down again, talking at the table. "This is not an area within my responsibilities. . . . Although those responsibilities are somewhat broader than they used to be." She went silent, leaving Toni drumming her fingers on her knees below the table.

After an awkward silence that felt longer than it was, Poloma picked up her half sandwich, pulled a paper napkin out of the dispenser, and made a neat package, tucking it in her purse. "I will have to consider what it would be feasible, and appropriate, for me to do. If anything. Now I have to go." She stood up, put on her gray wool sweater, and began moving toward the door.

Toni got up and followed, trying to keep up with Poloma, trying to think what else she could do. What occurred to her was not the brilliant piece of persuasion she needed, or a final tantalizing question to spur Poloma's curiosity. It was, far less satisfying, the decent thing to say. "Thank you for meeting me. I know you didn't have to, and could easily have said no."

Poloma stopped long enough to look back at her and say, "Maybe I should have. I've got to go."

Toni's mom looked as close to goggle-eyed as Toni had ever seen her. "Run that by me again. Slowly. You did what, and who said what?"

Toni had run half the way to her mother's house, with only a short subway ride in the middle to catch her breath. She panted a few more times before repeating herself. "I heard a conversation I wasn't supposed to hear, one that bothered me, so I called Poloma —"

Mom wrinkled up her forehead. "And since when are you on a first name basis with the designated representative of one of our adversaries?"

Toni just barely managed not to roll her eyes. "I told you about what I did about that dream of mine."

"Yes, after the fact. Just like this time. I would appreciate it if you thought about bringing me into the loop a little earlier, should a similar impulse strike you again. In any event, I apparently failed to grasp just how cozy the two of you became on that occasion. Go on."

Toni ground her teeth. "My *point* is, Poloma . . ." She ran through a recap, Mom leaning on her elbows and appearing to memorize every word.

When Toni finally ran down, Mom leaned back in her chair, lower lip pushed out in her somewhat silly-looking "crack legal mind at work" mode. She did not emerge from it until Toni plunked down mugs of tea for both of them, at which point she smiled in thanks and said, "The sixty-four thousand dollar question, as your grandpa used to say, is whether Poloma is going to stay employed, and retain her current assignment relative to the litigation, long enough for us to take advantage of what may be divided sympathies."

"Couldn't we anyway? Whether she comes there as a Bureau representative or not, she'll still be someone who worked there and knows a lot about what the Bureau has been up to."

Mom frowned. "Yes, but if she leaves in disgrace, or under any circumstances that might suggest disaffection, her testimony will be tainted by possible hostile motives. We need to keep her in place if at all possible." She leveled her stern Mom stare at Toni. "Which means no more approaches. No more heart-to-hearts, at least not any you initiate. And if she makes contact, talk to me *first*."

Chapter 14

Toni

Mom stopped filling the teapot with the pot half full. "You're almost done making a crib."

Toni refused to meet Mom's eye. She hadn't intended to tell Mom about the crib. She'd been searching for small talk, and it just slipped out. She'd been too distracted to do much self-promotion or searching for grants and such, and that left her with too much time on her hands, and hands too idle. Working on a crib didn't mean she was assuming success.

Which Mom, of course, assumed she was doing. "Honey, I'll do everything I can. You know that. But we're fighting an uphill battle here."

Now she did more than look Mom in the face, glaring at her, feeling herself slip into angry child mode. "I know, Mom. You've told me that several times. But I have to do *something* to get through these last three weeks. And a crib isn't a waste of time, even if I never get to . . . ." She'd thought she could finish that sentence. But if she did, she would cry, and that was the last thing she wanted to do right now. She shoved back her chair and headed for the door. "I'm going for a walk."

As she opened the door, she was able to glance back without making it obvious. Mom was still sitting at the kitchen table with her hands folded, an image of patience.

Toni growled as she flung the screen door open and rushed down the front steps, almost tripping, just managing to catch herself. She spit out a stream of curses and stomped toward the corner, kicking brown dried leaves and watching the wind blow most of them back in her path as if taunting her.

In a way, walking made things worse. If she hadn't donated, she would be very obviously pregnant by this time, and her body would feel much different. She'd be many pounds heavier, and the baby would be pressing on some organ or other. In fact, she'd probably have to pee right now.

Once she had turned the corner, already slowing down, she called Andy. When he answered, she told him, "I need someone to fume at. Got a minute?"

He looked a little sleepy, but not as if she had actually woken him up. "Sure. Fume away."

"It's Mom. I accidentally told her about the crib, and she started lecturing me about unrealistic expectations. Damn it, am I supposed to make it through all this waiting and suspense without sometimes hoping it's worth it?"

Andy wrinkled up his face in exaggerated nervousness. "Oh, boy. So it's my turn to say the wrong thing and get my head devoured."

She had to smile. "Go on. Take one for the team."

He grinned at her. "Okay, here goes." Then his expression turned sober. "You're already learning what it feels like to be a mom. She's been one for more'n twenty years, so of course she has mom reflexes. She wants to protect you and keep you from ever getting hurt. Even when that backfires and makes you feel bad. It's one of the oldest no-win situations there is."

Toni stopped walking. "Full points for a zinger there, bro."

Andy shrugged. "Just trying to be fair to everyone.

Wow, there's another no-winner."

"I should go back, shouldn't I."

"You could walk a little more first."

She held up her hand in the sign language abbreviation for I Love You. "Thanks, twin."

He blew her a kiss. "Any time."

She hung up and looked around her. She had almost made it halfway around the block. She would keep going and give herself a little extra time before going back. And apologizing, damn it.

* * * * *

Judge Rayner (Alex)

Alex made a brief prayer to any and all divine powers in praise of Fridays. She loved her work, but by Friday, she could see exhaustion lurking beyond the horizon. At least she had no hearings or trials today, just briefs and motions to read and reread, draft orders and opinions to write, and administrative tangles to prune.

She checked her mail for last-minute submissions or other business, and found a message from the Chief Judge to herself and all her colleagues.

Subject: Judge Hilbert's injury

As some of you have heard, Judge Alan Hilbert was involved in a freak three-car collision last night and sustained injuries including a shattered pelvis, a broken leg, and a punctured lung. The cars involved have been removed from service, and their models are being investigated.

Alex stopped, closed her eyes, and waited until the image of her first husband on a stretcher faded enough that she could go on reading.

While no detailed prognosis is yet available, it will be at least six weeks before Judge Hilbert is able to resume his duties. The impact on all your calendars will unfortunately be immediate and severe. Please go over your calendars as soon as possible and send our administrator a list of those hearings and trials that you believe should take precedence and those that may be continued without serious hardship to parties or attorneys.

So much for her morning. Poor Alan. She dashed off a quick message to him, though who knew when he would be able to read it, and then called up her calendar for the next two months.

This one could wait. That one had been waiting far too long already. Lead counsel on this case was pregnant and due in three weeks, but she had plenty of backup —

Oh, SHIT.

The donor/adoptive parent case was set for two and a half weeks from today. When was the baby due to be delivered? Was that date in any of the pleadings or motions or other papers filed so far? Yes, it was. The donor's filing during a tussle over discovery had mentioned it, in the course of arguing that any further stalling on the Bureau's part would be unacceptable.

She found the paper and scanned it for the date, tapping her foot. There it was. Less than four weeks from now, little more than a week after the trial was currently scheduled to conclude. Any substantial delay would land them all in an unparalleled logistical and emotional nightmare.

She called the Chief Judge. "I haven't finished my list yet, but we need to actually talk about one of my cases."

Three meetings, seven exchanges of messages, and six phone calls later, she had negotiated and log rolled and intimidated and promised and begged her way to a schedule that could work, after a fashion. They should finish the trial two days before the delivery date. When the baby came out of that incubator, they would all know where it was going, as long as she neither ate nor slept from the final fall of her gavel until she had a decision ready to issue.

And as long as nothing else went wrong.

* * * * *

Toni

Toni escaped Mom's home with relief. Mom was unrelenting in her intention to cheer Toni up in the wake of the postponed trial, one moment calling it only a short delay, the next pointing out how much more research she would now have time to do, or urging Toni to spend some of the additional time practicing for cross-examination. Toni was ready to burst with all the comebacks she'd suppressed by the time she reached the clinic for her visit and peeled off her jacket and scarf.

She paced back and forth in the waiting room, trying not to look at or eavesdrop on the two women, or rather, the woman and the girl, each sitting with an older companion, each probably about to do what Toni had done. Finally, an attendant took her to the visiting room, where the cheery rose-pink incubator was waiting as usual, and left with a cordial reminder of her available time. She waited until she could no longer hear footsteps before she went to the incubator and laid her cheek on its warm surface. She let herself slump against it, resting, almost dozing, for a few minutes before she straightened up and spoke into the microphone.

"Hello, sweetheart. I hope you're having a nice day in there. I can't feel you moving and guess what you're doing, the way I could if — if I hadn't separated us. But I can imagine it. Right now, I'm imagining you turning somersaults. I've heard little babies like you can do that, and that it feels pretty strange for the mommies.

"We were supposed to have the big trial, where everyone talks in front of the judge, in a couple of weeks. But another judge got hurt, and now they're all having to take on extra cases, so our trial got pushed back a little.

"I'm going to tell you a secret, baby. No one else knows it — not your grandma, not your uncle, not anyone. And I'm going to say it very softly, just in case someone is listening who shouldn't."

She leaned very close, right over the microphone, and whispered.

"I'm glad the trial got delayed. I'm glad things are going to stay just the way they are for even a little while longer."

Toni wiped a couple of tears on her sleeve, blew her nose, and went back to whispering.

"I'm glad, because I'm afraid that when the trial is over, I won't be able to talk to you any more, or to see you, even like this. I'm afraid we're going to lose."

Interlude – Mary and Jack

Jack had never told Mary that he always knew, pretty much to the day, when her period was due. She would get irritated over smaller things, and she ate extra bread and drank her tea with more milk in it. So he noticed, and tried not to show he'd noticed, when she failed to snap at him even though he'd spilled a soft drink on the floor. And drank her tea so watery and clear you could see the pattern inside the cup.

If she, in her turn, noticed that he smiled over his morning coffee and left for work with a bounce in his step, she didn't mention it.

But then he came home from work three days later to find her biting furiously at a piece of toast, and sniffling as she ate. He approached, cautiously, and put his hands on her shoulders. She leaned back into him, and he did his best to massage the tightness out of her. Even though, when she relaxed, her tears fell faster.

Chapter 15

Toni

At least the seasons kept taking their turns, ignoring any upheavals in the busy business of human beings.

Toni had spent the night at her mother's house. Her first look out the window made her wonder for one sleep-fogged moment if she'd been thrown back in time. How many mornings had she pressed her nose against a cold window, eyes and even mouth open wide in delight, watching the first snowfall piling up in the field behind the house?

She heard the clomping of Andy's feet in the hallway before he burst in, grinning, already dressed in parka and boots, gloves and knitted hat. "Time to go out and play! Get bundled up, twin!"

She laughed at the invitation to revisit their childhood, and then swallowed a lump in her throat as she decided to accept it. "Be down in five minutes!"

She made it downstairs in six, and they ran out into the yard. Toni studied the snow on the ground. An inch here, a little more there — not enough for a snowman yet. But plenty for a snowball . . . . She scooped up some snow and shaped it as fast as she could. Andy saw what she was doing, but she had a head start and was able to get her throw off first. The snowball burst against his hat; he yelped and returned fire, hitting her chest. She looked around for cover, found two bushes growing close together, and crouched behind them, scraping up all the snow she could reach into a pile from which to form her ammo. But when she looked up, snowballs ready, Andy was nowhere to be seen —

A snowball hit her from behind, knocking her hat forward. She whirled around, knees hitting the ground, and threw two snowballs at him, one with each hand. She got him on the arm and oh, joy! in the face. He dropped the snowball still in his hand, brushed the snow off his cheeks, and threw his hands up. "Truce!"

She still had three snowballs available. But her nose was cold, and she was starting to crave breakfast. "Truce, if you make the cocoa."

He stood up straight and bowed. "I accept your terms." Then he grinned again. "Race you to the house!"

Toni made the oatmeal while Andy tended to the cocoa. They made enough for Mom, but she hadn't yet appeared before everything was ready. Still asleep, or already out and active? Either way, it left them to a cozy breakfast, only the "twins," and Toni was just as glad. The two of them could avoid talking about anything emotionally charged.

Except her thoughts insisted on wandering in that direction, even as she spooned hot oatmeal and cold milk into her mouth.

She took an almost-gulp of cocoa and sighed. "Wouldn't it be nice if this was life. Snowball fights and then hot food, and no battles any more serious."

Andy finished swallowing a mouthful of oatmeal and nodded. "All conflicts to be settled by snowballs at dawn, with victory breakfast to follow. . . . I wonder how Adam and Grace would take that suggestion."

Toni's mouth twitched toward a smile. "I can't see

Grace going for it. But Adam might be tempted." She felt herself losing the smile. "Of course they wouldn't really. Both of them already love the baby. That's the hell of it."

Andy wiped cocoa from his lips with his sleeve and said, "From what little I've seen of them, they seem like good folks. It's a damn shame we ended up on different sides."

Toni looked at her unfinished oatmeal. It still looked delicious. But her stomach was clenching up again. She shoved it over to Andy. "Here, don't let it go to waste. I'm going to lie back down for a while."

He pulled the bowl toward him, but stood up and came over to pull her out of her chair and give her a bear hug. As she left the kitchen, she heard him sit down again, and his spoon hit the side of the bowl. The homey sound eased, just a little, the ache in her heart.

* * * * *

Adam

It was almost time for Adam and Grace to head to the clinic. The weather would require them to allow more time than usual: their and the other drivers' cars would be slowing down and leaving extra room because of the snow. He had put his jacket on, but Grace was sitting in her favorite armchair, her furniture equivalent of comfort food, looking out the window with her hands in her lap, and had not yet put on her boots or fetched her coat. He fetched it for her. "Here, hon. It's time to get ready."

She turned toward him, and he saw with dismay that she had tears in her eyes. "I don't know if I can. I don't know what to say to her, when we don't know for sure she'll ever be ours."

He dropped the outerwear on the couch, perched on the arm of the chair, and put a hand on hers. "Everything is in our favor. The law, the government, our situation as opposed to the donor's. We just have to stay strong. It won't be much longer."

Grace sighed, long and slow. "If I'd known what it would be like, I think I'd have turned this down. Just waited to get a baby whose mother was like most donors, glad to move on."

Adam shoved aside the vision of a simple, blissful road not taken. "We don't know whether we could have done that. The Bureau, maybe someone higher in the hierarchy than Poloma, might have put us even farther down the list, for being uncooperative. And besides . . . ." He pictured himself in that other reality, looking forward eagerly and happily to the day they would take their child home. A sob took him unawares, and Grace, startled, reached out to grasp his hand. He squeezed hers and went on, his voice husky. "It would have been wonderful, when the time came. For both of us, and I would have cherished your joy as much as my own. But . . . I might not have given the donor's state of mind a thought. Might not have wondered if she grieved her own loss. And I can't, not quite, wish myself that other man, who could take a woman's child that easily."

Grace bent forward to kiss his hand. "I think you would have thought about her, sooner or later. But you might not have wanted to tell me so. And if you had, I might have resented having any unwelcome intrusion on my own feelings. I don't, now. I've learned something. But it's taken a great deal out of me, love. I'm tired, so much of the time. Exhausted." She looked out at the snow again, as if not wanting to see his reaction.

Adam reached down and snagged Grace's boots, handing them to her one at a time. Once she put them on, he got up, picking up her coat and holding it out toward her. She stayed seated for long enough that he believed, and worried over, the fatigue she'd described; but finally she stood, slipped her arms into the coat, and turned to embrace him. "Thank you, my love. You'll get me through. You always get me through."

He hugged her back, but now he was the one reluctant to move. He murmured, "You know what I wish. I wish we could work this out somehow, without going through with the trial. Whatever Poloma and the lawyers say."

Grace's jaw set for a moment. Then she sagged against him, not so much agreeing as surrendering. He held her tight until she steadied, and then moved them toward the door, his arm around her shoulders. He didn't bother going back for his hat.

* * * * *

Toni

In the past, Toni might have accepted a call from Mom with pleasure, or impatience, or the knowledge of guilty secrets. Actual fear, fear of legal setbacks, was an unwelcome change. But while Mom's expression wasn't exactly a smile, it didn't have that careful calm that would have meant serious trouble.

"Mr. Voxsmith called to tell me that Adam and Grace want to talk to you. Just them and just you, with no lawyers present."

"What about?"

Mom gave Toni her use-your-head look. "It would be

uncharacteristic for them to try to intimidate you, and I doubt they have a purely social occasion in mind — though there might be an element of 'let's get to know each other as people rather than adversaries.' This may be some sort of settlement overture."

Though she would rather not admit it, Toni was uneasy at the thought of being alone and face to face with the older couple, who at least seemed so much more self-assured than she felt. "Do you think it's a good idea, meeting them without you there?"

"I think it could be, if you can find out what they want without making any promises or agreeing to anything. Be careful what you say, and if in doubt, don't say anything except 'I'll think about that and get back to you.'"

Adam and Grace had a large, tastefully decorated home. Was it paranoia to think that they'd invited Toni there to see just how much they could offer her daughter? It could just as easily be an attempt at a more relaxing and more private place to talk than, say, a coffee shop.

As if reading her mind, Grace asked, "Can I get you some coffee? Or tea?"

Hyper as she felt, she would probably have twitched, or even yelped, if Grace had somehow hit on offering cocoa. "Tea would be very nice, thanks."

Adam, sitting on a gray leather couch, leaned forward as Grace headed off to the kitchen. "I'd bet you're wondering why we asked you here. Would you believe we're not sure ourselves?"

Toni forced a chuckle. "That makes three of us, then."

Adam stood up to take two cups from Grace as she walked back in, keeping one and handing Toni the other.

"Please, won't you sit down? Grace, I was just telling Toni that we didn't have a clear agenda for this visit."

Grace hadn't brought a cup for herself, nor was there one on any nearby surface. Was she too tense, or too defensive, to drink anything? She certainly seemed less relaxed than her husband. Sitting close beside him and folding her empty hands, she said, "We did think that if there was any way out of, or around, the legal process we seem to be trapped in, we might be able to figure it out if we came together. Or rather, we probably wouldn't be able to figure it out separately, so we might as well try something else."

Toni gazed into her cup as if there were actual tea leaves there and she could find an answer in them. Without looking up, she said, "I'm sorry, but I still want to be my baby's mother."

"But —" Whatever Grace was going to say, and Toni had a pretty good guess about what it was, she stopped after that single word. Toni did look up then, to see Adam's hand covering Grace's as if it was a more gentle way to silence her than covering her mouth.

Toni sighed. "But I gave her up. And then the Bureau got you involved, and you had every right to start thinking of her as yours."

Adam cleared his throat. "Actually, Poloma did warn us about what we were getting into. So we knew it might not be smooth sailing."

That was new information, and Mom would be interested to hear it. It might even make some sort of difference legally. Meanwhile, Grace added, "Smooth sailing. No, hardly that. More like choppy seas and plenty of seasickness."

Toni tried a sip of her tea, found it not as hot as she

liked, and drank some anyway. "And here we are, all wanting to be the baby's parents, and what can we do short of fighting it out in court?"

Grace bit her lip. "I was hoping one of us could think of something new." She gave a bitter little laugh. "We could always get married. That'd simplify things."

Toni snorted. "Once, I'd have said we should do it just to see Poloma's face. But she's changed. Or maybe I'm learning to understand her better."

No one spoke for close to a minute, as Adam and Grace looked at each other and Toni tried not to look at either. Then Adam said slowly, "Maybe there's a way to come close to that. Not in how we relate to each other, but in relation to the baby. We could, I don't know, ask the court to let all three of us adopt her. Toni — if I may call you Toni —"

Toni waved acceptance.

"— Toni's already claiming the prohibition against donors adopting is overbroad and therefore unconstitutional. And plural marriage has been declared a protected right. So why not multiple adoption?"

She hadn't wanted to accept any settlement that would make Adam and Grace the parents and leave her with some lesser role. But having them all be parents together . . . that was different. And — Toni felt a smile steal across her face. "My mother would love arguing that."

Grace's face lit up. "Since you're already making a related argument, you might be able to amend your complaint to seek joint adoption, even as late as this." She paused. "But we need to talk about how this would work. Would we necessarily live together? And if you bring someone new into your life, would we have any say about the baby spending time around that person?"

Toni fought to keep from sliding into glare-at-the-grownups mode. It took about ten seconds, but then she managed to say, "That's a reasonable question, or set of questions. But we don't know enough yet to answer them, not completely. Everything would be simpler if we lived in the same place, but we don't know whether we could learn to get along, living together. And if we didn't live together . . . ." She almost trailed off, but shifted to thinking out loud. "I guess what we need to decide is, in case living together doesn't work, are you willing to have the baby spend part of the time with me? And . . . if not, how much am I willing to be apart from her?"

And there was no way they were going to decide all that on the spot. She stood up, ready to say as much. Adam stood up at the same time, a pleading look in his eyes, and said, "It's sunny out, and not too cold. There's a park down the street, and I've often found that a walk through it helps to clear my head. If you're willing, you could head there for a bit, and Grace and I can talk things over here." He glanced over at Grace, who gave a little nod, her body language not as tight as when Toni arrived. "Then we can see if we're close to figuring something out."

Toni needed to grab her coat and scarf, either way. As she did, she imagined giving up on this new effort and just slugging it out, and would have liked somewhere to spit out the sour taste in her mouth. Maybe once she got outside. "I'll see you in about half an hour, then."

Chilly wind, unruly, tugging at her scarf – welcome after the tidiness of Adam's and Grace's house. Snow sparkling in the sunlight; firm brick path under her feet. She walked through the park, following forks in the path this way and that, until she reached a fountain turned off for the winter, an abstract sculpture somehow suggesting carefree play, snow resting on the upper planes of it. It made her itch to be in her studio, with her mind on shaping wood and the smell of sawdust all around. But first she had to figure out what sort of future she could live with, one that Adam and Grace would accept.

She brushed snow off a bench and sat, the concrete not as cold as metal would have been. What would it be like, to live in her little house without her daughter? How different would it be than the way she was living now? How much worse – or maybe, how much better, how much easier, if she knew they'd be reunited in a few days' time.

They were going to try living together, it sounded like, unless Grace had talked herself out of it by now. Which might not work. And that wouldn't be so different from what happened when parents got divorced, or just separated. They were still parents. They made it work. And if they were good people, they put up with whatever inconvenience and pain came with that, to keep their children safe and secure and happy.

The thought reminded her of the call she had finally made to her father. He had been so glad to hear from her, and behind it, sad and sorry that she hadn't thought of telling him sooner. He had offered her any help he could give, to her or her daughter, now and in the future, and has asked her to come to lunch. He would make her favorite grilled cheese sandwich, cheddar on pumpernickel – "if you still like it." So much catching up they could do, if she chose to do it.

She had lost any anger at him somewhere along the way. But she could do better than Dad had done, and maybe even as well as Mom had, in her own very different way.

She stood up, blew a kiss to the fountain – would her

daughter play on it, splash in the water around it, blow kisses to it? Time to get back to the house and make sure she'd be there to see it. Her feet hit the path in a hard fast rhythm as she went.

While Toni's walk had energized her, Adam and Grace looked weary, as if whatever talking they'd done had worn them down. They looked up at her, startled, as she blew in. She took advantage of the moment before either Adam or Grace could recover and take back the initiative. "I realized something, out there in your wonderful park . . . ."

She'd said her piece, and now she had to wait and see if she'd said enough.

Grace had reached for Adam's hand while Toni talked. They seemed so united, whatever disagreements they might or might not have had. Toni pushed down a surge of envy. Maybe she'd have that someday, or maybe not. For now, her daughter came first.

Grace sat up straighter. It seemed she would be the one to speak for them, and Toni had to force herself to keep breathing. Grace cleared her throat and said, "We'll have to talk to Mr. Voxsmith about what our role should be, if any, in this change of approach."

Toni looked at the couple and gasped in relief. "So you're ready to try it?"

Adam and Grace relaxed against each other and nodded in near-unison. Toni stood up. "Then let's go talk to the lawyers."

After they all gathered at Mom's house, Mom and Mr. Voxsmith bundled up and went for a walk to talk through the legal ins and outs. When they returned, Mom headed straight to her stove, stirring spices into cider. The rich, festive smell filled the kitchen, as if to show they had something to celebrate.

Pouring the cider into mugs and putting out a platter of carrot muffins, Mom waited for them all to be seated around the table and then proposed a toast. "To the little girl waiting for her family. May she realize how lucky she is."

Toni looked up to see satisfaction in Mom's eyes. She gritted her teeth to hold back tears and lifted her mug in Adam and Grace's direction. "And to all those who leave themselves open to change."

The cider was not all that warmed her as she drank it down.

That left one enormous issue hanging. If this change in strategy delayed the trial, as Mom had warned her was likely, where would the baby live until the trial was over? Would Toni move in with Adam and Grace? There was certainly no room for them to move in with her.

As soon as she raised the subject, Mr. Voxsmith gave her a surprising wink and said, "As you know, my clients are people of some means. How would you like a vacation in a house in the country, with room for a small studio — and for a large nursery?"

Chapter 16

Judge Rayner (Alex)

Alex let out a long, low whistle. Her husband Harold, his easel facing the snow and ice outside, paused with brush raised and turned toward her. "What now?"

Alex looked up at him, mouth twitching. "The parties in the Greene case have decided to upturn everything by joining forces."

Harold scrunched up his forehead. "You mean they're settling?"

Alex laughed. "Oh, no. That would be too uneventful. No, they've both moved to amend their pleadings. The plaintiff is still asking me to hold that a donor has a right to withdraw consent until after delivery, but only as a conditional alternative stance. She's focusing on her claim that the policy flatly prohibiting donors from adopting is without basis in the enabling statute and/or unconstitutional." She teased Harold by waiting a few seconds before going on. "And both she and the adoptive parents are seeking to add a claim for a declaratory judgment that three-parent adoptions outside of plural marriage are legal and should not be treated with any disfavor."

Harold put down his brush to rub his hands together. "O tidings of great joy! That's got to be sending the Bureau into conniptions."

"Indeed. Their response came so quickly that they can't

have had much time to edit it. Unless the Bureau's lawyer gave sober thought to the matter and decided it would be a good idea to call opposing parties and opposing counsel names." She put her tablet down and came over to look at Harold's painting. "That's quite good, love."

He gave her a quick kiss on the cheek. "Yes, it is, isn't it? Thanks. When it's finished, I thought you might want it on the wall of your chambers for a while. . . . What about the schedule? Wouldn't this sort of shift require more preparation time or more discovery or both?"

Alex grimaced. "Aye, there's the rub. Without the Bureau's consent, I don't think I could grant these motions without a continuance to a date past the delivery. And what with our overcrowded schedules, we may have a longer delay than otherwise necessary. Where would that put the baby, literally?"

Harold had resumed his painting, but spoke over his shoulder. "Does the Bureau's response say anything about that?"

Alex scrolled up and down to be sure she hadn't missed something. "Only that they needn't address it since these motions are so out of order that I couldn't possibly grant them. Ha. But that if I do, they'll have a supplemental filing on that subject."

"Playing coy, are they?"

Alex shook her head. "You'd think their lawyer didn't know me. . . . I'm going to request briefing on the subject from all parties. This should get interesting."

Alex double-checked her research, checked the parties' filings one more time for any overlooked passages, and started dictating.

"This Court, having reviewed the submissions of the parties and considered those submissions and all matters pertaining thereto, now rules as follows.

"The motions to amend filed by plaintiff and by defendant adoptive parents raise new and complex legal issues. If granted, these motions may also necessitate additional discovery and/or witness preparation.

"Last-minute amendments are generally disfavored. However, settlements and partial settlements are generally favored. It is the opinion of this Court that the proposed amendments constitute a partial settlement.

"Granting these motions is feasible only if a continuance may reasonably be granted under the unusual factual conditions giving rise to this litigation. All parties have, at this Court's request, submitted proposals as to how the fetus, soon to be the infant, at the center of this case could be suitably cared for should a continuance issue. The joint proposal of plaintiff and of defendant adoptive parents would ensure that the infant would be in the custody of the two adults approved as adoptive parents in general and as this child's parents in particular, at a location under their control, as well as the only other adult with an asserted claim to parenthood of the child. Defendant Bureau of Reproductive Safety, on the other hand, objects to allowing the biological mother any role and instead proposes that it retain custody after the fetus is delivered, despite the fact that its clinic facilities are not designed for care of infants post-delivery. The Bureau's general claims to a capacity for such care are at once unconvincing and disturbing, for the statutes and regulations defining the Bureau's mission and covering its operations make no provision for any such facilities.

"This Court therefore grants plaintiff's and defendant

adoptive parents' motions to amend. This Court further adopts these parties' joint proposal as an order of this Court, here incorporated by reference. Any party desiring additional discovery will submit proposed discovery schedules and justifications therefor within the next five days. A discovery schedule, if required, and trial date will be set by further order.

"SO ORDERED."

* * * * *

Adam

It was still an unsettling novelty for Adam to receive a call from Toni. But given how soon they would actually be living together, he had better get used to this minor intimacy.

After a brief exchange of stilted pleasantries, Toni got to the point. "We'll have the baby with us for weeks before the trial even starts, and then for at least a little while before the judge issues her order. We'll need a name for her. And —" Her voice faltered. "— If the judge doesn't grant our request, if we don't all end up her parents, we should make the transition as easy for her as possible. So we should give her a name we're all willing to keep calling her."

Adam and Grace had been talking about this very issue. He should have been the one to reach out, to make this call. But at least he could be forthcoming now. "We've been talking about names. I have a few to run by you. Ready?"

Toni relaxed, and her eyes lit up in anticipation. "Very! I have some too, but let's see how I like yours first."

Adam fetched his list, not trusting his memory. "We came up with four. Two of them — Adia and Jessie — mean 'gift.' The other two — Kyra and Helen — mean 'sun' or 'shining light'. But please tell me yours."

Toni was beaming now. He'd barely seen her smile at all, before. "I had Jessie too! And a few others — like Amber, maybe because its color and feel remind me of some of my favorite woods to work with, and Katy, just because it sounds happy." She paused, pondering. "I do like Kyra, though — the sound and what it means. Though she'd have to keep spelling it for people."

"Let's get Grace in on this."

He fetched her over and summed up their progress thus far. She said nothing at first, but picked up a pen and a scrap of paper and wrote, in her most flowing script, Jessica Kyra, holding it up first to him and then to Toni on the phone. "Lovely, don't you think?"

Adam took her hand, kissed it, then kissed the paper. Turning his attention, a little belatedly, back to the phone, he saw Toni sigh before she shook it off and said, "Yes, it's beautiful. And our girl has a name."

* * * * *

Toni

The judge had accepted their proposal, and all the necessary rescheduling had happened. So it was three weeks until the trial.

It was two days until Toni's baby girl would come out into the light.

Toni spent most of her time jittering around her house. Occasionally she would visit Mom and fidget there, until Mom's eyebrows got high enough and her jaw tight enough that Toni figured it was time to give Mom a break. Today, she had only been there an hour when Mom grabbed her hands, pulled her to the kitchen table, and sat her down, still holding on. "Honey, I know it's hard to calm down. But I have something to say that might help a little."

Toni heaved a sigh. "Why not? Go for it."

Mom smiled wryly at the permission. "You've got two main sources of tension right now, the delivery and the trial. I won't tell you to relax and trust the clinic personnel, even though you almost certainly can. But I will ask you to leave the worrying over the trial to me and Mr. Voxsmith. We've got it covered. And you've done your homework. All you need to do is show up when I tell you to — which doesn't have to be every day, not with a judge, especially this judge, trying the case and no jury to impress — and testify the way you have when we've practiced. Soon you'll be bringing your baby, well, not exactly home, but something close to it. Look forward to that. And when she arrives, just focus on learning what it's like to be a mother."

Toni forced something close to a chuckle. "And I'm not supposed to be nervous about that?"

Mom laughed outright. "Touché. I was in labor with Andy for almost two days, and I firmly believe the main reason was how terrified I was to have a baby to look after. But your unusual situation may actually be a help. You'll have Adam and Grace there, maybe just as inexperienced, but in the same emotional boat. You can give each other moral support and learn together."

Toni blinked away sudden tears and said hoarsely, "I wish you were going to have more time to be there too."

Mom lifted her eyebrows in surprise. "But I will be, quite a bit — if you want me there. I can work anywhere." She paused and gazed thoughtfully at the tablecloth. "Though we will need to tread a little carefully, given my dual role. I can handle that. I can make a point of offering as much help — with the baby, that is — to Adam and Grace as to you. We can play it by ear whether I have any calls or meetings with Voxsmith from their house."

Toni gripped Mom's hands tight. "Will you be there with me at the clinic, for the delivery?"

Mom got her unstoppable-attorney expression. "That would be a very good idea. Though I may be waiting in the wings, as it were, near enough to scotch any attempt at funny business, but leaving the delivery room to you and Adam and Grace — if the Bureau allows you in. I'm still trying to get a straight answer on that."

Toni bit her lip hard enough to hurt. "If they won't let me be in there, then you have to be there, or at least observing. I don't trust the Bureau not to pull something — I don't know what, but something."

"Agreed. Now let me get you something hot to drink and give you a neck rub. I'm not as expert as Andy, but I believe I'll be better than nothing."

* * * * *

Adam

As he and Grace donned their scrubs in the dimly lit room, Adam quietly gave thanks that the clinic had longstanding procedures for deliveries. If adoptive parents were not routinely allowed to be present when the technicians opened the incubator and brought the baby out, he suspected he and Grace would have been kept at a distance. As for Toni, it had taken a judge's order to get her in the door. She had been waiting in the delivery room when he and Grace arrived, her face a mask of tension. She kept sending messages, probably to her mother-lawyer waiting somewhere nearby.

He had feared Grace would be a nervous wreck, but she was glowing, somewhere between joyful and serene. He, on the other hand, was sweating through the clothes under the scrubs.

He had half expected Poloma to be here with them, seeing to fruition what she had begun. But of course this scene, with its trio of parents, was not what she had intended or worked for. And yet he and Grace owed her so much, for choosing them out of all the couples she could have picked. If she could be comfortable in Toni's presence, they could invite her to visit. How would she cope with holding a baby? Maybe she'd surprise him and be a natural at it —

The door opened and a beaming technician wearing smock and mask wheeled in the incubator. This man, at least, did not appear to care how many parents this baby would have, or how unsettled their status might be, or how much they might have twisted the Bureau's tail. The woman and man who followed him into the room, similarly attired, one pushing a table with a heat lamp attached and the other a cart full of supplies, were more businesslike in demeanor. The first technician parked the incubator in the middle of the room, inside a circle inscribed on the floor, and came toward them. "Welcome, welcome! Isn't it a lovely day to come into the world? Let's get you situated. There are three of you, right? You two can stand together here, if you like, and you, miss —" He waved Toni over. "You can stand there." He pushed a button on a remote control, and a panel slid open on the ceiling, revealing a screen. "That'll give all of you the same view the technicians have. So you can see your baby just as soon as they do, on a screen at least. It's far enough up that the brightness of it won't bother the baby."

He looked at the three of them, nodded in satisfaction at their placement, and went back to the middle of the room. There was no more transition or ceremony than that; the technicians set to work.

First order of business was to don elbow-length gloves and then put their hands under a glowing purple antimicrobial field. After that, Adam couldn't see who was doing what, but the top of the incubator opened, opened out, opened like a flower. The segments, folded back, glowed a soft pink like sunlit petals. And into the space left by that unfolding, something was rising.

From Grace came a long, soft "Ohhhh." Adam looked at her, to see her looking up; following her gaze, he saw on the screen, between the petals, a flexible, translucent bag, moving in irregular ripples. Moving with the motion of what was inside.

Two sets of hands slowly unsealed one side of the bag. The third technician, the friendly one, reached inside. He did nothing sudden; he laid his hands gently on the baby's shoulders, saying, "Good morning, sweetheart! Ready to come out and play?" Then he shifted his hands, lifting her up a few inches, hands dripping amniotic fluid. One of the other techs grasped and lifted the placenta, while the third slid the bag out of the way.

Adam looked down, toward the incubator and technicians – and his daughter.

The cord hung in tight loops between placenta and baby, the baby squirming, wriggling, stretching her red-purple limbs this way and that in the suddenly empty space around her. Adam held his breath, waiting for the baby to breathe. The third technician massaged her tiny chest, pushing, a gentler version of the final contraction that would have thrust her out of the womb.

The baby breathed.

As they had already been told, their daughter had no need to cry. The dim lighting, the less stressful procedure, the soothing voice and touch, made for a transition not quite as gradual as a water birth, but not unlike it. The friendly technician was cradling the baby in his arms now, while the other two wiped her with heated cloths. At some point he realized that cord and placenta were gone, the blood from the cord to be stored against any future need. One of the techs wrapped the baby in a pale yellow blanket that looked as soft as sunlight. The light in the room was slowly growing brighter.

The friendly technician turned to face them. He spoke in something like a chant, saying what he must have said many times before. "Parents, come meet your daughter!"

Grace grabbed Adam's hand and clasped it so tight that her grip almost hurt. As they came forward, out of the corner of his eye, Adam saw Toni moving to the center as well, her eyes enormous, mouth open, her face the picture of amazement. The friendly technician was holding the baby now, cooing to her, patting her cheek; she was looking up at him — perhaps thinking he was her father? He might have spoken to her any number of times, through the microphone. Adam had fully intended to let Grace go first, but now he surged ahead and reached out. The technician showed no surprise, but simply handed him the bundle, the baby, the new center of the universe. Adam looked down into her eyes — gray-blue for now, skin already fading to pink. He spoke to her, finally, face to face. "Remember me, sweetheart? It's Daddy."

The baby was looking at him. She was seeing him.

Grace made a faint mewing sound. He had kept her waiting long enough, too long. He held the baby out for her to take. "And here's Mommy."

Grace received the baby, tears running down her face. Toni came close, eyes wary now, probably wondering whether they were going to revert, whether the sight of the baby would turn the recent allies back into enemies.

She might be right.

Toni waited, biting her lip. As Grace murmured loving words to the baby, Toni whispered to Grace, "It's hard, but I'll try to be patient. Please don't make me wait too long."

Grace looked up suddenly as if startled and said to Toni, "I'm sorry. I forgot. I forgot everything else."

Toni said softly, "I understand. Of course I do."

Grace took a deep breath, kissed the baby's forehead, and stretched out her arms just far enough for Toni to take the baby in her own. Toni held her awkwardly at first, then more firmly and naturally. She too kissed the baby's forehead and murmured, so softly Adam could barely hear it, "Welcome back, my darling, my own. I'm so sorry I left you here, but now we're together. You're my beautiful darling girl, and Mommy's here again." She looked up and saw Adam watching and listening. She stiffened for a moment. Then she held the baby up facing Adam and Grace, and said more loudly, "And there's your other mommy and your daddy. You're a very lucky baby. You have three parents who want to love you and take care of you. And one of your grandmas is going to make sure we get to do it."

Grace stepped closer again, pulling Adam with her. "Want to know your name, sweetheart? It's Jessica Kyra. Or you can be Ky, or Jessie."

Adam was finding it a little hard to breathe. "You can be whatever you want to be."

Then Toni. "You can learn things, and make things, and find things, and find things out. We'll help you, or you can tell us to let you do things for yourself."

Grace started to say something and then stopped short. One of the technicians had made some sort of noise, working at the incubator. They were cleaning it, getting ready to store it until the next embryo or fetus came along. Toni followed her gaze and grimaced in distaste before she looked back down at the baby and smoothed out her expression. "But first, we'll take you home. It's time to go home."

Out of the stacks of baby clothes they had accumulated, they had brought soft fleecy coveralls in three different sizes, to be sure that one would fit the baby, and knitted caps for warmth. All three of them had brought baby slings.

A nurse appeared and seemed inclined to dress the baby. Toni and Grace clearly considered objecting; Adam pulled them aside and whispered, "Let's pick our battles. We can let this happen, and no harm done." And the nurse handled the baby with gentle expertise, as the three of them got out of their scrubs, figured out the slings, and put them on.

Earlier, they had resorted to a quick round of rock-paper-scissors to decide who would carry the baby first. Adam pushed aside the feeling that he had cheated Toni by winning. It might be better, defuse any revived tension between the two women, if neither was first in possession. He let the nurse ease the baby into his sling. Toni, taller than Grace, laid his coat over his shoulders; Grace fastened the top button, turning it into an impromptu cloak. The sling bore the baby's weight, letting Adam use his hands to put on his hat. Both women were bundled up by now. They were all ready to go.

He saw on their faces the same sudden fear that it would all be a trick, that the clinic would never let them leave. He barely managed a quick smile and wave to the nurse and the technicians before he flung open the door of the delivery room and led the way out, Toni and Grace flanking him right behind.

As they neared the reception desk, the clerk got up and moved toward them. "You have some papers to fill out before you go —"

Adam stared her down. "You know who we are. You know where we'll be. Send the paperwork to our lawyers. We're out of here." He led his little phalanx past the desk and up to the exit. Toni and Grace drew even with him and then ahead, to open and hold the door; and they were out, out in the fresh cold air, and heading to the car.

Interlude – Mary and Jack

Mary came in, sat down next to Jack, checked what show he was watching, and muted it. He turned toward her and waited.

"I'm late again."

He put his arm around her and tipped her against his shoulder. "I know."

Mary sighed. "I didn't want you to feel like you had to pretend not to notice. We'll hope together, this time. And if . . . if it doesn't work out, we'll be disappointed together."

He kissed her cheek. "Thank you. It's better this way."

She kissed him back, on the mouth, and then sat up straighter. "I'm going to pray. I know you probably won't, and that's okay."

The next couple of weeks weren't quite like anything Jack had seen before. Mary didn't act the way she did before her period, or the way she acted during it — or the way she acted the rest of the time. Did the differences mean pregnancy, or just her hope that she was pregnant? He tried not to wonder too much.

The morning she first threw up, he held her head, rubbed her back, and couldn't stop himself from grinning from ear to ear. Once he'd handed her a washcloth to wipe her mouth, flushed the toilet for her, and helped her up from the floor, he asked, "When will you go for a test?"

Mary clutched his hand tight. "Not until I know anyway. Not until I'm sure."

Chapter 17

Toni

Mom had been right. It was easier this way.

If Toni had kept the baby, or the Bureau had let her take the baby back, the two of them would be alone now, unless she had moved into Mom's house. In which case she and Mom would have driven each other crazy in no time.

This way, she had two people older — but not too much older — and somewhat steadier than she was, also good at working together, to step in whenever she got too frazzled. True, they tended to step in a little more often than that, especially Grace. But so far, Adam had defused any building tension, at least enough that Toni had time to bite her tongue. And miraculously, while none of them was getting enough sleep, none of them was horrendously sleep-deprived either.

A couple of Adam's and Grace's relatives had shown up as well. Adam's dad was a shorter version of Adam, a slightly stooped sweetheart of a man, like a particularly appealing gnome. And Grace's mother had flown in — a mixed blessing, at least for Grace, given that she cried easily and carried on about how she'd almost given up hope of a grandchild.

Toni's own father had actually dropped by a couple of times, tentative, almost tiptoeing, as if the days when he lived in a family with babies were too long ago to have left a trace. And he always made sure Mom wasn't expected before he came over.

Mom spent a good deal of time visiting, sometimes helping with the essential baby chores, more often either playing with the baby or working on her laptop. She never volunteered updates about the pretrial maneuvering, and when asked, kept those updates short and bland. For hours at a time, Toni was able to forget — almost forget — that the trial was coming so soon. Though it would have been easier if this improvised living arrangement were not a constant background reminder.

But there was Jessica Kyra. Little Jessie. Who still had no last name, and wouldn't have one until some time after the trial was over. Jessie, who loved to be carried — who, in fact, hated to be put down, or even to be held by someone sitting down. Was it a reaction to all those months in the incubator? Or would she have demanded constant contact and constant motion anyway? In any case, the three and sometimes four of them — no, make that five, with Andy's occasional visits — were a baby-carrying tag team.

Speaking of Andy! She would know that knock anywhere. Adam was carrying the baby through the house, Grace bagging up used diapers, Mom frowning (what about?) at her tablet. That left Toni, currently minding a pot on the stove, to answer the door before the pot boiled over. She stepped quickly out of the way as Andy blew in, covered in snow and shedding the stuff in all directions. She darted in once he was mostly snow-free to give him a quick hug before returning to the stove. Andy followed her, sniffing. "What's that? Smells too good to be something you made."

She cuffed his head lightly and took a taste, smacking her lips in over-the-top enjoyment. "It's a joint production.

Butternut squash stew. Stay long enough, be good, take Jessie for a while, and you might get some."

Andy affected confusion. "Jessie?? Oh, you mean Kyra, queen of my heart, empress in training! I ask you, what sort of a name is Jessie for an empress? At least give her the dignity of 'Jessica,' you prole, you."

Adam came in on cue, bouncing the baby in front of him, to the tune of her delighted giggles. "Did I hear some humble visitor request an audience with the empress? What do you say, Your Grace? Will you grant the petition?" He held his ear close to her lips; she blew a spit bubble in his direction. "I believe that was a gracious assent! Here you go."

Andy took the baby in the crook of his left arm and made trilling motions with his right hand. The baby followed the motion of his fingers, then yawned and closed her eyes. Toni snorted. "No fair, Your Grace! You should keep him on his toes, not let him off the hook by falling asleep."

Mom threw in her two cents from the table of the breakfast nook. "I protest at this reversion to undesirable and outmoded power norms." She looked up at Grace's emergence from the baby's room. "Grace, honey, lead the revolution, please. I'm too busy."

Grace sat down across from Mom, her serious expression an implicit rebuke to the clowning all around her. "Actually, I was hoping to hear more about what you're busy with."

Toni moved closer to Andy and gently stroked Jessie's hair to calm herself. Mom turned her laptop to show Grace the screen. "I'm responding to the Bureau's witness list, in particular their list of experts. They're really pulling out the stops, or perhaps I should say scraping the bottom of the proverbial barrel."

Grace sighed. "I won't ask for details. Where is Mr. Voxsmith in all this?"

Mom gave Grace her battle-grin. "We've divided things up so we both get juicy targets, and are cross-referencing each other's papers."

Jessie added her opinion by spitting up on Andy's sleeve. Andy jumped; Toni laughed and took the baby. "The sonic cleaner is on the bathroom counter." Andy blew a kiss to the baby and headed to the bathroom.

Mom finished typing something and closed her laptop. "I'll take a breather before I proofread. Toni, do you feel like getting some fresh air?"

Adam caught Grace's eye; some signal passed between them, and he faced Mom, saying, "You don't have to go out in the cold to get a little privacy. Andy's dying to show the baby how to vaporize alien invaders, a skill any empress may need. We can all spend some quality time playing video games."

Mom gave him her warmest smile. "That's kind of you. Toni, which would you prefer, bracing winter breezes or hot cocoa indoors?"

Toni glanced out the window at the blue-tinted scene. "I believe I'm short of my minimum daily requirement of cocoa. Thank you, Adam, Grace. Go show Andy he's got a lot to learn about defending the planet."

Mom waited to hear the opening music of the video game before leaning the doorway between the rooms almost shut and foraging in the fridge for milk. Toni, more familiar with the layout, produced the cocoa powder, handed it to Mom, and sat down, feeling sleepy again, to enjoy the luxury of being served. Mom got to work at the stove.

It seemed an instant later that Mom set a steaming mug in front of Toni and tapped her on the shoulder to wake her up. Toni jumped a little, managing not to spill the cocoa, and smiled sheepishly. "Caught me napping, literally. Thanks."

Mom sat down, took a cautious sip from her own mug, and looked Toni in the eye. "How's this arrangement working out?"

"Pretty well, considering. Grace and I are a ways from being soul mates, but she and Adam are both great with Jessie. And yeah, this is a good deal easier than going straight from living alone to being a single mom, even a single mom with a lovely, supportive family." She drank some cocoa and then got to the hard part. "This isn't really answering your question, but I'm terrified. The contrast between the way things are now and what might happen — well, actually, I guess part of what's helpful about living here, with them, is that I have to hold myself together. If I were on my own with nothing but stuffed animals watching, it'd be hard not to freak out, even with the baby to look after."

Mom suddenly had a twinkle in her eye. "That reminds me." She reached for her large boxy briefcase, rummaged around in it, and brought out something soft and coiled, stretching it out. "Jessie's first stuffed buddy! . . . Or is it? Did someone else beat me to it?"

Toni blinked away tears, the better to admire the green and orange caterpillar. "No, you're the first. So it's a family tradition now! Let's go find Jessie, and you can give it to her."

Mom stood up and held the toy toward Toni. "Want to give it a squeeze first?"

Toni studied her face for any hint of mockery. She found a smile, but one of loving understanding. She took the caterpillar, snuggled it up against her face, handed it back, and gave Mom a hug of her own before following her toward the living room.

* * * * *

Poloma

Poloma had expected, ever since her promotion, that she would be called upon to appear in court representing the Bureau. Had she ever been told as much? She thought so, but she hadn't made any contemporaneous memo of the relevant discussions.

As her view of the donor had moderated, and her concerns about undisclosed information had increased, what had been nerves about adequately representing the Bureau had become something more complicated. And queasier. So she should have been relieved, as well as surprised, when the latest DD memo — to a host of recipients, not to her alone — mentioned the colleague who would be taking on that responsibility, with no hint that Poloma had previously borne it.

What she felt, mostly, was indignation at being shunted aside, along with a tinge of regret at not seeing Judge Rayner in action on a case Poloma actually understood. And then, moments later, some apprehension about whether this meant she would be, or had been, demoted. Not that the duties that had come with her new position were so appealing, but the salary had finally kicked in, and she had been so imprudent as to make some plans for spending it. There was a puzzle convention she had never attended, held at a resort previously beyond her means . . . .

Why the change? It could have resulted from the

complaints the DD had passed on to her. Or it might be due to her role in choosing Adam and Grace as the adoptive parents. Their unexpected change of course had, of course, infuriated and dismayed those above her in the hierarchy. Poloma could well be tainted by association.

And she had not even done what she had hinted she might do, or at least thought of doing – checking on the phone call Toni had heard. Toni had confided in her, and she had done nothing. It would have been risky before, but so much more now, when she might already be under suspicion.

She tried to concentrate on her work, without knowing how much of it remained her work, for the rest of the day, awaiting clarification of her status. None came by quitting time. She spent the trip home wondering why, if she had lost the confidence of her superiors, she would be left in place.

The only answer that came to her had a bitter taste. Her work on the case, with its avalanche of confidential files, might be considered as placing her in a position to strike back, were she dislodged. Undoing her promotion might be viewed as imprudent. The fact that she would never consider making use of such information for personal gain, or personal revenge, might be entirely outside the world view of whoever had made this decision.

She almost detoured to a pub for a beer, but she suspected her roiling emotions would show in her face or her body language. Instead, she went home, grabbed the last bottle of her favorite brew, and settled down to brood in privacy.

Half a bottle later, she had resolved only one of the tangle of worries and quandaries facing her. She would no longer be attending the trial as the face of the Bureau, but no one had thought to order her to stay away. When the trial began, she would wait until everyone's attention should be on the proceedings and make an unobtrusive entrance. And if anyone attempted to bar her way, her credentials should see her past that obstacle.

Interlude – Mary and Jack

It wasn't often that Mary and Jack hosted both sets of parents at once. Their dining table could fit six people — if everyone squeezed close to leave enough room for her father and his mother. They chose to make such a gathering work, rather than make the announcement twice. But there was no helping the fact that their parents would know something was up.

And they'd probably guessed what it was. But Mary waited until she brought in the dessert, Jack's family cheesecake recipe, and passed around the slices before she sat back down in front of her empty plate, another clue, and took a deep breath.

"We just wanted you all to know that I'm pregnant."

Jack's mother elbowed his father hard enough to make him jump. "I told you! I knew it!" She beamed at Mary as if all her wishes had come true, which was likely close to the truth. Mary's father's eyes were shining, and he blinked hard. Mary's mother, however, bit her lip before she forced her mouth into a smile and reached across the table to grab Mary's hand.

"Oh, I do hope you'll be all right. How are you feeling? Is everything . . . going right so far?"

Mary didn't try to smile. "Yes, ma. Everything's just fine. I do hope you won't go worrying yourself." Or me, Jack knew she was thinking. Mary's father may have guessed the same. He whispered in his wife's ear.

An awkward silence fell. Jack reached for the cheesecake, to pass it around and hope it inspired some new subject, just as his father-in-law said, "You two deserve all the best. And we'll be praying you get nothing less."

Mary got up, leaned over her father, and kissed his bald spot. "Thank you. I'll be praying some myself. Now help us eat up this cake."

Chapter 18

Judge Rayner (Alex)

The trial would start tomorrow, and a good thing too. Alex was more than ready to get to it.

First would come preliminary fencing over witnesses. The plaintiff wanted to call an expert in maternal psychology, and another in the history of adoption in the U.S. The latter was possibly unnecessary, but more efficient than the alternative methods of getting that history into the record. The designated adoptive parents, bless them, had no experts in their arsenal. The Bureau, on the other hand, wanted to call a psychologist, a sociologist, its own historian, and a private investigator.

Alex preferred to run a tight ship, so to speak. But the odds of an appeal in this case were so high that it might be prudent to err on the side of allowing testimony. Careful drafting of her eventual order, making clear what evidence had persuaded her, would reduce the odds that an appeal claiming improperly admitted evidence would succeed. An appeal based on the refusal to hear evidence that might have changed her mind would by its nature have a better chance.

So she denied, one after the other, all the motions to exclude any witness wholesale. But she would ride herd on those witnesses and keep them from wasting her or anyone else's time.

* * * * *

Toni

Mom had pulled Toni out of the shared residence for some final trial prep. Toni had more or less refused to go all the way to Mom's place, so they met over double-decker grilled cheese sandwiches at the only restaurant within ten miles of the country house. It was late enough that whatever lunch crowd frequented the restaurant had mostly dispersed, and they had enough empty tables around them for relative privacy.

"The judge wants to start with the testimony of the three individual parties, instead of having all your witnesses go first." Mom spoke around a bite of sandwich; she had never accepted or enforced the rule against speaking with one's mouth full, and Toni had lifelong practice in understanding her. "She thinks we can get all three of you in and out in one day, which means she'll make sure it happens. And she made a point of saying you can bring the baby to court, as long as someone takes the baby out if she starts howling."

Toni gulped down some sandwich before responding. "That would make things easier, but it's an unnerving idea."

Mom twitched an eyebrow. "It should be. Judge Rayner doesn't make idle suggestions. I'm guessing she wants to see some or all of you with the baby. It'll be in the nature of an audition. Are you up to it?"

* * * * *

Alex

Few people knew that Judge Rayner's chambers allowed her to stand at a particular spot and see at least part of the courtroom. It was often useful to see how parties acted without the constraint of a judge's presence. Her colleagues had varying reactions, from amusement to envy at her nerve to several levels of disapproval, but she had discussed the matter with the judicial ethics board, which had so far accepted her assurance that she would never base a decision on any impression so gained unless her experience while actually on the bench corroborated it.

Now she watched Grace Allen pass the baby to Toni Greene, Ms. Allen's body language showing only slight reluctance. This pretrial period of cohabitation might have been at least somewhat transformative. Would the rapprochement prove temporary once that period ended, if the three-party adoption took place?

The donor-mother's face lit up as soon as the bundle touched her arms. She kissed the baby's forehead; her posture suggested murmuring or cooing. The designated adoptive father, Adam Brown, looked on with a somewhat paternal air that seemed directed more at Toni than the baby. He might well be functioning as the bridge between the two women. If true, that spoke of impressive talent for diplomacy.

There came Mr. Voxsmith, sticking his face close to the baby, an exaggerated smile on his face. Was he saying "cootchie-cootchie-coo" or some other string of nonsense? The judge took a moment to relish the incongruity, almost tempted to take a picture.

That man behind Mr. Voxsmith – his eyebrows, and something about the jaw, resembled the donor's. Her father, perhaps? She had neither seen nor read anything about him up until now, but at least he was there to support his daughter.

Enough of playing the voyeur. The judge pressed the button that alerted the bailiff of her impending entrance, waited thirty seconds, and then passed through the door to the courtroom. As she took her seat, she suppressed, as always, her amusement at being elevated and robed like some sort of monarch, and benignly granted her permission for everyone else to sit as well.

Alex ran through the agreed arrangements: individual parties first, testimony from the non-expert Bureau witnesses next, then experts for both sides. The order differed from the typical witness progression, but Alex exercised to the full her authority to hear witnesses in whatever sequence she thought intuitively useful.

Within these groupings, however, the plaintiff would go first. Her attorney, whose clear resemblance to the plaintiff underscored their familial relationship, called her to the stand. The donor-mother gave the baby another kiss and handed off to Mr. Brown before making her way to the well-upholstered chair at the side of the bench. Alex had used a substantial portion of her discretionary budget to ensure its comfort.

The lawyer ran quickly through the preliminaries of name, age, (self-)employment. Meanwhile, the baby, too young to actually crawl, gave it her best attempt, squirming and flailing, socking Mr. Brown in the cheek. Grace Allen bravely relieved him about the time the lawyer got to questions of substance.

The plaintiff explained her not uncommon reaction to learning she was pregnant: fear, shock, the sense of being overwhelmed. The public service announcements from the

Bureau had made her feel that trying to cope would be a selfish effort, and implied it would be a futile one.

The lawyer handed the witness a photo. "Is this a still shot from one of those announcements?"

"It looks like it."

The lawyer showed the photo to the other lawyers and then handed it to the judge. "Exhibit A for the plaintiff, Your Honor." After the exhibit was appropriately marked and stowed, she pulled out a transcript. "I'm going to read this aloud, and you tell me whether the PSAs you heard included any with either these words or something similar."

"Objection!" called out the Bureau's attorney. "Lack of proper foundation."

Plaintiff's lawyer gave the Bureau's an "Oh, really" expression. "If necessary, we will introduce a recording substantiating this transcript."

The judge studied the lawyer's expression briefly to confirm that she could do just that. "Proceed."

The witness's face grew more rigid and still as the lawyer read.

"'Alone and pregnant? Confused and afraid? Do your circumstances make the prospect of pregnancy difficult at best? Are you too young, too poor, too inexperienced to take on the lifelong challenge of supporting, protecting, and guiding another human being?

"'You may feel there's no way out, but you're wrong. We're here to help you. And by letting us help you, you'll be helping others, fulfilling the dreams of those well prepared for these challenges, but for whom pregnancy has proved impossible. You can return to your own life path, while grateful parents, carefully chosen, will honor your courage as they raise your child in love and plenty.

"'Give the gift of love. Give it to your child, and to the future.'"

The witness's eyes had filled with tears. "That sounds like some of the PSAs I heard."

"Did anyone you spoke to at the clinic or the Bureau, either in person or otherwise, offer you any assistance or suggestions about ways to cope with raising your child?"

The Bureau's lawyer stirred as if considering an objection, but apparently decided against it.

"No."

The lawyer took the witness through the process of deciding to donate, the day of the donation, and its aftermath. None of this testimony was particularly surprising or unique, but the detail of the donor's dream the night after the procedure came as a jolt. Alex had had a similar dream the night before her abortion. She had almost canceled her appointment when she awoke from it.

She shook off the memory before it could further distract her. The witness had started to say something about her discussions with her mother aka her attorney, who deftly cut off that response with a new question before the witness could waive attorney-client privilege. "What is it you want, now, for yourself and your baby?"

"Objection. Phrasing assumes the outcome of this proceeding."

"Overruled. Think twice before you raise objections that assume this court is so emotionally suggestible. The witness may answer."

The witness took a deep and somewhat shaky breath. She had been facing her lawyer, but now she turned toward Alex. "I want more than anything in the world to be my baby's mother. To take care of her, to show her the world, to share the world with her, to protect her, to love her."

Another breath. "But I realize that, because of what I did, the choice I made, these two good people —" She gestured toward the designated adoptive parents — "have attached their hopes of doing all those things to the child I carried. It would be cruel to tear apart that bond. It would be unfair to do it if I had a better choice. I hope I have that choice. I hope you will tell us that we can all, the three of us, give Jessie, Jessica Kyra, the best love and care we can give, the widest options, the safest childhood, the best education, the broadest scope for creativity, that we can come together to provide."

Alex had not expected this level of fluency or this mature a demeanor from a young woman who had rushed almost blindly into her initial decision. This passionate and forthright woman had potential.

Mr. Voxsmith arose for what, technically, would be called cross-examination. "Based on your observations over the weeks you have spent co-parenting, can you describe Grace Allen as a parent?"

The witness looked at Ms. Allen and chuckled. "She's energetic. And efficient. She can change a diaper or clean up baby barf or get Jessie dressed more quickly than Adam or I can. She plans ahead. She already has recipes concocted for when Jessie starts eating solid food. She's stronger than she looks — she can carry the baby almost as long as Adam can before she gets tired. And she's terrific at finding reading material. Adam and I read the baby our favorite stories, but Grace finds nonfiction on all sorts of fascinating subjects, written at a level a young child can understand. It'll be fascinating to see, later, whether any of it is sinking in."

"And Adam Brown?"

The young woman's expression changed to something short of affection, but along the same spectrum, colored with respect. "He's kind. He's patient. Boy, is he patient. Of all of us, he's the one I can imagine coping with parenthood by himself. He never seems to get frazzled. . . . He comes up with more fun games than Grace or I do — physical games the baby can already understand. He sings to her — so does Grace, and so do I sometimes, but he sings the most and has the best voice."

After a few wrap-up questions and a short recess, it was time for true cross-examination. The Bureau's lawyer would have had an easier task before the lawsuit had changed direction, questioning the young woman's fitness to cope with parenthood alone. Now he chose the best remaining avenue of attack. "Ms. Greene, you have described the admirable parenting skills of the mother and father the Bureau chose to be the parents of this child. What do you contribute to her present and future well-being that they cannot?"

The witness's glance toward her lawyer suggested that the latter had foreseen this question, and while Ms. Greene was too experienced and cautious to have scripted an answer, her feedback had no doubt helped to form one. Toni looked back at the Bureau's lawyer with something close to confidence as she replied. "I'm my own person, and I'll love my daughter in all the ways that my individual qualities make possible. Adam and Grace will show her love; I'll show her love with a face that looks more like her own. I'll be able to introduce her to the rest of her biological family — on my side at least — and to share stories with her that'll make the earlier generations of that family real to her." Toni paused, as if not sure how to put the next statement. "Adam and Grace can teach her to appreciate art; I can show her what it's like to create it. I can show her how to make the most of a chunk of wood, to turn it into something that she or others can use, or something to delight the eye or move the spirit, or all these at once. And . . . I'm younger, and closer to my own childhood, which may help me understand how she feels and what struggles she faces as she grows up." She gave a self-deprecating smile. "I won't have to guess or imagine or project how she feels when she gives her heart to an armful of wool and acrylic shaped like a rabbit or a dog or a bear or a unicorn. I haven't yet left behind my own love of these, and I can remember how they helped me learn what giving love was like." She looked back at her lawyer-mother, probably seeking a nonverbal hint if she had forgotten anything. Alex shifted her eyes to the lawyer, letting her see that she was under observation, then back to the witness, who shrugged and said, "That's all I can think of right now. But I'll still be thinking and trying, every hour of every day, if I'm allowed to — to *contribute* whatever I can."

Adam Brown, testifying about Toni Greene:

"Honestly, she's a delight to have around. She has a playful heart. If she's part of our family, one of our daughter's parents, our daughter will grow up familiar with joy." He blushed a little. "And I must confess it's a relief, in several senses of the word, to have someone who loves our little girl so much, available to be with her when my wife and I want to revisit the relationship we had before we were parents."

Grace Allen, testifying about Toni Greene:

"I didn't have the best first impression of Toni. A lot of that came from my assumptions, and from what I was told — that she was too self-centered or too immature or both to raise her own child. There may have been a grain of truth in those notions. She's young, and she has some growing up to do. But she's done a lot of it since she gave up the baby. She's learned some very important lessons the hard way, or one of the hard ways. She's growing into parenthood. And she loves the baby with all her heart. I think Adam and I can help her become the parent she is dedicated to becoming. And that will be good for our daughter."

The Bureau's lawyer, on cross, scenting potential to drive a wedge: "Would you say your daughter would thrive, even in the absence of this proposed third parent?"

Ms. Allen's expressive face showed her thinking through the question before, some seconds later, she replied, "I think Adam and I will be good parents. And if Toni had never had second thoughts, had gone cheerfully on with her life, we would have made a good life for our daughter. But once we knew that Toni so desperately wanted to be reunited with Jessie, we ultimately had two choices. We could find a way to include her in our family. Or we could become the kind of people who learn not to think about the pain of someone intimately connected to their family. And that would have been very bad indeed for us, and ultimately, for our daughter."

Alex had to fight to maintain her detached and authoritative expression.

Which showed her that she was taking sides too soon. She would have to make a special effort to consider the Bureau's position as the trial continued.

Alex was not often taken aback by the direction of a witness' testimony. She had correctly assumed the investigator had been deployed to dig up dirt on the plaintiff, the donor. Nor was she surprised at what the investigator had been able to find: a citation for use of recreational drugs too close to a school, a misdemeanor charge of operating an automobile on manual inside municipal borders, a short-lived romance with an unsavory local character, and the like.

But she had underestimated the Bureau's chutzpah.

Before the plaintiff and the defendant parents had so drastically changed course, the Bureau had, in public pronouncements and filed papers alike, stoutly defended its procedures for choosing adoptive parents in general, and in papers filed under the seal of confidentiality, it had been just as laudatory about these adoptive parents in particular. But now that this admirable couple had decided to join forces with the donor, the investigator had been told to target the couple as well.

This was one of the fairly frequent occasions when Alex was glad not to have to worry about a jury. She could halt proceedings and provide a reality check without any cumbersome people-moving delays. She waited for the expected objections from plaintiff's and the couple's attorneys, waved them to their seats, and leaned forward to stare at the Bureau's attorney, still on his feet. "Counsel, I could send you all away to get coffee — or perhaps, in your case, a cold shower. And I could research the technical applicability of the legal terms the other lawyers have just used, to see which, if any, properly cover this about-face. I will do that in any case. But it may save a little time if I allow you to proceed, on the understanding that unless that imminent research surprises me as much as this line of questioning has done, you and this witness will be wasting your breath. I predict that no case law or other rule will require me to give any significant credence to your attempt to tarnish the characters of two people who have already received your client's enthusiastic endorsement after every opportunity for scrutiny. Now — do you wish to continue with your direct examination?"

The lawyer's face looked a little redder than it had a few minutes ago. "If you will allow me a moment to confer with my client —"

Alex gave a minimal nod and sat back, silently counting seconds while the lawyer had a muttered exchange with the Bureau representative sitting at the counsel table. Mr. Voxsmith, she noticed, was using the same interlude to confer with his own clients, probably to check their skeleton inventory. Alex had only gotten to twenty-two when the lawyer straightened up again and faced her. "No further questions."

Which meant whatever the fellow had dug up wasn't worth further annoying Alex, even to get it on the record for use on appeal. She allowed herself one roll of her eyes before turning toward Mr. Voxsmith. "Cross-examination?"

Mr. Voxsmith, never one to resist the call of instant karma, ran through a litany of what the investigator had not discovered. "Any felony convictions?" "Any felony charges?" "Any substantiated investigations for abuse or neglect of children?" "Any unsubstantiated investigations for either?" "Any rejected credit applications?" "Any outstanding warrants of any kind?" The witness rather sullenly gave his negative responses, and Voxsmith finally stepped back as if to let him go, then paused and faced him once again. "When did the Bureau hire you to investigate Adam Brown and Grace Allen?"

The date was two days after the couple had moved to amend their complaint.

"No further questions."

Now plaintiff's counsel had her turn. "Did your instructions include any provision for finding positive information about Mr. Brown or Ms. Allen?"

They had not.

"In the course of your investigation, did you in fact come upon any such information? I refer to activities of apparent benefit to the community or to individuals outside their immediate social circle."

"Well. Ms. Allen used to teach art at the community college. But she got paid for it."

"Is it your assertion that no one can benefit the community unless they are wealthy enough to do so without financial compensation? No, I withdraw the question. Your views on the subject are immaterial."

Alex gave her a warning glance. "Less gamesmanship, if you please, counselor."

"My apologies, Your Honor. . . . Anything else?"

"I don't remember anything else like that."

(*Careful, counselor. If you imply the investigator failed to find information, that raises the question of what else, less favorable to your client, he might have failed to find. . . .*)

Ms. Greene had a facility at picking up cues that sometimes bordered on mind-reading. She wrapped up her questioning and sat down, aiming a polite smile at the Bureau's lawyer. That gentleman looked back at her with a sour expression he would have done better to conceal.

The second day brought the battling experts, with detailed cross-examinations of each. Then came the closing arguments, weaving stronger and weaker threads in their attempts to create a rope strong enough to bind Alex to their side's view.

Finally, Alex thanked all and sundry, whether or not

they deserved thanks, and promised to issue a decision in short order. She headed home for a massage, a meal, a drink, and a good night's sleep. Tomorrow would be soon enough to untwine and assess the strands.

Chapter 19

Toni walked out of the courthouse in a daze. She had been nerving herself up for the trial for months, and now the ordeal was over with nothing decided. She felt as if she were drifting through uncharted waters, despite Mom and Andy by her side, Andy carrying Jessie, and her new allies Adam and Grace somewhere nearby.

It didn't help the feeling of unreality to see Poloma Clark standing on the steps of the courthouse and looking up in her direction. Toni had given up hope that Poloma would get back to her about that ominous phone call – and Poloma's manner now didn't suggest the suspense or excitement, or even dread, she would expect to go along with any revelation. What was Poloma even doing here? Toni hadn't seen her in the courtroom, at the Bureau's table or anywhere else — but then, she hadn't been looking around at spectators.

Poloma came up to meet Toni and the others as they started to come down and spoke to Toni. "May I talk to you for a few minutes? Is there anywhere you need to go immediately?"

The Poloma Toni had first met would not, she thought, have asked that second question. It would not have occurred to her that Toni might have her own business of any importance. Toni and her family and Adam and Grace had been planning to grab an early supper together at a coffee shop nearby before going their separate ways. She explained as much and added, "We can head that direction, and talk on the way."

Toni waited on the steps for the rest of the group to reach the sidewalk and go halfway down the block before she started down herself, Poloma falling into step beside her. Mom and Andy both glanced over their shoulders at the two of them. Mom looked somewhere between curious and worried; Andy paused and turned partway around, ready to come to her rescue if necessary. She waved them on. Poloma waited for them to reach the sidewalk, firm level footing with the snow cleared away, before saying, "I just wanted to apologize."

Toni glanced at Poloma's face and then back at the sidewalk ahead. The woman did not look awkward or embarrassed, only steadfast, as if performing some difficult duty without letting herself flinch. Toni replied, "I don't want to jump to conclusions. Apologize for what?"

"For letting my preconceptions cloud my judgment." Poloma paused, cleared her throat, and went on. "Or rather, for letting my preconceptions drown out my judgment. When I first met you, I liked you."

Toni stopped in her tracks and turned toward Poloma, who stopped as well. "You liked me? Even though I'd donated my baby? But wait, you wouldn't have known that when I first showed up."

"No, but I assumed that's what you were there to do, and it didn't stop me from having a favorable first impression. Remember, I believed — believe — in the good donations can do. I thought I could help you, and beyond that, you seemed interesting. If you hadn't startled me by upending my assumptions, I might have wished that we were friends. And then . . . ." Now she did show some discomfort, shifting her weight back and forth. "It upset me to have been wrong about why you were there. I'd . . . I'd assumed I was in control of the situation, that I knew all about it, and I was rather pleased with myself, coming down from my office to solve people's problems. It made me feel foolish to realize I'd misunderstood your purpose. And to realize you were going to be a problem for me instead. I resented you for that."

Toni blew out a frosty cloud. "It's cold. Let's keep walking." They started moving again. Toni mulled over Poloma's apology, or confession, or whatever it was, for half a block, Poloma walking silently beside her. As they made it across the street, she asked, "What difference would it have made if you'd felt any different? If you hadn't resented my surprising you?"

Poloma took a few moments, and a few steps, to answer. "I don't know, really. The rules are clear. I don't think I could have found a way to work around them." Another few steps, and then, "I could have suggested you talk to Adam and Grace. Even served as an intermediary. Things might have gone differently if I'd — if I'd described you differently when I spoke to them."

Toni mulled that over. "If that had happened, I don't know whether we'd have ended up trying for the three-way adoption. Adam and Grace might not have been willing, that far back. And if we lose on that, well, we'll be in pretty much the same situation as if you'd brought us together earlier. I won't say 'no harm, no foul' — it's been a rough time, in some ways. But if I thought it all over for a while, I suspect I'd decide it had been a growing experience. And I had some growing to do, when all this started."

Poloma sounded as if her throat had tightened up.

"Thank you for saying that. You've been — gracious."

Toni shrugged. They had almost reached the coffee shop. "Well, I'll be going in to join the others." She paused, examined her feelings, and decided to go on. "I hope you'll stay in touch." She smiled a little. "Maybe we would find out whether we can be friends after all."

Poloma smiled back. Had she ever seen Poloma smile before? Maybe the day they met, before she threw such a curve ball Poloma's way. "I'd like that. Goodbye, then." Poloma waited for nothing more before she walked away.

* * * * *

Judge Rayner (Alex)

Alex looked up from her notes, saw the time on the old-fashioned travel clock on her desk, and whistled. Harold must have gone to bed by now. She vaguely recalled his presence behind her, an hour or so ago. Had he kissed her hair? Probably, but she had been so immersed in her work that the moment had failed to lodge in her memory.

She had resolved to decide this case on legal principles, rather than becoming mired in the factual weeds, but that left open the crucial question of whether she would push those principles in novel directions. Though there were, of course, established principles for determining when to go beyond established principles.

She got up to make herself a cup of tea. When it was ready, she would bring it back into her home office and bang out a draft. She would get up an hour earlier than usual, read the draft, and see whether a night's — or rather, a partial night's — sleep had changed her thinking.

It did not.

Alex tweaked a word here and there, proofread, fixed the single typo, hit "file", and sighed. It would have been gratifying to provide the earnest and intriguing young mother some greater relief. But gratification, of her own desires or those of the parties who came before her, was not her job. At best, it was a fringe benefit of doing her job.

Not this time.

*****

Toni

It was almost warm out if one wore layers and stayed in the sun. Adam and Grace had taken Jessie to the playground to give Toni a good stretch of time to work in her studio. Toni was using her electric sander, a noisy enough tool that she might have missed the first knock on the door. The one she did hear was loud enough to be a second attempt.

She turned off the sander, brushed sawdust off her smock, hurried from the studio through the front room, and opened the door to find her brother. The smile froze on her face as she took in Andy's sober expression. She knew he came with bad tidings before he said, "Mom sent me. She wants to talk to you, and she wanted you to have someone here."

She slumped into his chest, knowing he would catch her and hold her, letting him steer her toward the beat-up sofa she had managed to fit into the studio for impromptu naps. She said nothing as he shrugged out of his jacket, made the call to Mom, and said, "I'm here."

Toni pulled herself upright and leaned against Andy's shoulder to look at the screen. Mom was waiting, her laptop open beside her. "We got the decision, honey. It isn't good." She waited in case Toni had something to say, but the very idea of speaking seemed impossible, something out of another time. Mom went on. "I'm sending it to you, but I'll read you a few bits first."

Toni tried to make sense of the legal language, tuning in and out like an old-fashioned ham radio operator on a stormy night.

This court is not authorized to rewrite either statutes or regulations, nor to interpret them in a manner clearly inconsistent with their authors' intent . . . applicable statute and regulations do not address or purport to modify existing statutes, regulations, or case law concerning voluntary termination of parental rights . . . not necessary to reach the general question of three-parent adoptions outside plural marriage . . . . What this court might have determined if the designated adoptive parents had petitioned for adoption with a party new to the situation is not . . . donor did not seek to withdraw her consent until after the period had expired within which a birth mother in her state would have been entitled to withdraw a post-natal consent to adoption prior to the advent of fetal donation . . . .

Toni fumbled for a tissue and blew her nose before asking, "How long did birth mothers have? How close did I come?"

Mom's arms twitched as if she longed to reach out and give Toni a hug. "That second visit, when you asked me about trying, was four days too late, the way the judge sees it. But that by itself may not have made a crucial difference."

Toni buried her face in Andy's shoulder again. He squeezed her against him as Mom said, "We didn't come out of this with nothing. There's something like a suggestion in the order. *There is no impediment to the donor and the designated adoptive parents entering into any sort of visitation agreement or living arrangement they choose. The Bureau should take note of the likelihood that any attempt to change the adoptive parents' status as a result of such an agreement or arrangement would raise serious procedural and substantive questions. Any such action would doubtless be challenged, and such a challenge would, in this court's view, have a substantial likelihood of success, such that preliminary injunctive relief might well be available . . . ."*

Toni pulled herself out of Andy's hug and reached for his phone. He let her take it. She waited for her hand to stop shaking and then said, "That would just put us back where we decided not to be, when we decided early on not to settle. Except worse, because Adam and Grace could change their minds. Unless this agreement is whatever you call it —"

"Enforceable?"

"That. Unless it's enforceable, it wouldn't really mean anything."

Mom chewed her lower lip. "I wouldn't say that. It would show their intentions, that they wanted you to stay part of the family. It would show that they've accepted your moral claim, if not a legal claim, to be part of Jessie's life."

Andy spoke up for the first time since the start of the call. "Isn't there some way to make this kind of agreement enforceable, even at this stage?"

Mom stuck her tongue out the side of her mouth in the way that meant she was thinking especially hard. Toni held her breath. She had to gasp for air before Mom said, slowly, "There might be something we could do. But we'd want to make sure Adam and Grace knew why we were doing it."

Chapter 20

Judge Rayner (Alex)

Alex checked the afternoon filings and did a double-take. A Notice of Appeal, already?

Oh. Oh, yes. That must be what they were up to. Alex's smile grew into a grin.

Well played.

She jotted down a note to record her prediction. It would, she figured, take less than two weeks before the plaintiff and the adoptive parents reached a settlement and the plaintiff dismissed the appeal. Or she might wait to dismiss it until she saw how the Bureau responded.

The settlement would not, because it could not, constitute a tripartite adoption, with adoption's extensive benefits and protections (not to mention responsibilities) for the adoptive parent. But it would, she suspected, come reasonably close – on a day to day level, and assuming the continued good will of all parties.

Would the Bureau join in the settlement, accepting a status quo much like the arrangement preceding the trial? They wouldn't like it. But if the alternative was an appeal that could establish a precedent they'd like even less, bureaucratic prudence would probably prevail.

* * * * *

Toni

Mom had made blueberry muffins, but Toni's stomach was twisted up too tight for her to eat. And the more they talked, the worse it got.

"The problem is, I have to trust them." She jumped off the bar stool she had just perched on and started pacing again.

Mom had on her I-can-be-patient-a-little-longer face. "To some extent. But that would be a much more serious problem if you hadn't been living, and parenting, together for all this time."

She could really have used a larger room to pace in. Which may be why Mom had steered them into her relatively small kitchen. "It's one thing for us to get along, and for Grace to tolerate me, while I had a chance of being named Jessie's parent. Now she doesn't have to. And being in their vacation house is different from being in their real home, where they have their routines that don't include me."

Mom tapped her fingers on her knees. "They don't have routines that include the baby and exclude you, or not entrenched ones. In any event, the settlement will have language that lets you go to court to enforce it. And Grace is sensible enough not to want to raise Jessie in an atmosphere of acrimony."

Toni stopped pacing. "I suppose she is."

"You realize some people would assume that the three of you are a polyamorous triad. Would that trouble you?"

Toni had been clenching her teeth, or grinding them, or struggling not to cry, for so many hours straight that she hardly recognized how it felt to smile. "After all that's happened? I really don't care what people think."

Mom got up, took Toni's hand, and squeezed it. "That

is one of the most transformative lessons you can learn in life. Congratulations! Just don't lose sight of the possibility that what people think will, in some circumstances, have a practical impact."

Toni squeezed back, extracted her hand, and sat back down. "Is there any practical – or legal — downside to that assumption? That we'd be a triad?"

Mom gave a mulling-it-over series of small nods before saying, "No legal downside that currently comes to mind, or practical ones, unless the cultural winds shift against such arrangements. But you'd need to make sure the prospect of people misunderstanding your living arrangements doesn't trouble Adam or Grace more than it does you."

Toni rolled her eyes at the thought of Grace's likely reaction. "Should I be the one to suggest the arrangement, or should it come from you?"

More small nods, before Mom said, "I see a role here for both of us. The proposal to come from me, as an implicit indication that it's feasible, and because I can hint delicately that there are less favorable options in reserve. And the warning about any appearance of a triad from you, so you can make plain you have no such intention."

* * * * *

Adam

Adam and Grace sat in the big armchair that let him hold Grace on his lap. She had been wise to insist that they move it to the country house. (Though they would have to move it back when they returned home.) There was no better spot for this discussion. Now if only the baby would keep napping a little longer . . . .

Grace got them started. "So do we keep doing this joint parenting, and commit to it indefinitely, even though we don't have to?"

Adam kept his voice as soft as a lullaby. "Would you really feel better, day to day, knowing we'd thrust Toni out, that she was somewhere longing for Jessie?" It would be more like grieving. But that word would likely bring a protest neither of them needed right now.

"I don't know." Grace curled herself up a little tighter in his arms. "Maybe not. And it probably wouldn't be that simple. She'll pursue the appeal if we don't settle. We'd be in suspense for a long time yet. And she might be able to get some sort of visitation while the appeal was pending."

Adam doubted that. Mr. Voxsmith thought it unlikely. But Grace had not been part of the phone call in which Mr. Voxsmith said so. Adam had called him when Grace was napping with the baby. He hadn't known how to bring it up. And he didn't want to do it now.

Grace sat up and grasped the arms of the chair. "If we do this, if we settle on these terms, I don't want us to stay here. I want to go home, and bring Jessie home. Toni can move in with us."

Adam mentally walked through the rooms of their house. "The guest room would be all right for her bedroom. But there's no studio."

"She has a studio. She can go there whenever she likes."

Adam didn't know how far it was from their house to Toni's studio. But it was probably near the subway. And if it wasn't, they could always help her out with transportation costs, or turn taking her there into an outing. He'd enjoy seeing what the studio looked like.

Grace, meanwhile, was frowning. "This business of looking like a triad. I don't care, or not very much, if it looks that way. But . . . is there . . . might you . . . she's young and pretty . . . ." Her voice dropped to a whisper. "And — vital."

Even whispering, she couldn't bear to say what he knew she meant. The doctors had told them that of the two, Adam's fertility challenges were less serious. She would never forget.

He pulled her back against his chest, and after a moment's resistance she yielded to the pull. He waited for the tension to fade from her shoulders, and then gave up waiting for it to fade entirely, saying softly, "You are my great good fortune, and my life's best choice, and my ideal woman, and Toni Greene will never be any of those things. And I find her youth . . . intimidating rather than attractive."

She let go the rest of the way, snuggling against him. "What do you feel for her, then?"

Adam gathered the impressions he had, without conscious attention, been collecting, and tried to put them into words. "I would say I feel rather as if she were something like a relative, except met only recently. Someone a little wayward, emerging from a troubled period, but with potential and in need of guidance. Almost like – what was that religious term? A sort of goddaughter."

Grace squirmed around to study his face, then looked down at her hands. "If I can learn to feel like that, or closer to it, I imagine I'd be a good deal happier about all of this." She looked back up at him and asked quietly, "Do you think I can?"

He bent his head to kiss her, and lingered in that kiss, awakening and accepting her response. By then, he thought she might be ready to believe him when he said, "I believe you can. I know you can. So now, what do you want us to decide? About this settlement proposal, about having Toni live with us for an indefinite period, raising Jessica Kyra with her?"

Grace laid her head against his chest, and stayed in that position, breathing evenly, for long enough that he wondered if she could have somehow dropped off to sleep. But finally she said, "I have to remember that we've already done this. Been doing it. Even knowing it was a temporary arrangement, I could have found it . . . unbearable. Or more difficult. We managed. So we can keep managing. And if anything, it should be easier without the trial looming."

The wave of gratitude that swept through him told him how unsure he'd been of her answer. "So if she'll move in with us, we have a deal?"

First a whimper, then a wail came from the nursery. Grace gave him a quick kiss on the cheek and shoved herself off him. "Yes. You can let them know the answer is yes." And with that, she strode off to tend to their daughter.

* * * * *

Poloma

Poloma read the news item and sat back to ponder it.

At least the trial was over. And given the settlement of the appeal, nobody was left too unhappy, with the possible exception of some people in the Bureau hierarchy who couldn't be content with what amounted to victory unless the adversary was suffering in defeat.

Now she could get back to what had been her work, free of all these distractions. Or at least, as much of that work as she could still do in the more senior position she apparently still held.

Some part of her remained uneasy. But surely, as she readjusted to her routine, the feeling would fade.

Interlude – Mary and Jack

Jack came home from work to find Mary already there, and what's more, lying on the couch. As he closed the door, he heard what might have been a sniff. He hurried toward the couch and saw Mary stuffing a tissue under her back to hide it. Her eyes were red. He squatted down next to the couch and pulled the tissue out. "What's wrong?"

She came up with a smile that would have looked real to someone who didn't know her so well. "It's nothing. Just hormones, probably."

He shifted to his knees and stroked her hair, keeping it up until she relaxed against the couch and let the smile fall away. "It's Ma again. Whenever she calls to see how I'm doing, she always ends up telling me about all the trouble she had between me and my little sister. Three miscarriages, and then she almost lost Sis too."

Jack clenched his teeth. "I know." Though he'd been trying not to think about that family history. "But that was years and years ago. The doctor said things are different now, didn't she?"

Mary went stiff again. "Not exactly. She just said I shouldn't borrow trouble, and that she'd take good care of me. Talking to me like a child, the way they do."

Well he knew it. And while he hadn't been able to get off work to go with her, he could guess she'd given the doc an earful about it. Not such a good idea, when they needed the doc on their side, but that was Mary, standing up for herself, and he loved her for it. "You're not bleeding or cramping, are you?"

There, finally, a small smile. "No. Just sick, like I'm supposed to be. Ma did say she was sick as a dog with me, and everything turned out fine."

"All right, then. Now —" It was her turn to cook, but he could smell that nothing was cooking. "Let's go out for a bite, shall we? Whatever you want — whatever you think you can handle."

Mary scooted away from him and got up from the couch. "That's sweet of you, honey ,but we shouldn't spend the money. I've got yesterday's ham I can warm up." She went a little paler, and he saw her throat move as she swallowed what must have been bile.

He scrambled to his feet and took her hands in his. "We can afford it, this once, the way we've been saving up. The place on the corner has soup. Chicken soup, and remember all the people who say chicken soup will fix whatever ails you? I'll get your jacket."

Dinner out had cost as much as Mary had feared, but it had still relaxed her a little. They had been home about half an hour when Jack heard his phone, looked at it, and did a double-take. Mary's father — or Pop, as he liked Jack to call him — was calling him. Why hadn't he called Mary? Mary was reading in the living room, so he went into the kitchen to take the call and leaned the door almost shut.

Pop tended to pause between words, as if wondering whether he had the right ones, and he was doing it now. "Ma and I, we've been talking about something. You know how Ma's been worrying, and why."

He could hardly help it, the way she went on. And after all, she had some hard history behind it.

"Well, we heard something. There may be nothing to it, but we thought you maybe should know about it. You and Mary."

"Okay, Pop. I'm listening."

"You probably know about those clinics they have nowadays, the ones women can go to if they don't want their babies. Where the babies get put in some sort of tank until they're ready to be born? And then people adopt them."

"I think so." Jack had heard about it some time or other. In fact, now that Pop mentioned it, he'd wondered whether Mary would consider adopting if they couldn't get pregnant.

Pop paused even longer before going on. "Well, somebody told me the fellow who invented those tanks had wanted them used to keep women from losing their babies. That the idea was, if things started to go wrong, the woman could go to her doctor or a hospital or somewhere, and they'd take the baby out and put it in the tank. It should work, shouldn't it? It's the same thing, really, whether the woman doesn't want the baby or she can't hang onto it because her body isn't working right."

That made sense, but — "So why don't we hear more about this? Why hasn't Mary's doctor mentioned it?"

Pop shrugged. "Maybe you have to ask. Maybe you can't have that done, whatever the inventor wanted. You could try to find out."

Various online pregnancy groups had plenty to say about this supposed news. But what with all the different claims and warnings and guesses and arguments, there was nothing there to grab onto.

Mary's doctor had nothing to add. "But if such a use is approved, I'll make sure to let you know."

Chapter 21

Adam

The problem with giving your daughter two names you liked was settling on which one to use. Adam hadn't yet settled. Just now, he was combining the two. "Jessie-Ky!" (It sounded almost like Jessica.) "Bath time!"

The baby bounced up and down in her high chair and clapped her sticky hands. Bits of strained carrot went flying. Since he was cleaning Jessie, could he leave the location cleanup for Grace or Toni? He'd decide that later.

He eased the baby out of the high chair and carried her to the bathroom. As he peeled off Jessie's yellow overalls, now spotted with the reasonably harmonious orange, he wondered how much of the stuff had ended up on his own clothing. Well, no matter. He had plenty of clothes. He might change if he took Jessie out for a walk to look for crocuses. Or he might not bother.

He took off the baby's shirt and diaper and lowered her gently into the tub. She kicked and splashed and crowed. Settling her against one end of the tub, he gave her a couple of minutes for pure enjoyment before grabbing a washcloth and wiping off the parts of her not underwater.

Was that carrot blending in with Jessie's few strands of strawberry blonde hair? Yes, the shade was distinctly different. He was just reaching for the shampoo when he heard what might be the chime of the doorbell.

He gave up on the shampoo and grabbed the measuring cup they used for sluicing Jessie down, pouring it carefully over the back of her head. The doorbell — no mistaking it this time — rang again, twice. Adam cursed under his breath and ran the washcloth over the rest of Jessie's hair. "Sorry, sweetheart. Looks like bath time's over."

The baby squirmed in protest at being lifted out so soon. By the time he had wrapped a towel around her, she was crying. He had no choice but to answer the door with a still dripping and loudly indignant baby in his arms.

A man and a woman stood at the door holding tablets. They were almost a matched set, similar in height, both with dark blond hair, the man's short and the woman's pulled tightly back. Something in their manner said officialdom even before the woman announced, without introducing herself or her companion by name, "We are here from the Department of Child Services."

Was this some sort of followup to the adoption? Well, presumably they would tell him their errand. "Please come in." He waved them toward the living room. "Make yourselves comfortable. I'll just get the baby dried off and dressed."

"You were bathing her?" The woman's tone suggested disapproval.

"Yes, she was something of a mess after her lunch."

"Was she," the man said, as if doubting either the mess or Adam's response to it. "Yes, you'd better get that little girl dressed, hadn't you?"

What the devil was the man implying? Adam marched out of the room without replying. At least the energy in his step pleased Jessie, who stopped crying and started babbling a little two-note song.

He reached the baby's room and hesitated. Would they draw some sort of malign conclusion from his closing the door? On the other hand, they might decide he was improperly exposing his daughter if he left the door open. He was coming to believe that they would find a way to interpret whatever he did as some sort of shortcoming. Making up his mind, he closed the door and fumbled with his phone. While he collected a clean outfit with his left hand, he managed to open his list of contacts with his right and scrolled down to Mr. Voxsmith. He needed two hands to finish drying Jessie off, but every few seconds he tapped out another word or two of his message. *DCS is here and acting hostile. What the hell?*

He had just steered Jessie's arms through the clean shirt when the phone's text alert chimed. *I'll find out. In the meantime, watch your ass. But don't act like it.*

Great.

The baby yawned. Her babbling was more like mumbling now. Maybe she was ready for a nap? He picked her up and went back into the living room. "I'm going to put her down for her nap, and then we can talk."

The woman looked at the man and then back at him. "You're going to leave her by herself?"

He forced back a growl. "Would you like to see her room first?" He could swear they would find nothing to criticize in the safety-certified crib with its firm mattress, in the top-of-the-line baby monitor whose speaker sat on the living room bookcase, in the blinds safely distant from the crib with their cords secured up high.

Unless the recommendations had changed again, and he and the others were doing something wrong.

Both of the visitors (or investigators, or intruders, or whatever they were) inspected the room and everything in it. They said nothing, but both made notes on their tablets as Adam put the baby in the crib. When they all returned to the living room, the pair sat down on the couch while Adam was considering whether to invite them to do so. The woman studied her tablet and then said, "We have received reports of the infant's loud and continued crying."

Adam frowned, trying to remember any time when Jessie had been particularly cranky or inconsolable. "I don't think that's happened."

The man looked down his nose at Adam. "Really."

The woman said, "Perhaps you were out at the time, and your wife or the . . . other woman was in charge of the infant."

Couldn't these people say the word "baby"? And was he supposed to leap at the suggestion that Grace or Toni was a negligent parent? "I have full confidence in both of them. They love Jessie as much as I do, and look after her just as carefully." The man's smirk upon hearing this statement made it that much harder for Adam to control his temper. "Who made these so-called reports?"

They both started to speak at once; the woman subsided to let the man finish. "That information is confidential."

Of course it was. Well, to be fair, you wouldn't want people to keep quiet about possible child abuse or neglect for fear of retaliation. Was there some point in the process where the parents learned who had accused them?

After another twenty minutes Adam spent describing Jessie's diet, sleep schedule, and elimination habits, as well as his and Grace's and Toni's work schedules, the two from DCS stood up, nodded to each other, and headed for the door. Adam's voice rose in an undignified and embarrassing squawk. "Wait! What happens now?"

The man said over his shoulder, "Now we file our report."

And with that, they left.

As soon as they were out the door, Adam started to slam it, caught it in time to close it less loudly, and called Voxsmith. "They're gone. Did you find out anything about why they came here? I thought we had everything taken care of!"

Voxsmith, not for the first time, gave Adam a look Grace had labeled "Ah, The Innocence of Childhood." "DCS has opened a file, which is supposed to happen only after they receive a report. I wouldn't bet against one of their people having solicited or invented that report. The Bureau decided not to fight your and Toni's settlement, but did you think they were happy about it? You made the Bureau look bad, and bureaucracies, when they aren't feuding with each other, tend to support each other."

"So it's harassment. How far do you think they'll take it?"

Voxsmith chewed his lower lip thoughtfully. "Just a guess, but I suspect they won't do anything else this time. They're probably jerking your chain to remind you it's there. If you don't find a new way to make trouble, they may not make any back."

Toni's mother, however, received the news with a frown of concentration. When Toni questioned her, Valerie shushed her and said, "My iceberg detector is pinging. Not loudly, but — give me a while to think about what might be lurking below the water."

Chapter 22

Ad agency personnel

The ad agency's sales manager did her best to negotiate a higher rate than federal departments usually paid. She was, however, somewhat surprised to succeed. She would have thought some regulation or other would set a strict limit on such expenditures. But on the other hand, who knew how many different categories, classifications, and priorities were involved?

In the end, the spots were so easy to write that she could have accepted a lower rate without serious regrets, or flak from the VP for Sales.

The creative director met with someone from the Bureau, who accepted her recommendation on which spot should run first. And it ran with unusually little delay.

The scene: a home that might have been typically suburban, if not for details like shabby furniture and worn rugs. The front door opens and emergency medical technicians rush in, carrying a stretcher. The view changes to show the couch, where a pregnant woman lies gasping, frightened or in pain or both, with a man crouched by her side, gripping her hand. The man stands and backs away as the EMTs reach the couch, but he whispers anxiously to the nearest one, "Is she going to lose the baby?"

The EMT does not take his eyes from the woman, reaching to secure a strap across her legs. "We hope not."

The scene freezes and is replaced by the solemn face of another woman, impeccably groomed. "Once, there was nothing you could do to keep this potential tragedy from happening." Then, slowly, she smiles. "But now, there is."

Cut to a room full of incubators in a pastel rainbow of shades, cheerful music playing softly in the background. The same couple stands next to one of the incubators, relaxed, holding hands, beaming at each other, and in subtle ways better dressed than before. A voice-over, with the familiar advertisement tone, drowns out the music. "A simple, free procedure will protect your baby from the possible complications of pregnancy . . ." A list of such hazards as maternal anemia, gestational diabetes, placenta previa, and preeclampsia scrolls by slowly on the right side of the screen. " . . . leave you free to prepare for your baby's arrival, and be healthy, strong, and well rested when you welcome your little one."

Final scene: the couple, holding a yellow-wrapped bundle, radiating happiness, with a website and phone number displayed prominently above them, and a few lines of minuscule verbiage at the bottom of the screen.

* * * * *

Toni

Toni usually ignored ads with the ease of long practice. But these days, anything about pregnancy or incubators forced its way to her attention. She watched the ad and knew how it would have seemed to her before, if she'd noticed it at all. Intriguing. Promising. Benign.

Now, she tried to imagine what scheme might lurk behind this new application of Bureau-controlled technology.

It sounded like a wonderful idea, saving babies from

dying or being born prematurely, saving parents from grief. Maybe she was getting too cynical, to assume there was more to it. But she might see what her mother thought, next time they talked. They were due to talk sometime, about the DCS harassment. Though if Mom had figured out what was setting off her alarms, she would probably have called Toni to let her know.

* * * * *

Jack

Mary was sitting on the couch when Jack opened the door, a magazine upside down beside her. She looked up and reached toward him with a gasp, as if he'd been gone for weeks, not hours, and then made it home sooner than she'd hoped. "Ma called again. She said something new this time — about what Pop told you. It sounds like it's actually happening — she saw some sort of ad about special incubators, about how if you're having trouble with your pregnancy, you can have an operation where they take the baby out and put it in one of these incubators."

Jack sat down next to her and put his hand on her belly. The idea had sounded less scary when it was just Pop talking, and not something they would have to decide about. "They'd cut you open? How long would you be laid up?" And what if she lost her job for taking time off?

"I've saved up a few days of sick leave. I could use it. They say — at least, Ma says the ad said it's simple, that it wouldn't take long to get over it. And it's free."

It would have to be, for them to manage it. But — "Wouldn't you miss having him with you?" With the both of them. He'd been looking forward to feeling the baby move for the first time, and all the times after that.

Mary teared up again. He handed her the squashed-up tissue as she said, "But we'd miss him so much more if . . . if anything . . . ."

He pulled her against his shoulder and held her. "Maybe we should do it. I just don't know."

They waited three days, trying to decide. And then Mary started spotting, and they went to the clinic within the hour.

Chapter 23

The Bureau

Once the regulation was proposed, those who reviewed it first wondered only why it had not already been promulgated. Of course the incubators should not be used only for the convenience of expectant mothers. Of course any woman who could not carry a fetus without exposing it to toxic chemicals should be required to transfer that fetus to the Bureau's care for the remainder of her pregnancy.

After all, even though smoking tobacco cigarettes was almost everywhere prohibited, a black market in such cigarettes persisted. And women who lacked the minimal good sense to avoid poisoning themselves with nicotine and its byproducts could not be counted on to refrain from smoking during pregnancy. For that matter, women careless enough about their own health to allow members of their household to smoke might well continue that path of least resistance, even when the secondhand smoke could irreversibly harm the child they were carrying.

As for alcohol and other recreational drugs: some states, to be sure, had made ingesting them while pregnant a misdemeanor at the least. But scofflaws were certain to exist. And the ads touting the greater freedom a mother would enjoy, should she leave the concerns of gestation to the Bureau, would practically write themselves.

But then, bean-counters and other naysayers started in

with their objections about enforcement costs, jurisdictional battles, and other such practicalities. The proponents reluctantly shelved the idea for the time being. When the process of accepting embryos or fetuses for temporary safekeeping had further matured — when the regulatory environment had developed as the safekeeping mission made desirable — such rules would be a mere detail, easy to incorporate. But it was high time to get that development underway.

* * * * *

Poloma

There was nothing quite like watching a young child arrive at the clinic, about to become a big brother or sister. Some were solemn, eyes wide, almost holding their breath. Others bounced every which way, rambunctious and loud, announcing their new status to all comers.

So when she saw the tall, hard-angled woman approach the front desk tugging a little girl by the elbow, harsh commands interspersed with muttered insults, she could barely contain her rage at how such a special moment was being defiled.

And of course, the infant waiting to emerge, so carefully nurtured and tendered and guarded, would be turned over to this same monstrous mother, to be berated and abused in its turn.

How many parents like this, and worse, had Poloma seen in her days as a social worker? And how few had she been able to coax into parenting lessons, and how few of those had made the most of that opportunity? How many children had she been unable to help, let alone rescue?

The Bureau, with its clean, calm corridors, its sweetly colored incubators, its carefully chosen adoptive parents, had been a refuge from all that. But now that parents were encouraged to use the Bureau's resources to ease their own pregnancies, the refuge had been breached, and barbarians like this woman had forced their way in.

Could anything be done to stop them?

Poloma rarely vented about work to anyone, and especially not over a beer, when she and her coworkers were all looking to relax. But that evening, after she'd been biting her tongue all day, the second beer was enough to loosen it. When a woman she had only seen at a distance sat down next to her and started making conversation – a woman old enough to have developed parental instincts, even if not actually a parent – she found herself telling the story and saying, "How can the Bureau be making it *easier* for an abusive mother like that to have another child?"

"It's a terrible shame, isn't it?" The other woman looked Poloma in the eye, her expression curiously intent. "And yet, if that woman hadn't had her older child with her, you might never have known what sort of mother she was."

Poloma found she was clenching her teeth, and relaxed her jaw enough to drink some more of her beer. She should have chosen a less bitter brew.

The woman went on, her tone not so much sympathetic as passionate. "If the Bureau is going to take responsibility for the well-being of children, shouldn't that responsibility include ensuring the children leave us for safe homes and responsible parents, whether or not the Bureau is choosing those parents?"

Poloma was certainly inclined to agree — except . . . . "How?"

Her coworker took a careful sip of white wine. "We screen potential adoptive parents. That procedure could be adapted for, or at least inform, some procedure for ensuring that any child who leaves our care goes to a safe and appropriate environment."

Poloma took a less careful gulp of her beer, taste notwithstanding. What she was hearing . . . it was unprecedented. Could it possibly be authorized?

And what did "appropriate" mean?

But remembering the woman that morning, and the pained, hopeless eyes of the child, she could not bear to ignore this possible alternative. "Please tell me more."

Poloma sat at her desk at home, tablet at the ready. Despite the beer she had drunk, her head felt remarkably clear. It might be excitement at an unlooked-for opportunity, or the thrill of starting down a path that felt, but apparently was not, forbidden.

Where to begin?

Guidelines

Or should it be *Parameters*?

But either title presumed too much. She was being allowed — had been invited — to contribute her ideas, but whatever the administrative structure of this confidential project, she was surely at a bottom rung.

Suggestions as to Possible

What were they planning? Screening? Analysis? But she needed to face facts. There would be no purpose to such analysis, to examining parental capacity, unless the results would be used to protect the helpless children in the Bureau's care.

Suggestions as to Minimum License Requirements

Maybe the beer was having some effect after all. She found it hard to call forth the bureaucratic language in which she was usually fluent. For now, she had better content herself with making notes to be refined later.

No violent or abusive behavior

. . . How could a violent or abusive temperament be discovered, absent conveniently obvious evidence? Had that woman shown up without her child, Poloma might well have overlooked any more subtle warning signs. But surely those in charge were consulting with experts, psychologists, who would know how to flag such tendencies.

No violent or abusive behavior demonstrated or tendencies identified

So much for abuse. But neglect, if less blatantly culpable, could be just as dangerous.

No negligent tendencies demonstrated or identified

Of course, negligence need not be a general character flaw. It could arise from ignorance.

Basic knowledge of infant care confirmed

But not only infant care, surely. It would be wishful thinking to assume that a parent who knew how to care for an infant necessarily how to handle the more complex and wide-ranging needs of a toddler or older child.

Necessary knowledge concerning the care and rearing of children from infancy through adolescence

That should be enough. It would, in fact, require a great deal of work to craft and implement the necessary procedures.

With so much to do, Poloma might be called on to play some additional role. She jotted down one last note.

Indicate availability

Chapter 24

Poloma

Poloma had tried telling herself that she was content to have offered input on the parameters of any future licensing program. She did her best to ignore her belief that her training and skills would allow her to be useful in that process, beyond simply submitting a single preliminary set of ideas.

When she finally received the notification of a secure message, she felt the relief and satisfaction of patience rewarded for as long as it took to go through the necessary steps and see the message. And only that long.

Apparently, the work of designing the program had proceeded without her. Her assistance was now desired, not for any psychological or sociological insights she might have, but because of her tactically useful place in the Bureau bureaucracy. The licensing program, it seemed, occupied a somewhat ambiguous — perhaps even precarious — position. How could it be introduced as unobtrusively as possible?

There was, as it happened, a pragmatic answer to that question. Poloma still had primary administrative responsibility over the screening of prospective adoptive parents. She could assimilate content from the proposed licensing program into that process. It would then seem logical and natural to use that content more broadly, whenever the proper permissions came through.

She started to send a message to that effect and then hesitated. She had better review the questions to be asked and procedures to be followed. It would be irresponsible to replace all or part of her own longstanding and fine-tuned procedure without ensuring the quality of the replacement.

Poloma went through the material, taking note of how various questions would either fit within or adequately replace questions she was already asking. That left a fair number of additional questions whose inclusion she found mystifying, with little obvious connection to the qualities, positive and negative, the process was meant to identify. But the language used, and the subtle repetitions to be found among the questions, suggested the involvement of one or more psychologists, just as Poloma had recommended. She had also received a list of investigative inquiries, presenting a similar dichotomy between obvious and obscure purposes.

Poloma extracted the questions and inquiries for which she had no clear explanation and put them in a separate document. At some point, she could follow up, asking what made these items necessary to the Bureau's new mission.

For now, she had enough to do, working the material that posed no such problems into her usual procedures.

* * * * *

Chairman of a Bureau committee

The committee with no name — a name being potentially detrimental to security — had issued its update concerning the proposed license exam for those who had made use of Bureau clinics as an alternative to in vivo pregnancy. Much to the chagrin of the chairperson, however, the update came accompanied by a minority report. Until almost the last minute, the chair had expected to be able to dissuade the committee member in question. A minority was one thing, but a minority of one?

In the end, however, the chair decided that including the report was a more prudent course than calling the man's bluff. A public release would do far more damage. She begrudgingly made do with alerting those higher in the hierarchy to the report's existence and emphasizing the eccentricity and recalcitrance of its author.

The likelihood that the public will accept the state's status as in loco parentis, where temporarily placed fetuses are concerned, must be seriously reduced if the requirements for parental retrieval go beyond those addressing an infant's future safety and security. In my opinion, the exam adopted by the majority does just that. The argument that ideologically extreme parents will be more likely to endanger their children in unpredictable ways is itself destabilizing, in that future Bureau management may apply this principle in ways current management would find unacceptable . . . .

* * * * *

Valerie Greene (Toni's mother)

Valerie Greene, attorney at law, also known to two people as Mom and to much of the legal community as Oh God Not Her, had two assistants, sometimes a third, and none of them was idle. They had many duties, varied enough to keep them interested if sometimes overburdened. One such duty, usually scheduled for the first of the month, was to review matters in which the office had received no filings the month before, so Valerie could decide whether they required action of some sort. The list Valerie had just received included the file DCS had opened concerning Jessie. If the allegations had been investigated and found to be groundless, Valerie's and Voxmith's offices should have received a report declaring the case "unsubstantiated." No news was not always good news.

Valerie stuck her head out of her office and told her current assistant, pecking away industriously at her computer, to check up on the matter. She had barely sat back down when her assistant buzzed her. "Still pending."

"Thanks. That's all for now." Valerie closed the connection and cussed, quietly enough that her assistant wouldn't hear. DCS appeared to be playing a game Valerie had heard called "the sword of Damocles." Keep trouble hanging by a thread, so the subject of the inquiry would fear every slamming door, every gust of wind, that might sever the thread and make the sword descend.

The buzzer sounded again. Valerie rolled her eyes, then frowned as the other assistant said, "Your daughter, on line 2." She would rather have had, if not better news, at least something more conclusive to share.

Valerie picked up. "Hello, darling. Are you calling about the DCS investigation? I'm afraid there's nothing new so far."

"That's what I figured." Which suggested there was another reason for the call. And indeed, Toni went on to say, "I wanted to mention something else. Have you seen any of those new ads about using incubators for problem pregnancies? To help the parents, with no donation involved?"

Toni started to say something else, but Valerie interrupted her. "Hold on a moment. There's that pinging again."

Toni chuckled, if not without a hint of strain. "Your iceberg detector?"

Valerie nodded. "But there's nothing actually wrong with using the incubators that way. In fact, I heard something years ago suggesting that was the original idea, was what the people who developed the incubators in the first place intended. So why are both of us reacting as if there's a problem?"

Toni replied, grimmer than Valerie had often seen her, "Because we don't trust the Bureau."

"True enough." Valerie tried to track down exactly what was troubling her beyond that general distrust, and failed. "I suppose we'll just need to wait and see. To keep an eye on things, until these interrupted pregnancies reach their conclusion."

$$* * * * *$$

*A Bureau of Reproductive and
Infant Safety administrator*

The couple who came into the administrator's office did not look much alike — he was tall and skinny and red-haired, while she was short and curvy and had stiff black hair that didn't match her eyebrows— but they had similar befuddled expressions on their faces. Clearly, they had not read the updated paperwork carefully enough, or understood it well enough, to know what this "exit protocol review" appointment was actually for.

The administrator started by putting them at ease, asking them how the last few months had been. The mother perked right up. "It's been so *nice* being able to keep up with all my activities — and to eat and drink whatever I want!"

She giggled. "I didn't have to be a stick-in-the-mud on New Year's Eve after all. And Steve here —" She jerked her head in his direction with a look halfway to a leer. "He's been glad I was able to keep my figure, haven't you, baby?"

The father had the grace to look embarrassed, but he managed to recover and smile at her. "I always love how you look, baby." He turned toward the administrator. "Are there more papers for us to sign or something? And can we go visit the baby when we're done?"

First things first. "There's nothing for you to sign today. But you're not that far off track. You see, as the facility you entrusted with the care and protection of the fetus, we have a number of related responsibilities. Those responsibilities include making sure that when the fetus, or rather the baby, leaves our care, he or she —" He paused and glanced at the file on his screen. "He, that's right, will have the best chance we can give him to thrive, to grow into a happy and productive citizen. So we've adopted some procedures to maximize that chance."

The father knitted his forehead. "You mean you're offering us some sort of help with the expenses of raising him? Do we have to do anything special to get that help?"

The question provided the administrator with a segue. "It's not about expenses, exactly." Or at all. "But yes, there is something we're asking you to do, some questions for you to answer at this stage of the process." He opened a desk drawer and pulled out two tablets. "These have the questions loaded on them. You just click that green START button when you're ready. I'll show you to a room where you can work undisturbed."

The couple was looking confused again, but they would understand the procedure better once they took part in it. He finished up by saying, "The tablets will tell you when you've finished. Then you can visit the fetus, and come see me afterward. And by the way, it's perfectly all right to help each other answer the questions." After all, that was how parenting worked. It was only fair.

The administrator looked at the couple's test results and spat out a couple of his mother's Polish oaths. He'd known his luck would run out sooner or later, and now it had happened. The couple were probably downstairs right now, in one of the visiting rooms. And he would have to explain why they would no longer be welcome there. Not until – not unless – they completed a more successful retest.

He'd been given a suggested script for the upcoming conversation. He dug it up and looked through it again, wincing at the stilted bureaucratic language. He could do better on his own, but winging it had its hazards . . . .

The knock on his office door told him he was out of time. He ushered the couple in, trying not to wince at their expectant faces.

As they sat back down, he made the spur-of-the-moment decision to forget about the script and let the proverbial chips fall where they might. It was unlikely, anyway, that the couple would have occasion to quote him word for word to any of his superiors. He took a few breaths to stall and to plan before he leaned forward, folded his hands on his desk, and looked at neither of them.

"I'm sorry, but the results of the test you took weren't what we hoped. That means we'll have to proceed differently than we would have if your scores had reached the desired threshold."

They both looked disappointed, the man crestfallen, the woman petulant.

"I didn't describe the test in any detail beforehand,

because we get the most accurate results if you take it without preconceptions. But as I suggested, the test has to do with our responsibilities as caretakers of these fetuses. Part of our mandate —" (That was overstating the degree of consensus, but no matter) "— is to ensure the well-being of these fetuses beyond the point of delivery. Accordingly, we ask parents to answer some questions designed to ensure that when infants leave this facility, they will be going to safe, appropriate, nurturing environments."

The woman looked confused; the man, quicker on the uptake, had gone tense, his elbows tightening against his sides, his chin lowered toward his chest.

"Toward that end, we will be offering you some free classes, designed to help you improve your test performance. I can call up the schedule right now and get you signed up. If it's feasible for you, you could start next week."

The man relaxed a little, and his face brightened. It was the woman's turn to shrink back into her chair. "I don't want to take any classes! Why should I?"

The man looked not at his wife but at the administrator. "It's important, isn't it."

"Yes, very important indeed. We take our responsibility for these children very seriously. We're duty bound to do everything we can to safeguard them, even after they leave these premises. That includes providing the classes you —" He bit back the phrase he had been going to use and substituted, "— that will help you give your baby the best possible care. Now let's get to work on that scheduling." The administrator opened the scheduling program. "How about next Tuesday at 7:30 p.m.?"

The man shook his head. "My sister's getting married next week. I'm in the wedding. We leave town tomorrow and won't be back until Wednesday."

"Oh, what a shame. That makes things rather difficult. There are six classes, one per week, and it's normally required to take them in order."

The man gazed up at the ceiling, probably doing mental arithmetic. The administrator could see the moment when he reached the crucial realization: he went pale, and hands closed into fists. "If we have to wait until the classes start over, that'll be after our baby is delivered."

The woman tossed her head. "So we finish the classes later, if we have time."

The man gulped. "That isn't how it works, is it?"

The administrator struggled to appear relaxed and businesslike. "I'm afraid not. If you haven't completed the classes and achieved the required score on the test by the delivery date . . . ." (Just spit it out.) "There would be a delay in our releasing the infant into your custody."

The woman gaped at him and then turned to her husband, asking in a shaky voice, "What did he just say?"

The man looked as if he were fighting back tears. "She said that if we don't take this class and pass their damned test, they won't let us have our baby." He turned back toward the administrator and said through clenched teeth, "We have to talk about this."

"Of course." The administrator got up. "I can take my lunch hour now, so you can stay here and discuss the matter. Leave me a note, or send me a message, telling me what you've decided."

Not that it was likely to make much difference — unless they had the wit to decide that the man would give all the answers next time. He would have to make a note of the necessity of preventing that, despite his earlier naïve approach to the matter.

If he had been a betting man, the administrator would have bet that this couple would fail the test again. It was a shame, but at least the shakedown period for the new facility was almost over. The infant to be delivered in six weeks' time would have the chance to thrive in more capable hands.

* * * * *

Ad agency Creative Director

The creative director had brought the ad campaign's copywriter and art director to this meeting, but the creative director did the talking while the other two set up for the presentation. "We believe we've struck an appropriate balance between over-promising and intimidating. As you requested, we avoided any direct reference to the licensing exam. And production costs should be quite reasonable."

The Bureau rep shifted in his chair. Most clients, at this stage, either looked eager, or presented a cultivated air of boredom or skepticism or both. This one seemed almost . . . embarrassed? The creative director had a good guess as to what might be happening, but she forged ahead. "As you'll see, there's plenty of room for tweaking the details." She nodded to the art director, who started the video playing on the conference room screen.

For visuals, they had a series of sketches where the actual ad would use video with actors. The sketches of the parents, a traditional man-and-woman pair, did not so much show as suggest some non-Caucasian ethnicity. The man smiling and welcoming them bore a faint resemblance to the Bureau rep.

The voiceover was already in place.

You chose the best, safest way for your baby to come into the world. Now it's time to prepare for the next phase. We can help you acquire the knowledge and skills you need so you can say with confidence, when the time comes, "We're ready to take our baby home!"

A second sketch showed the same couple as part of a small group, sitting in unrealistically comfortable chairs in a sunny classroom, a motherly teacher at the front pointing to a whiteboard. The accompanying voiceover provided reassuring promises as to the frequency and convenience of classes. The final sketch showed a baby wrapped in a green blanket, with a smiling technician handing the baby to the beaming parents. A banner at the top showed contact and web site information as the voiceover practically crooned, "Bureau of Reproductive and Infant Safety Classes — Helping You Become a Parent."

The final image stayed on screen as the copywriter and art director looked expectantly at the Bureau rep. The creative director kept her expression calm and neutral.

The Bureau rep waved a hand at the screen. The creative director murmured a direction to the art director to turn off the video.

The Bureau rep cleared his throat and said, "It's excellent work, just as we expected. I commend you on capturing our brief so well." A pause, with more throat clearing. "It's just that some, ah, discussions have been taking place recently about whether the time is right for this promotion, and whether a revised brief is indicated."

The creative director greeted this news with a hint of an ironic smile. "Are we looking at payment of the kill fee, then?"

The Bureau rep waved his hands in denial. "That would be premature, I believe. These discussions should wrap up quite soon. If we decide to proceed with the current brief, I believe your schedule can accommodate the short delay, and if not, we would adjust our delivery expectations."

The creative director allowed herself a slight frown. "I believe the contract includes specifics about the circumstances under which the kill fee will be due. Your legal folks can review those. In the meantime, please keep us in the loop." With that, she got out of her chair, her team following her lead.

"Certainly." The Bureau rep looked as if the word had a sour taste as he opened the door for their exit.

Back in the street, the copywriter asked plaintively, "What did all that mean?"

The creative director looked around before responding in a lower voice. "Just guessing, mind you, but I'd say there's a faction in the Bureau, or maybe higher up, that isn't so sure they want to help parents who would otherwise fail the test to squeak by."

The creative director opened the message with some reluctance. The agency's financial interests notwithstanding, she would rather the Bureau dropped the campaign and paid the kill fee.

If not for her misgivings, the message would have been cause for relief. The single rejected spot was to be replaced by two.

One spot should feature a female of undoubted attractiveness, though not a type appealing to sophisticated tastes. She should suggest membership in the lower socioeconomic strata, with a presentation far removed from the innocent or virginal. She is to be shown in conversation with a comparable male. The male's appearance and body language should imply the possibility of brutish behavior. Their dialogue should focus on the degree to which pregnancy would make the female less desirable for, or less apt to engage in, sexual congress. The final sequence should relate or illustrate a recent donation, with sexual congress as likely in the near future.

Another spot should feature a female similar to the first, but less carefully groomed. She should be shown in a posture and living quarters evidencing a reluctance to engage in any housekeeping activity or physical exertion. She should express dissatisfaction at her recent increase in fatigue, and at the inconveniences to be expected from her recently confirmed pregnancy.

Satisfactory completion of these spots may result in extension of the series.

The creative director shoved herself back from her desk and took two gulps of lukewarm coffee, grimacing at the temperature and taste. Water would have been better. Or mouthwash.

These spots weren't aimed at parents who could use a little help to meet the new standards.

They were aimed at parents who never would.

Chapter 25

The comm buzzer — still too loud, and likely to wake some napping infants — jolted the facility director out of what must have been an unscheduled nap of her own. The gate guard sounded both nervous and defensive. "Trouble on its way. Three men, all big. And I think at least one of them is packing."

"Packing?"

The guard made a noise that probably came with rolling eyes. "Armed. Carrying a gun."

And the guard hadn't felt up to stopping them. Understandable, if frustrating. "What do they want?"

The guard mumbled something she couldn't quite hear. "Speak up!" she ordered.

He yelled this time. "One of the children!"

The men were already banging on the front door; two babies started crying. The director ran to the break room across the hall, hoping to find reinforcements. Two nurses, one man and one woman, neither physically formidable, were drinking the mediocre coffee. She pointed frantically down the stairs and ran on, hoping they would follow.

The front door shook from the hammering. If she didn't open it, the intruders would probably break it down, and she would have to spend money getting it repaired. She unlocked it, opened it, and backed up barely in time to avoid the three men who burst in. The guard had been quite right:

they were big, both tall and broad. All had dark curly hair and either untidy beards or rough stubble. They looked alike enough to be brothers.

The one with stubble rather than beard moved close to her, glared down, and growled, "I've come for my boy."

She pulled herself together and replied, in her most official tone, "Please explain yourself. We do not care for other people's children here."

"The hell you don't!" The taller of the bearded brothers stepped up to loom over her as well. "They talked my sister-in-law into putting her baby in one of those boxes, and then they wouldn't give the baby back!"

Now she understood. The woman in question must be one of the involuntary donors, unable to meet minimum parenting standards. She should have realized something like this might happen. She would have to request additional security. In the meantime, where were the nurses, and the rest of the staff? She looked quickly around and found an audience, rather than allies. No one wanted to get in the way of these men. No more did she, but that was her job.

She stood as tall as she could manage, her chin up, looking the self-proclaimed father in the eye. "I'm afraid I am not authorized to admit visitors to this facility. Please remove yourselves before I'm forced to call the police."

The man laughed in her face, a harsh bark of a laugh. "Move a finger toward a phone, and I'll be forced to remove it — the phone, that is. At least for starters. No, you're going to tell me where my son is, and we're going to take him out of here and back home where he belongs."

What would he do if she spit in his face? Best not to find out, much as she longed to do it. "I have no idea to which child you're referring."

The shorter — though not much shorter — brother

crowded in. "Where's your office?"

She folded her arms and stood mute. He sniffed, an incongruously delicate sound. "You'd rather I start opening doors until I find it?"

She gnawed her lower lip, searching for an alternative, and came up with nothing. She spun around and led the way, fists clenched, back up the stairs. The men thundered along close behind.

When they reached her office, the shorter brother pushed his way ahead of her, sat down in her chair, and addressed himself to her computer. Her jaw dropped and she sputtered in inarticulate protest, but he ignored her, finding his way to the intake files with disconcerting ease. But there, surely, he would hit a snag. The data base did not include donor names.

The man pulled out a slip of paper on which he'd written some numbers and typed them in. In a few seconds, he spun the chair around and gave the others a thumbs-up. "Found him!"

The director stared at him. "But — how?"

The man who claimed to be the father came forward and clapped his brother on the shoulder. "He hacked your precious Bureau, that's how. He got my wife's fucking 'donor number' and used that." He bent over, peering at the screen. "They've got a photo, don't they?"

"It should be . . . here."

The father's hand tightened on his brother's shoulder. "Oh, my God. There he is." He let go and faced the director. "Get him. Or we'll go through this place until we find him."

She looked past him at the computer, and the picture on the screen. They still had few enough children that she recognized him and even knew in which room he'd been placed. But what should she do? Did she even have a choice?

She walked stiffly to the door of her office and turned left. "This way, *gentlemen.*"

The boy had the crib near the window in the second room down. Of the three other babies, one appeared to be napping, while two were standing in their cribs, watching as the caregiver held the one these men wanted and pointed out the window. "Look at the squirrel! See how it jumped?" The baby laughed and pointed.

The men had stopped short, just inside the doorway. The father moved slowly forward; caregiver and baby turned toward him. The caregiver, seeing the director's tight-lipped frown, breathed in sharply; the baby, all unaware, studied the new face, and after due scrutiny, gave the man a beaming smile.

One of the brothers said softly, "He's got Ma's eyes. And Pa's dimple."

The other came back toward the director and whispered in her ear, "We're taking him whether you like it or not. Make it easy, and no one gets hurt, and none of the kids get scared."

Meanwhile, the father held out his arms and said to the baby, "Come to Daddy. Time to go home." The director could hear the tears thickening his voice. "We have squirrels there too, lots of them. I'll show them to you, and so will your mother. She'll be so happy to meet you." His voice faded away, and he dashed at his eyes with one hand before stretching it out again.

The caregiver was stammering objections; the director came closer and said stiffly, "Go ahead." The caregiver looked from director to father to baby in obvious bewilderment, but put the baby in the father's arms.

Next time, they would have better security in place. As for this child . . . maybe they could get him back. If the family planned to stay in one place, gawking at squirrels, there must be some forces available to find and confront them.

The director backed out of the men's way as they moved in a tight phalanx out of the room, into the hall, down the stairs, and out the door.

Chapter 26

Poloma

Poloma stood by the door of the delivery room, watching as the incubator unfolded and the technicians opened the bag and lifted the baby free. Adam and Grace stood close by, clutching each other's hands, waiting in breathless eagerness for the technicians to hand the baby to them. Toni Greene stood in a corner, tears streaming down her face.

The technician cut the cord, wrapped the baby in a surprisingly colorless blanket somewhere between khaki and gray, and carried the baby past the expectant parents as if they were invisible. Grace reached out and grabbed the technician's arm, but was shaken loose. Adam appeared frozen in horror. Toni wailed aloud. Poloma tried to follow the technician out the door, but when she reached the corridor, technician and baby had utterly vanished.

She started awake, panting, eyes wide, sitting up in the bedroom just starting to pass from the darkness of night to the warmth of dawn.

Poloma rarely bothered about her dreams, if she even remembered them. But the dream from this morning refused to fade away in daylight. It kept creeping into her thoughts all day, distracting her from her work, even disturbing her digestion.

She finally gave up on matching her usual productivity and left an hour early. After all, she had a ridiculous amount of leave time saved up. She may as well go home.

The fresh air, carried to her on a soft breeze and smelling of cut grass, should have made her feel better. Yet it failed to do so. In fact, she was getting a headache. Whatever was wrong with her, leaving the office was doing nothing to ameliorate it. When she had almost reached the subway, she sat on a bench near the entrance and put her head in her hands. After five minutes, she got up, headed back to the Bureau, and made her way through the mostly deserted corridors to her office.

Much as she wished to, it appeared she could not indefinitely avoid confronting what Toni Greene had heard, back before the trial. Toni might be immature and impulsive, but nothing about her suggested a dishonest character. And if the proposal to set up some sort of facilities had not, after all, been abandoned, it was all too plausible that after Poloma's inquiries had been brushed aside, she would be left out of the loop from then on. As someone positioned to investigate, did she not have a responsibility to do so?

That memo, the one she'd been told to delete months before, had had one or more appendices that she hadn't read. She should have read them, or at least skimmed them. It might not be too late to do so.

Everything she did on her desktop was recorded, of course, and her superiors could access that recording at any time. Unless she finally used the some of the software her cousin had given her, an assortment of dubious programs, the gift no doubt intended to tease her for being so straitlaced. This one would hide her keystrokes and her file access, and was disguised as an antivirus program. She might conceivably get away with using antivirus software other than what the Bureau supplied. She closed her eyes and gathered her resolve. Then, with the sense of stepping into an uncharted void, she engaged the software and searched her personal files.

There.

She had been right. There were two appendices. The first included more detail, charts and graphs and formulae, about the projections. She looked them over for any information not included in the preliminary summary, and found nothing of importance. On to the second, titled, "Scale Projections Depending On Scope of Implementation of Evaluation and Filtration Procedures."

A few years ago, that language might have stymied her. But she had spent those years wading through and using such language. The title sounded like a reference to the licensing program.

Which was supposedly a recent development, to whose planning Poloma had been asked to contribute. But which had been contemplated, and possibly underway, more than two years ago, and was here described as "integral to the details for implementing the third proposal in the main body of this document." And now that she thought back, the body of the memo might have made reference to licensing, in the proposal she had failed to finish reading.

But she had set out to investigate what Toni had overheard, not to brood over having been played for a fool. If the proposal to establish some sort of institutional infant care had in fact been approved, who would be tasked with developing and implementing it? It could, of course, be under the Bureau's aegis. But it seemed unlikely that with all the file review that had brought the initial proposal to her attention, Poloma would have come upon nothing more recent. Where else, in the vast network of federal agencies and departments, might matters somehow related to donated fetuses be handled? She should start with those under the same overall Health and Human Services umbrella as the Bureau. Of which there were plenty. She called up the list.

No, no, not there, no, probably not . . . Maybe. Though it would be a stretch of that agency's authorizing legislation, to the extent she understood it.

And she had never received access to that agency's files. But the Deputy Director, and others above Poloma in the hierarchy, might have broader permissions installed on their computers; and they had just received new computers. The old ones would be in the storage room. Their batteries probably hadn't run down. And they might not have been wiped. Tech services of that kind tended to receive low budgetary priority and were therefore understaffed.

Of course, she wouldn't have the necessary login information. But one of the programs from her cousin could bypass many obstacles of that kind. Only if a user was particularly diligent about security would she be stymied.

Time for another step into the void, or closer to the cliff.

She had no key to the storage room, but the janitors' changing room was unlocked. With growing excitement, rather than the fear that would have been more rational, she picked a hanging coverall pocket, left the room, and sauntered past the storage room as if heading to the stairwell beyond. Entering the stairwell for good measure, she waited a couple of minutes and reemerged, walking past in the other direction. No one nearby; no footsteps, not even from the floor above.

She had to try several keys, of course, but she succeeded on the fourth. She slipped inside, locked the door again, and used her phone as a flashlight to look around, shading the light with her sleeve to keep the illumination at a minimum. There were the old desktops, all shoved together on top of a discarded desk. She would have to move at least three of them to have access even to one. And none had keyboards attached. She looked around, her pulse racing, and finally found a stack of keyboards on a shelf.

Forty minutes later, she took stock of herself and had to laugh. If she had ever imagined entering the world of espionage or other intrigue, she would not have expected it to be such a sweaty and disheveled business. But she had managed to go through five desktops, hooking up a keyboard to each in turn, and eliminate them as possibilities. On to the sixth.

She connected the keyboard, powered it up, and identified the former user. Senior enough, this time, but so had two of the others been. She stretched her aching back and neck, and for the sixth time she ran a search.

Finally, pay dirt.

She tiptoed to the locked door and listened through it. Footsteps! Her stomach leapt into her throat. But the footsteps went on by, and she chided herself for excessive nerves.

Still, she had better hurry.

Fingers fumbling, she opened the file and looked quickly through it. But the dense bureaucratese defeated that first attempt. She took a few deep, cleansing breaths and started over more slowly.

It didn't seem to be a document describing a project or proposing one. It had more to do with routine expenditures and approval of same. Expenditures including various personnel. Personnel including pediatric nurses.

And other expenditures including cribs. And a high-priced security system.

She went back one screen to the list that had yielded this file. Was there anything else worth reading? The list included several committee reports. Odd — here was one that failed to name the committee. And it included a minority report, infrequent nowadays with all the institutional pressures against such.

She opened the file and skimmed the main report, and then the report of a lone dissenter. And with this, her investigative foray became surreal. The author of the minority report might have been tapping into all the doubts Poloma had been suppressing ever since she received the licensing questions and procedures.

She copied the relevant files onto the portable drive she had taken from her office, then double-checked that she had not missed anything significant. She was sufficiently deep in her task that it took her several seconds to register the approach of more footsteps. She yanked out the drive and stuffed it in her pocket, hoping it was robust enough to withstand such treatment, as she heard the jangle of keys.

Poloma had at around five seconds left to think and act before the door creaked open. It found her turning off the desktop with a satisfied nod and turning toward the door. "Oh, hello. I'm all done here. You can carry on with —" She gave a supercilious sniff. " — with whatever it is you're here to do."

The janitor — presumably not the one she'd stolen keys from — was pushing a large dolly. "Here to move this crap out. They won't let movers in here for security reasons, so we deliver it all out back. Not that that'll make any difference, security-wise, as far as I can see." He glanced at the desktop she had turned off and then back at her. Thinking about security — not good.

She forced herself to smirk in satisfaction. "Good timing on my part, then. I suspected my assistant hadn't done a thorough job cleaning up my old hard drive, and I was right." She walked past him without another word, out the door, and down the corridor to the stairwell. She entered it and leaned against the wall, hands shaking.

Had he bought her act? Would he tell anyone? Would whomever he told check her story?

Perhaps. But there was nothing she could do to prevent it. All she could do was make her escape and hope for the best.

And then, decide what to do with the information she had taken such risks to obtain.

After a night of restless and interrupted sleep, Poloma finished getting dressed and called up her calendar. How early did she need to get to work? The thought made her feel slightly nauseous. She sat back down on the bed to consider why.

She still believed in her work. At least, she still believed that the clinic, the incubators, the publicity reaching out to unprepared and panicking women, saved innocent lives and helped women go on with their own. But might not some of those women, if offered the chance to stop panicking and to prepare, have chosen to raise and cherish their own babies? And now there was the licensing program, a program she had naively believed would stay within its initial boundaries.

What was her share of responsibility? At what point did doing her job become complicity in things that she would never have accepted if she had been told about them when she accepted that job?

Poloma looked at her calendar again. A full day, yes,

but full of routine tasks, work that could be done either sooner or later, and much of it by other people if necessary.

She needed a mental health day. A day to relax, to rejuvenate.

Or a day to think.

She sent off the message, tried lying down again (though not going so far as to undress), got back up and made a cup of ginger tea. She drank the tea in her rocking chair and watched the leaves on the trees seeming to dance in the rain, wrapped in the giant shawl her oldest aunt had given her on her 21st birthday. (Would she ever learn to knit? Could she ever be that patient, give herself that much time?)

The mug warmed her hands, the warmth comforting, even though it would be a warm rain outside. There was something hypnotic about watching rain on leaves. She could almost empty her mind . . . .

She sat bolt upright, her heels hitting the floor and stopping the motion of the chair. Where had that thought come from? In what depths had she been hiding and nurturing so perilous, so explosive, a notion?

She would lose her job, and that would be just the beginning. Though there might be ways, and reasons, to delay that inevitable consequence.

She shrugged out of the shawl and went to find a pen and paper. She needed to think in writing, and these words must not be digitally accessible. In fact, she would start a fire in the seldom-used fireplace, the better to destroy the evidence as soon as it had helped her decide what to do.

Chapter 27

Jack

Jack held Mary's hand tight as they walked into the clinic and checked in with the receptionist. It had been a sickening shock to receive the "reminder" message and realize that, in the mind-numbing process of going through all that paperwork, and with Mary dashing to the bathroom with morning sickness in the middle of it, he had neglected to read all the fine print. At least, he assumed — and maybe he was being naive — that somewhere along the line, they had agreed to take this infernal exam before they got their baby back.

Mary was annoyed, even offended, by what she saw as an unnecessary nuisance; but that was all. The message had, after all, come almost six weeks before the designated delivery date, and they had been able to get a time slot a few days later. If any governmental snafu caused complications, she thought that would be long enough to untangle them. Her imagination had gone no further. It was Jack who had been waking up at three in the morning with barely remembered nightmares about dimly lit mazes, or more literally, testing locations he was unable to find. Some instinct, developed over generations of ancestors dealing with ever larger and more complicated power structures, was warning him of trouble ahead.

He and Mary sat next to each other at a table, in a room with the same pastel walls as elsewhere in this place. They'd been told they could talk to each other about the questions. But as they started the third and final portion of the exam, they both stopped, at almost the same instant, and stared at each other in speechless dismay.

Your child is fourteen years old. You find illegal drugs in his room. Do you: (a) leave them in place; (b) throw them away; (c) call the proper authorities?

Your child's teacher sends home a report that your child has been talking back in social studies class. Do you: (a) ignore the report; (b) contact the teacher to defend your child's actions; (c) remind your child to respect the teacher's expertise and avoid disruptive conduct?

Mary pointed to the final option on both questions. "I wonder if the right answer on this part is always (c)." Her finger was shaking. So was her voice.

Jack grabbed her hand and squeezed it, wondering if she could feel his pulse racing. He leaned close and whispered, "What should we do?"

Mary had never been one to whisper. She swallowed and said softly, "One of us has to answer the way they want."

His other hand tightened into a fist. "And then what happens? They might make us split up, so only the *approved* parent —" He was forgetting to speak quietly. He didn't bother to finish the sentence. The rest of it was obvious.

Mary lifted their joined hands and kissed his knuckles. "It's only for now. We'll do something. We'll get help." She freed her hand, turned back to the screen, and touched option (c) on both questions.

Jack glared at his own screen as if he could melt it. He stabbed option (a) on the first and (b) on the second, so hard he jammed his finger. Finally he let himself swear. He didn't stop until they both had finished and hit "submit."

The administrator looked genuinely sorry. "I'm afraid neither of your results were satisfactory."

Mary gasped. "*Neither* of us?"

The administrator wriggled a little in his seat. "We allow parents to take the test in concert, just as parents are able to help and reinforce each other in meeting the challenges of parenthood. But we monitor the testing facilities to guard against use of outside sources or other inappropriate activity."

If Jack had tried to speak, or even move, he would have leaped across the man's desk and grabbed him by the throat. Mary glanced at him, saw the danger, and asked quickly, "What happens next? What can we do to, to satisfy your requirements?"

The man shook his head and stood up. "I'm sorry. If you had failed to pass under other circumstances, you would have been given the opportunity to take classes that could improve your scores. But a deliberate attempt to subvert the testing process is a different matter."

"Meaning what?" Jack growled. "Are you planning to just *keep* our baby? We — we won't let you!"

The man almost managed to hide how nervous Jack's manner made him. "There is, of course, a process by which you can contest your results. If you'll consult the message we sent you, you'll find the particulars. For now, you'll have to leave."

Mary stood up, grabbed Jack's hand, and pulled him upright. She was right, of course. The first thing to do was get out of here. Then they would figure out what to do next.

There had to be something. And he doubted it would involve the Bureau's "process."

* * * * *

Toni

Toni had her hands full of tools and covered in wood dust when her phone played its new-caller tune. She could let the call go to voice mail — but what if Adam or Grace was calling to tell her something had happened to Jessie? She blew dust off her hands, dropped the tools on a table, and shoved her sleeve up.

An unidentified caller, and no video. Not Adam or Grace, then. And the absence of video suggested some scam, or maybe a reporter. Still, now that she'd let the call disturb her work, she may as well find out who was calling and whether she could yell at them for it. "Hello?"

The video came on: Poloma, looking nervous and tense. "Toni. Thank you for taking my call. I need to talk to you."

Toni rubbed the remaining dust off on her overalls. "My lawyer — my mother —" It felt odd to call her either when speaking to someone who was neither a friend nor a stranger. "She told me to talk to her if you made contact."

"She knows. I called her first. She said she couldn't talk to me, only to the Bureau's lawyer, but that you and I could talk if you were willing."

Should she double-check with Mom first? It wasn't likely Poloma was lying. And this might have something to do with what Toni had overheard at the clinic, even though so much time had passed. "Come to my studio, then, if that's all right with you. I'll send you the address."

Toni had put a hot plate and mini-fridge in the studio, and allocated one section of cupboard to snacking supplies. When Poloma arrived, looking even more uneasy than she had on the phone, Toni waved her toward the one respectable chair and asked, "Would you like some tea? Or —" It was midafternoon, not necessarily too early. "— a beer?"

Poloma hesitated. "A beer does sound awfully good, at that."

Poloma chugged half the beer in one go. Toni managed not to do a full-fledged double take, but she did twitch in that direction. Poloma looked up at Toni and sighed. "This is difficult."

Toni did her best to hide her impatience as she waited for Poloma to start talking. It took another couple of minutes and the rest of the beer. Putting the empty bottle down, Poloma looked at Toni with eyes wide and face pale. "I've followed up on the matter you brought to my attention, and reviewed what I found in the light of my knowledge of recent . . . changes in the Bureau's practices. I now know things that you, that parents, should also know. I want to tell you about them."

Toni abruptly discovered herself to be her mother's daughter. "Wait a minute. Aren't there laws about what government employees can reveal?"

Poloma pressed her lips together tight, then loosened them barely enough to say, "There are. I assume I'll be breaking them."

Toni held up a hand. "Just let me call my mother. You should really talk to a lawyer first, and she can help you find one." Without waiting for Poloma to answer, she got up and walked to the other end of the studio, calling her mother and speaking as quietly as she could manage. She summarized the situation and asked, "Was I right?"

Her mother's mouth twitched in what was probably amusement, but she answered promptly. "You were right, both about Poloma's legal jeopardy and about my being able to recommend someone suitable. Note this name down." She rattled off the name; Toni jotted it down with pencil and paper rather than her phone, in perhaps unnecessary caution. She read the name again; it was unfamiliar. "Why this fellow?"

Her mother gave a rather evil chuckle. "Because he knows the law in this area intimately. And because he used to know the government's attorney intimately, and would be delighted to make the latter's life miserable."

Toni thanked her mother and returned to Poloma, who had picked up the bottle again and appeared to be reading the label over and over. She handed Poloma the note. "Here's who you should call."

Poloma took the note and tucked it away inside her slim purse. "Thank you. I will. But I'm going to talk to you anyway, even after this attorney tells me why I shouldn't. So I may as well go ahead and do it now."

Poloma started chronologically, one memo and conversation at a time, while Toni balled her hands into fists on her lap and tried to let Poloma make her revelations in her own way. Soon, however, she could not help interrupting. "I'm sorry. You know what you're going to say, so you understand it. But I'm not following all this."

Poloma grimaced, an expression Toni had never imagined she would see from this woman. "All right. I'll just sum up what I think has happened and is in the process of happening."

And now, the sentences fell like blows.

Tests, required tests, that parents had to pass to claim their babies. Tests going beyond parenting skills and even parental temperament to parental politics.

Institutions, not just for children for whom no adoptive parents could be found, but for the children whose parents failed the tests.

Plans for longterm state custody and education of all these children, with room for more and more to join them.

When Poloma ran down, Toni sat stunned, staring at her. She had trouble pulling her thoughts together, let alone putting them into words. What came out first was, "I have to call my mother again."

But when she got to her feet, she found she had to do something else first. She ran into the small studio bathroom and threw up.

* * * * *

Valerie Greene (Toni's mother)

Valerie chewed on her stylus and reread her notes for the third time. She had suppressed her emotional reactions while talking to Toni, and set them free during readings one and two. Now, sadness and apprehension and rage behind her, she could consider tactics and legal constraints.

First: did these revelations give her any basis for getting the settlement set aside and aiming for some better result, with true adoptive parent status for Toni? Was Poloma's information directly relevant to the issues raised in their pleadings? If not, would the judge have allowed more amendments to those pleadings in order to take aim at the Bureau's secret programs, and would Toni, or Adam and

Grace, have had standing to do so? Or could Toni, or could Adam and Grace, credibly claim that they would have declined to settle or insisted on different terms if they had known about these programs?

Against all these uncertainties, she had to weigh the predictable consequences of rocking the proverbial boat. The Bureau – assuming it was behind the DCS harassment – had already leaned on the family in a clear warning not to make further trouble. Blowing the whistle on these Bureau activities would certainly qualify. Just how nasty would things get if she or Mr. Voxsmith ignored the warning?

And now, finally, she could see the connection that had been eluding her. The Bureau intended to vet every parent who left its facilities with an infant, regardless of biological connection between parent and child, using either the preexisting adoption process or its new licensing program. But by joining forces with Toni, Adam and Grace had created an unprecedented situation. Rather than simply accept it, the Bureau had enlisted DCS to provide additional scrutiny. Who knows – they might move on to monitoring other adoptive families in the future, to make sure they conformed to whatever requirements the licensing scheme was meant to impose.

Time to consider the options. She shouldn't speak to Poloma, but Toni could — though Valerie might be risking trouble with the bar by using Toni as a conduit. Poloma might have access to lists of parents who had been unable to pass the exam. Theoretically, Valerie could represent such parents, as long as both they and Toni understood about the possible (if unlikely) conflicts of interest and agreed notwithstanding. But then the Bureau would probably strike at Toni in order to pressure Valerie. It would be better, once she found a new plaintiff or plaintiffs, to refer the case to another lawyer, one independent of her . . . .

Independent. The word echoed in her mind, and brought back memories she'd buried years before. Neja Patel. Her protégée, the rising star of her boutique law firm, a fearless and ferocious litigator after Mom's own heart, who had shocked her – though she shouldn't have been surprised – by leaving the firm for one across the state. She'd told Valerie at the time that so long as she worked in Valerie's firm, or even in the same city, the legal community would see her as a younger, more junior Valerie. And off she went.

Valerie took the stylus out of her mouth and stared at it. What better choice than a lawyer known throughout their legal circles for having insisted on independence, spurning an offer of partnership and moving halfway across the state to ensure a fresh and separate start? Would that disappointment – that painful rupture – unexpectedly bear fruit?

Of course, she couldn't be sure Neja would take such a case. But a chance to poke self-important bureaucrats with a stick, learn important and heinous secrets, and garner plenty of publicity? Neja would have a hard time turning that down.

Well, she was getting ahead of herself. The first order of business was to look for such alternate plaintiffs, through Poloma or if necessary some other way. And if that search failed, she could still file a motion directly on Toni's behalf.

Time for another phone call — a short one. She had better discuss all this with Toni and Adam and Grace in person.

Chapter 28

Jack

Two days had passed since the disaster at the clinic. By the second day, when they could go hours at a time without either Mary or Jack cursing until they got hoarse or bursting into tears, they were able to think and to plan.

They started by calling in sick. It was harder for Jack than for Mary, and the last thing they needed was to lose either of their jobs, but they had no choice if they were going to make phone calls during the day. They worked together on a list of lawyers who handled "family law" and "civil rights," the two categories that seemed to apply, and took turns phoning them. So far, they were getting different frustrating responses from the two types of lawyer. The family law attorneys did not handle cases against government agencies, or required fees well beyond what Jack and Mary could possibly scrape together, or saw the couple as some kind of troublemakers. The civil rights lawyers were swamped with work already, or had a long application process full of hoops to jump through.

None of the lawyers had expressed outright disbelief. Their assumption that this was how government could be expected to work made Jack almost too angry to talk.

Mary ended her latest call and shook her head. Jack picked up his phone again, which was overheating from too much use in too short a time. He should take a break, but he hated to wait, feeling helpless, with so much at stake. Then the phone flashed an incoming call, with no image or ID. Could one of the lawyers be calling back? Mary came over and looked on as he took the call and said, gruffly, "Hello?"

The voice on the line was female, refined, and tense. "Mr. Connor, my name is Poloma Clark. I work for the Bureau of Reproductive Sa — of Reproductive and Infant Safety, and I'm not supposed to be speaking to you. Is there somewhere we could meet, you and me and your wife, after 5 p.m.?"

5 p.m. Government hours. But this woman could be anyone. "You'd better show me what you look like. Unless you plan to wear a red carnation in your buttonhole."

The video came on, showing a woman with a thin face, brown eyes, and long black hair. And if she was setting him up somehow, she probably wouldn't look so nervous. Or she might, if she was a coward as well as treacherous. But it was take the chance or keep doing what wasn't working. He looked over at Mary. She lifted her chin and nodded.

"We could meet at —" Jack gave the address of a local dive where no self-respecting government employee would spend time. "— at 5:30. What is this about?"

"I'll tell you that at 5:30, if no one stops me." And she hung up.

He and Mary were sitting with iced tea and a basket of cheese fries when the woman slipped through the door. Once inside and away from the grease-coated windows, she stopped, stood up straighter, and walked with short tight steps to their table. Mary produced something like a smile. "Please sit down. Would you like some fries? Or something else?"

A wistful look passed over the woman's face, as though there was something she would have liked but couldn't allow herself. "I'll take a cheese fry, thank you." She plucked one daintily from the basket and laid it on a spare cocktail napkin.

Jack bit a cheese fry in half with a snap. "Why did you want to talk to us?"

The woman — Poloma, had she said? — pushed the napkin and cheese fry to one side and folded her hands in front of her. "My position at the Bureau gives me access to various confidential files. So I am aware of your results on the recent custodial capacity exam. Including the particular responses that were deemed — disqualifying."

Mary was looking at Poloma with wide eyes, as if she held the promise of some sort of escape from this nightmare. As if she would say it had all been a mistake. Fat chance. "And?"

Poloma twitched once as if she had started to look back at the door and restrained herself. "And I believe you may have a basis for legal action."

Jack gripped the edge of the table and leaned forward. "That's all this is? Telling us we should sue? We've been calling lawyers all afternoon!"

A faint blush added color to the woman's pale skin. "If you already have counsel, I would not do anything to interfere. But if you have not yet found legal representation, I know of a very able young attorney who would be interested in discussing your case. An attorney trained by Valerie Greene, an extremely able and widely respected attorney herself."

Jack had been, until now, safely distant from the world of lawyers and courtrooms, but the name rang a faint bell. "And what would you get out of this? A finder's fee?"

Poloma's chin jerked up. "Mr. Connor! I am jeopardizing my job and risking criminal prosecution by even contacting you. I will gain absolutely nothing by doing so — except . . . ." Whatever was fueling her indignation seemed to run out. She looked down at the table, and her next words were almost inaudible. "I will, to some extent, cease to be complicit in policies I oppose."

A silence fell, broken by Mary's saying, "Will this lawyer be expecting us to call?"

Poloma looked up, and said with the first hint of humor she had shown, "She'll be hoping so, at least. May I take it you won't disappoint her?"

The receptionist who answered the phone at the lawyer's office was dressed like a model or a movie star. Her manner, as she put Jack and Mary on hold, suggested that she was withholding judgment about whether the caller was worth her, let alone the lawyer's, attention. Instead of either silence or elevator music, the hold screen played a fusion of classical and classic metal, along with almost hypnotizing abstract visuals.

After about two minutes, a woman in a less fashionable but equally expensive suit appeared, her features some sort of Eurasian mixture. "Good morning. I'm Neja Patel. Thank you for getting in touch."

The phrasing, as if they were doing her some sort of favor, made Jack wonder just how dim she thought he and Mary were, but he let it pass. "A woman whose name I maybe shouldn't mention told us you might be able to help us."

"I spoke to our mutual acquaintance at some length. If she will help me, as she seems prepared to do, I will do my best to help you. And while no attorney can guarantee success, especially in cutting-edge litigation against a formidable opponent, my best is very good indeed."

Jack had no idea what to say to that. "Says who?" would hardly be appropriate. Fortunately, the lawyer wasn't done. "The first order of business is to decide on your goals. Are you seeking an opportunity to retake the test? The Bureau personnel admitted to you that other parents get that opportunity."

Mary broke in. "Excuse me, but isn't the first order of business actually — business? What would your help cost? Could we be on some sort of payment schedule?"

The lawyer's smile was close enough to condescending to raise Jack's hackles. "Ms. Connor, I'm willing to take this case pro bono. Which means 'for the public good,' and also means you pay nothing. Our firm makes a point of doing a fair amount of pro bono work, and this would be just the right sort of case to approach on that basis."

Mary turned to Jack, face tight with distress. She came from folk who never asked for help and never let anyone know they might need it. Jack's family had been either more practical or less determined. He'd eaten many a can of donated tomato soup with stale donated crackers. And they were going to need the best help they could possibly get. He looked at the phone instead of at his wife. "Thank you. Very much. About your question — if they let us take the test, what would keep them from simply flunking us again? Or is the rest of the test, the non-political part, so straightforward that there'd be no room for funny business with the scoring?"

The lawyer's eyebrow twitched as if it surprised her that he could think of the question. "Unfortunately that isn't the case. Along with what you're aptly calling the political portion, there are aspects of the tests designed by psychologists to assess a wider range of parental attitudes and inclinations. Aside from whether those questions are based on anything better than junk science, the scoring involves a confidential algorithm."

Mary still sat stiffly at his side, but had apparently resigned herself to going forward. "What else could we aim for, then?"

The lawyer started ticking off possibilities on her fingers. "We could ask to have the Bureau ordered to treat you as passing, on the basis that Bureau personnel admitted reasons for your disqualification that were arbitrary and unreasonable. Or you could seek to be exempted from the testing requirement, on the same basis. Or we could mount a broader attack on the testing process itself, on any of several grounds: as outside the Bureau's mandate, or as inconsistent with the agreement under which you ceded physical custody of the fetus, or as violating one or more constitutional rights."

Jack ground his teeth. "I don't know how to begin to think about legal tactics. What do you think would give us the best chance at getting our baby back — and getting him back before he's born, or delivered, or whatever they call it?"

The lawyer's confident expression became something more intense. "Ms. Clark didn't mention the delivery date. When is it?"

"Around four and a half weeks from now."

"Then we'll have to start with a motion for preliminary relief, requesting an order that you get custody of your baby pending any further proceedings. We'll point out the potential for irreparable harm to your relationship with your child if the baby is placed anywhere else while the process grinds on."

Jack tried to focus on anything but the picture of their

baby being handed over to foster parents, or kept in some sort of ward. The image that replaced it was not much better. "Won't they claim that our test results show us to be —" He spat the words out. "— dangerous people, who could do more harm than their oh-so-carefully-selected replacements?"

The lawyer got the somewhat glazed look of someone multi-tasking, and they heard the clicking of keys. "We'll also request an immediate freeze on your file, so no one can adjust your scores in that direction. If I can get this in front of the right judge, they'll have to at least come forward with evidence rebutting the presumption that you are the best custodians for your child."

More clicking. "I'm having our contracts prepared now. My assistant will go over the details with you. But as far as the case is concerned, you'll be working directly with me. Assuming you've decided to proceed."

Jack glanced at Mary. No reluctance now. She leaned in and fairly growled, "You bet we've decided. Let's turn those so-and-sos inside out."

Half an hour of mind-numbing legalese later, Jack fixed Mary and himself double scotches, set them on the cinder block coffee table, and turned on the gas fireplace. He flopped on the couch, making the springs squeak; Mary thumped down next to him and laid her head back, exhausted. He handed her one of the glasses, and she pried her head up enough to take a good long slurp before she set it back on the table and collapsed again. Jack took a swig of his own drink and stared into the glass. "I'm afraid to hope. But I'm hoping. That lawyer's a firecracker. She could get things moving in the right direction."

He settled back in the couch, and Mary shifted over to rest her head on his shoulder, saying softly, "I'm hoping too.

We should get in touch with that woman, Poloma, and thank her."

Jack frowned. "That reminds me. Her number never did show on my phone, and when we met, she didn't give us a way to get in touch with her."

"That's too bad," Mary said. "But maybe she'll call to find out what happened."

Chapter 29

Poloma

Neja called Poloma on a Saturday evening. "Am I correct that you've sent me all the relevant documents to which you have access?"

"Yes. I don't think I forgot any."

Neja nodded but didn't smile. "Very good. Now we need to talk about what may happen next, or soon. I don't know how well you covered your tracks, to the extent that was even possible. You must have done reasonably well, or there would have been repercussions before now. But there is a possibility that your breach of security will be discovered, or has recently been discovered. And as I believe you know, much of your investigation, and your revealing what you found, could be characterized as violating one or another federal law or regulation. So it's not improbable that you'll be arrested."

Poloma swallowed the bile welling up in her throat. She had stalled on calling the attorney Valerie Greene had suggested, partly because of the financial burden of paying one. And there might have been some uncharacteristic magical thinking involved – that if she didn't hire an attorney, she would escape without needing one. The man might not be available after all this time, if he ever had been. "If I'm arrested, could you be my attorney? Do you even do that kind of work?

Neja's smile had an edge to it. "In fact, I did quite a bit of white-collar criminal work when I first joined my current firm. It served to broaden people's expectations of me. So I know my way around the criminal justice system. There is, however, a complication." Neja chewed her lower lip, a mannerism Poloma would not have expected of her. "There would potentially be a conflict of interest between my representation of you and my representation of Mary and Jack. Whether such a conflict actually exists depends on whether there are ways you could assist Mary and Jack in their litigation beyond what you've already done. If so, any plea bargain for you might well include a guarantee that you would take no further part in their case, or even that you would be available to help the Bureau defend against it."

Poloma tried to put herself in the place of her future self, threatened with prison time, subjected to whatever forms of intimidation might be tried. When she was fairly certain that present and future Poloma were in agreement, she replied, "I won't help the Bureau against Mary and Jack, no matter what — unless I learn something about them that changes my views. As far as helping them, all I could do is testify about how I found out about the first documents and tracked down the rest."

Neja didn't smile, but something in her expression conveyed as much warmth. "Hmmm. If you're willing, it'd be a good idea for you to write all that down in detail in an affidavit. I'll send you the language it has to include as soon as we hang up. That language will make it the equivalent of testimony for some purposes. And I suggest we still find you another lawyer in short order."

Where had Poloma put the information about that other attorney? "Hold on a moment, please." She searched the purse she had been carrying when she visited Toni and found the slip of paper, wrinkled and creased, in one corner. She read Neja the name, Chase Alister, and asked, "Do you think I could hire him?"

Neja pursed her lips. "He's in much demand, and this is awfully short notice. But I can call in a favor, and he'll take you on if he has time."

Poloma's chest went tight. "I would hate to impose on you in that way, to reduce your future options."

Neja gave a quiet snort. "I'll earn more favors soon enough. It'll be my pleasure." Her expression shifted toward stern. "But I may not be able to reach him over the weekend. I think you'd better take Monday off, and possibly more time after that."

Poloma heard nothing from Neja on Sunday. As she sent off the message that she would be taking a day of leave, she was surprised at the rush of gaiety that flowed through her at the idea. The feeling lasted until she fell asleep, but Monday morning brought back the burden of worry she had learned to ignore, more crushing for the respite.

She was finishing her second cup of coffee, contemplating an unprecedented third, when her phone trilled its first-time-caller chimes. The screen showed her a man about her age or a little older, well-groomed almost to the point of becoming conspicuous for it. "Ms. Poloma Clark?" At her nod, he went on, "I'm Chase Alister. Neja Patel tells me you may be needing help soon. And she summarized your situation, to the extent she's aware of it, which should save us some time. Time being, I gather, of the essence."

Poloma hoped the flinch she felt wasn't visible. "I'm sorry I didn't get in touch earlier."

Mr. Alister nodded and moved on as if her apology,

whether or not appropriate, was of little importance compared to the tasks before them. "Here's what Neja told me . . . ."

Listening to his recital, she realized that Neja knew all the pertinent facts, and very little about the emotional realities behind them. The realization saddened her somehow, but there was hardly time to discuss it. More, she lacked the energy. She felt suddenly tired, as much because of what might lie ahead of her as what had gone before. When it became clear Mr. Alister had finished, she asked, "What should I do now?"

"Now, or rather tomorrow, you go to work and act the way you normally would, as much as possible." He paused, listened to some unseen employee ask a question, tossed off a brief instruction, and went on briskly, "And it's possible nothing dramatic will happen. But in case something does, I'd like to give you some idea of what you should expect if you're arrested. First of all, are you familiar with the expression 'good cop, bad cop'?"

"Vaguely. One cop acts nasty and the other acts sympathetic?"

"That's right. And the way you deal with it is the way you deal with everything else that happens. You say nothing except 'I want to speak to my attorney.'"

It seemed too easy. "And if I say that, they'll let me talk to you?"

The cynicism in the attorney's face and voice made him seem older. "We'll have to do a little arranging beforehand to ensure it. Police sometimes like to play 'hide the prisoner.' When they want a nice long uninterrupted go at someone, they don't record the prisoner's presence at the facility and give, shall we say, uninformative answers if a lawyer calls and asks about them. So I need you to contact me, let's see, twice a day to tell me that nothing's happened yet. If I don't

hear from you when I should, either I or one of my associates
—" He paused at something in Poloma's reaction. "I'll show
up myself, if at all possible, for any significant court
proceedings. My associate or I will start checking the likely
lock-ups, in person. We have enough weight to throw
around that they won't stonewall us for long. And in the
meantime, all you know how to say is, 'I want to speak to
my attorney.' Got it?"

Poloma took a deep breath, shakier than she would
have liked. "How difficult is that likely to be? Are things
going to get rough?"

"Physically? Not very, would be my guess. They may
keep your cell brightly lit at night, or otherwise deprive you
of sleep. There might be other attempts to put you off
balance, such as giving you ill-fitting or soiled clothes to
wear, or delaying your meals or your access to bathroom
facilities." Mr. Alister tapped his clean-shaven chin. "Let's
make that check-in three times a day instead of two, if you
don't mind."

Poloma gave a small, humorless chuckle. "I don't mind
at all."

Her bosses let her get through all the annoying
messages and accumulated busywork before the police
appeared, handcuffed her, and took her away. She
wondered, as she stumbled along surrounded by armed and
uniformed figures, whether the timing had been on purpose.

"You're in a whole lot of trouble, girl. Hope you took a
good deep breath on your way in, because you're done with
fresh air."

"I want to speak to my attorney."

"That's a laugh. You think we care what you want?"

"I want to speak to my attorney."

"Look, I admire your idealism. And your guts. Lots of us want our public servants to have those qualities. I want to help you, if you'll let me."
"I want to speak to my attorney."

"What do you expect some lawyer to do for you? They'll throw doubletalk at you until you're cross-eyed. Or they'll grandstand and get their face on all the feeds, and never mind what happens to you."
"I want to speak to my attorney."

"We call it the Precinct 37 diet plan. It's a 'back to basics,' traditional sort of diet. Bread and water. Except for the bread part. And the water."
"I want to speak to my attorney."

"Off the floor, you! Sitting on the floor is against the rules. In fact, I don't believe you're allowed to sit, period. And if you lie down, well, things could get really ugly."
"I want to speak to my attorney."

"Awww, are you crying? Not so superior and tight-assed now, are you?"
She had no tissues. She wiped her eyes, and her running nose, on the scratchy yellow-green uniform. "I — I — w-want to sp-speak to my att-t-orney."

She later found out that it took only four hours for the lawyer to find her. But it took rather longer for him to push his way in. Mr. Alister must have overestimated his law firm's pull, or underestimated the police determination to keep squeezing her.

In the meantime, they gave her a cellmate. A cellmate who was twice her size and much amused by Poloma's apparently obvious unfamiliarity with her surroundings. "Get used to it, darlin'! It might even get better, after a while. I might even let you share the toilet sometime soon. For now, you can use that corner. Oh, and I get restless at night, so you'll be leavin' both bunks for me, so's I can change back and forth."

"Gee, you don't look so hot. You start being a little more cooperative, and we can find another cell for you. One that smells better."

It was hard to remember what she was supposed to say. "I want . . . I want to . . . I want to speak to my attorney."

When the lawyer finally gained access to her, they let her use a toilet and wash up — which gave her a chance to drink as much water as she could quickly gulp — and even gave her a fresh uniform, though not a mirror or a comb. She untangled her hair with her fingers as best she could and tried to straighten her shoulders despite her exhaustion.

She dragged into the windowless little room, dully noting the squeak of the clear plastic shoes on the floor. The man who stood as she entered wore an unobtrusively expensive suit with a lilac shirt and a dark gray tie. She suppressed embarrassment at the contrast between this elegant ensemble and her own attire. Obviously he knew she had had no choice as to the latter, and he must be accustomed to it.

He waved her to a sturdy, blocky wooden chair. "It's

bolted down, I'm afraid." She collapsed into it with a little moan of pleasure at sitting down.

"I'm Matt Hamilton. As Mr. Alister told you, I'm with the same firm. And I want to start by saying you've done a good job so far. You've got them frustrated as hell. Now tell me everything that happened from the moment you were arrested."

When she had reported everything she could remember, he gave a satisfied nod and said, "Most of that isn't too surprising. But much of it could be useful."

When Mr. Hamilton left, they put her in what must have been a regular cell, with a less alarming cellmate, a bunk bed, and a toilet she could actually use. She had just enough time to accept her new cellmate's ultimatum that she take the top bunk before a loud bell rang from a speaker in the wall and the cell doors opened. She followed her cellmate and the others to a cavernous room with long metal tables and bolted-down metal benches, and a serving line through which they all filed. The trays were not metal, but laminated cardboard, presumably too lightweight to be used as weapons; the flimsy plastic spork was similarly limited in potential, and proved adequate to eating the grayish stew and overcooked mush of unidentifiable vegetables.

Then it was back to the cell, whose reek she now had time to appreciate. Her cellmate showed no interest in conversation, instead pulling out a worn paperback with a title suggesting pop self-help mysticism. Poloma used the toilet with more gratitude than she would have imagined a few days ago, then hauled herself up to her bunk and lay there, facing away from the ceiling light, until she fell asleep.

The next morning, after a breakfast actually recognizable as oatmeal and bitter black coffee, Poloma was rounded up and taken in a van with eight other prisoners to a tall slab of a building that proved to be the courthouse. They were unloaded and herded into a large and barren cell in the basement, already half full of prisoners and echoing with the noise of multiple conversations, cursing, and complaints. After about half an hour, Poloma and another dozen prisoners were sent out of the cell and up a well-guarded elevator, and then to a courtroom furnished with an incongruous splendor of dark red leather and polished wood.

Poloma saw neither of her lawyers until she had been sitting on a bench at the side of the courtroom, with a gradually shrinking row of other prisoners, for almost an hour. The judge, a pudgy balding man in his forties who slouched enough that his robe appeared too big for him, droned his way through one plea after another — mostly guilty pleas — and calendaring of further proceedings. There were only two prisoners left next to Poloma when Mr. Alister slipped through the door and made his way to the row of seats behind the table where prisoners and their lawyers had been sitting. He saw her staring at him and gave her a reassuring smile. The woman at the other table, presumably the prosecutor, stared also, her shoulders going stiff. Poloma recalled, now, what Toni's mother had said about bad blood between them.

Ten minutes later, a bailiff escorted Poloma to the polished table at which Mr. Alister awaited her. He whispered one hasty instruction. "Don't say anything unless the judge is obviously asking you to. If you're not sure of the answer, ask for permission to consult me."

The judge read her name, or rather, a mangled version of it, from a screen in front of him. Mr. Alister identified himself as counsel for the defendant, waived reading of the charges, and when asked for Poloma's plea, said "Not guilty" with notable firmness. The prosecutor cleared her throat and said, "Given that the defendant is charged with serious breaches of government security, and is likely to have additional information that must not be disclosed, we ask that bail be set at five hundred thousand dollars."

The judge pointed his nose at Mr. Alister, who had raised his eyebrows as if in disbelief. "Any response?"

"Your Honor, we can if necessary present evidence that the authorities holding my client have obstructed her access to counsel and made repeated attempts to interrogate her despite her requests for counsel. They have also subjected her to a variety of illegal, degrading, and injurious conditions designed to make such improper interrogation more productive. Bail on the order of that requested by the prosecution will facilitate the continuation of such tactics." He looked the prosecutor over, his expression suggesting suspicion that she had been complicit in those tactics. "Nor has the prosecution shown my client to be a flight risk — unsurprising, as she is well established in this community and has absolutely no criminal record."

The judge looked wearily at both lawyers and then at his screen again. "I see that Mr. Alister has filed a motion to change venue for this case to Judge Rayner, who is already presiding over what he describes as a related civil proceeding. Does the prosecution have any comment on that motion?"

The prosecutor started. "Your Honor, we are not prepared to respond to this motion at this time, having anticipated —"

"Yes, yes, you anticipated filing something. But if this case is going to end up being Judge Rayner's problem, the issue of bail would be likely to arise again at that time. For the sake of judicial economy, do you consent to addressing the motion now?"

The prosecutor looked glum, but said, "Yes, Your Honor." Poloma longed to ask her attorney what was going on, but instead bit her lip and folded her hands in her lap. She tried to follow the discussion that followed, gaining a general impression that the judge was looking to unload a hot potato, and that the prosecutor was fumbling for some compelling argument the other way. After about ten minutes, the judge rapped his gavel on the desk and announced, "I'm granting the motion for change of venue. Which means the question of bail is Judge Rayner's problem. Bailiff, return the defendant to holding while counsel check Judge Rayner's schedule."

As the bailiff approached, Mr. Alister muttered quickly, "I've already checked Judge Rayner's calendar. She has an opening in a couple of hours, and I should be able to get us in. Try not to worry. Things went well here."

Back to the big cell in the basement. There were only a few other prisoners there; one was bored enough to approach Poloma and ask, "What you in for?"

Hoping she understood the question, Poloma started to answer and then stopped short. The space was almost certainly being videotaped, and anything she said would probably be thrown back at her in the future. She fell back on a terse "I didn't do anything wrong." Legalities notwithstanding, it was a summary she would defend.

Poloma no longer had any way to tell time, and there was no clock visible from the cell. It might have been midday or later, and her stomach felt both hollow and unsettled, when two guards came to fetch her out again and lead her to a different elevator that rose to a higher floor. Mr. Alister was already seated at the counsel table when one of the guards brought Poloma in. Poloma did not have time to sit before the bailiff commanded, "All rise," and the judge entered from the back of the courtroom.

Poloma had not been sure until now that "Judge Rayner" meant the judge who had made such an impression on her during Toni's lawsuit. The judge's name had not been what stuck in Poloma's memory. She found herself glad to confirm that guess. But should she be? If the law was against her, on the question of bail or the question of guilt, Poloma had no doubt that this formidable woman would apply it without hesitation.

The judge aimed her keen glance at the prosecutor. "I see you're requesting bail in the amount of five hundred thousand dollars, based on the assumption that Ms. Clark might, if released, commit further offenses similar to that with which she is charged."

The prosecutor looked relieved at this beginning. "Yes, Your Honor."

"Can you point me to the language in the relevant statute authorizing bail as a form of preventive detention as regards future criminal activity?"

The relief fell away, replaced by wariness. "Your Honor, it is commonly considered appropriate to —"

The judge snorted; the prosecutor stopped in her metaphorical tracks. "If it is commonly considered appropriate to make up for the absence of statutory language by pretending it exists, I do not consider that a trend I should encourage. There is statutory language indicating that release on bail may be denied, or may be hedged about with conditions, where the judicial officer determines that such release will not reasonably assure the defendant's appearance at trial, or would endanger the safety of any person or of the community. It is my practice to treat the setting of bail at an impracticably high level as equivalent to denying bail. Do you have an argument as to how this standard has been met?"

In the three-way conversation that followed, the chief point in contention seemed to be whether the reckless revelation of such federal secrets as Poloma might possess would endanger "the community," with Mr. Alister eloquently pointing out the speculative and amorphous nature of this claim. Finally the judge held up one hand. "I am ordering bail set at seventy-five thousand dollars. The prisoner is remanded to custody until bail is paid."

Poloma sat, stunned; Mr. Alister stood up and tugged Poloma's arm to pull her upright. The bailiff approached; Mr. Alister said to him, "A moment, please, for me to confer with my client." He hovered nearby; Mr. Alister threw him an annoyed glance. Poloma, afraid she would lose the chance, said hurriedly, "I can't pay anything anywhere close to that!"

Her attorney seemed to be fighting back a smile. "Don't worry. You only have to come up with ten percent of that." The trace of a smile fell away. "Although that ten percent pays the bail bondsman, so I'm afraid you won't get it back."

Poloma tried to remember the combined balance of her bank accounts. "I'm not sure —"

"Try not to worry. I believe I know someone interested in being of assistance."

And with that mysterious hint, Mr. Alister turned her over to the bailiff and trotted out of the courtroom. In less than an hour, Poloma was back in her cell. She had missed lunch.

Poloma was on her way to dinner when one of the jailers waylaid her. "Your bail's paid. You're being released."

She was weak and lightheaded from hunger, but she stumbled after the jailer, almost stepping on his heels. They thrust her clothes at her and told her to change in a small room opening off the intake area. She signed the inventory of what she had in her possession when arrested — her phone, wallet, and keys — and found herself facing the door with nothing in her way and no idea what came next. She should call her attorney and find out. Which reminded her —

She turned back. "Who paid my bail?"

The clerk gave an amused snort. "People always ask that, even when it should be obvious. In your case, it was some hot-shot lawyer — not yours, not even in the same firm. Maybe she owed your lawyer a favor or something."

Poloma had an educated guess as to which lawyer it might be. But for now, she had a more urgent question. "Where's the closest place to eat?"

Chapter 30

Mary and Jack would finally be meeting Neja. Well, it hadn't been that long — the hearing on their motion was set for only a few days after Neja had filed the petition — but it had been the longest few days Jack could remember. They'd tried to pass the time by going for long walks to admire the autumn leaves, but they always ended up talking about the case, or the Bureau, or their baby and how much they wanted to be with him. How scared they were that the Bureau would succeed in taking him away. And they would come home without Jack being able to remember looking at a single tree.

Jack hadn't been sure they would even be allowed to show up at the hearing. On that, at least, Neja had been able to reassure them — and to recommend that they be there. "It's not technically mandatory. But as long as you can show up looking respectable and mature and generally parental, it'd be a good idea."

So only hours after Neja had flown in, here they were, the three of them grabbing coffee two blocks from the courthouse, with Mary and Jack too nervous to eat anything and Neja cheerfully chowing down on a large chocolate croissant and lecturing between bites. "As I told you, there's a presumption that parents are the best custodians for their child and will do what's in the child's best interests. I'm sure the Bureau would love to get rid of that presumption, but it's not going to happen today, if ever. So they'll be trying to rebut that presumption any way they can." She peered at Jack. "If they want to call you as witnesses and the judge allows it, you absolutely must not let them provoke you into saying anything intemperate."

Jack supposed she was justified in aiming this warning at him. When they'd done some practice Q&A on the phone, he'd been the one to lose his temper. But Neja had never seen Mary riled up. When that happened, she could make Jack look like a sweet spring lamb.

"Your Honor, as to the presumption favoring parental custody, there is no clear precedent applying that presumption where custody is challenged prenatally. Moreover, the petitioners' test results serve to rebut any such presumption."

Jack glanced over at Neja to see whether this argument made any sense or constituted a surprise. Her expression answered neither question: she looked somewhere between grave and stern as she said, "Respondent's argument is both revealing and, for that reason, disturbing. Authorized only to ensure the safe delivery of infants to their parents, the Bureau has, with no statutory authorization, set itself up as a gatekeeper, ready to deprive parents of their fundamental rights based on standards of its own devising."

Back to the Bureau's lawyer, like a game of legal ping-pong. "Like all parents to whom my client provides this service, petitioners acknowledged the Bureau's responsibility to ensure that infants would be released to a safe and secure environment. Individual inspections being both impractical and intrusive, the Bureau has substituted the examination on which petitioners performed so poorly."

The judge's thin lips twitched as though she would have liked to respond, but she merely turned toward Neja, whose fingers were rapidly drumming together as she spoke. "Your Honor, even in commercial transactions, waivers must be unmistakable in wording and highlighted so as not to be missed. The Bureau's assertion that its general language about safety and security constituted a waiver of parental rights speaks volumes as to the weight it assigns those rights."

The judge tapped a keyboard and peered at whatever came up on her screen before saying with obvious distaste, "Counsel's characterization of the language in question is accurate, and even somewhat generous. And now, I will hear from counsel for respondent as to why they object to petitioners' request for their test results. May this court assume that those results, and any other contents in petitioners' files, have been preserved intact and unaltered, as ordered?"

The lawyer drew himself upright. "My client has, of course, obeyed the court's instructions. As for the test results, it would be impossible for this court to properly assess those results without expert testimony concerning the development and intent of the questions and the means used to evaluate the responses."

It sounded like evasive doubletalk to Jack, but the judge was nodding along. "As you may know, my calendar does not allow for a full evidentiary hearing on these points until after the scheduled delivery date. What does the Bureau propose to do with petitioners' child?"

Jack clenched his fists on his lap. Mary, sensing or predicting his surge of rage, put her hand on the fist she could inconspicuously reach and pressed down hard. Meanwhile, the lawyer was saying something about finding "suitable facilities." Mary pushed down harder as his fist went to rise up. But the judge arched a gray eyebrow and replied, "And yet you have shown this court nothing concrete to indicate that the parental home would be 'unsuitable.' Despite your dismissal of it, the presumption in favor of parental custody does apply. But I will appoint a guardian ad litem to inspect petitioners' residence and interview them, and to file a report with the court no later than ten days before the delivery date. Unless and until the GAL's report rebuts the presumption favoring petitioners by indicating the necessity of placing the child in temporary custody elsewhere, the Bureau is ordered to allow petitioners to be present at the child's delivery and to remove the child from the Bureau's facilities at that time." The judge sat back and studied her screen again.

Neja stood up and said, "Thank you, Your Honor." To Jack's puzzlement, the Bureau's lawyer did the same. Mary muttered, "What's going on?"

Neja gestured toward the door and led the way toward it. They followed her into the hallway, where she stopped, shook her head as if releasing tension, and beamed at them. "We just won the first round. Lawyers say thank you regardless. It's courtroom etiquette." Then she lowered her eyebrows and stared at each of them in turn. "Now it's up to you. Get your house looking clean and comfortable and cozy, and practice answering nosy questions. Don't screw this up."

Neja called Mary and Jack after work five days later. "We've agreed on a guardian ad litem. He might call to set up a visit, or he might just appear on your doorstep. I've told him you both have daytime jobs outside the home, so if he does arrive unannounced, it should be in the evening. He might come more than once, after he thinks you've let your guard down, so —" She smirked. " — no orgies or drug deals until I tell you the report has actually been filed."

Mary frowned. "If he's such a suspicious person, why did you agree to him? Was everyone else worse?"

Jack wondered whether to signal Mary to back off, but Neja appeared unruffled. "Intuition played a role. This man didn't strike me as someone who would take kindly to government meddling in his own life. And he was the youngest and probably the least jaded one on the list. As for a possible second visit, that's my professional paranoia talking, not based on anything about this particular GAL."

At that moment, the doorbell rang. Neja's eyebrows shot up. "If that's him, be pleasant and patient. And offer him some refreshment, if you have any. Good luck! Call me after."

The man at the door was almost painfully clean-cut, and young enough that he might have graduated college (he definitely looked like someone who'd gone to college) within the last couple of years. Jack reminded himself not to react to the man's likely history as some sort of attack on his own.

Mary's manner welcoming the man in had a faintly maternal flavor that seemed to put him at ease. He introduced himself and showed them the order appointing him, then said a little awkwardly, "I'm not quite sure about the circumstances of my appointment. The order didn't explicitly mention adoption, but are you prospective adoptive parents?"

Jack clenched his jaw and then made himself relax, trying for a tone somewhere between cheerful and matter-of-fact. "Oh, no. We're the biological parents. Mary had to have the procedure — to have the baby moved to an incubator

— when she was three months along, and our baby is due to be delivered pretty soon." He shrugged. "We certainly weren't told at the time that our baby would have a GAL appointed, but we'll be happy to answer your questions and show you around."

They had cleaned the house every night since the hearing, but left just a little clutter for a lived-in look. The baby's room, on the other hand, could have been a show room in one of the department stores that still existed when Jack was little. They had replaced the secondhand crib from Mary's aunt with a new one guaranteed to satisfy all federal and state regulations; the rest of the furniture was used, but freshly painted in the same range of pastel colors found in the clinic's visiting rooms. The matching curtains had no draw strings, and the mobile that had hung from the ceiling was now hidden away in a suitcase in the master bedroom, in case the GAL thought it would tempt the baby into trying to climb the crib sides. A teddy bear night light smiled near the doorway.

The GAL took notes on his tablet throughout the tour. But in the baby's room, he stood looking around, tablet apparently forgotten, and Jack thought he saw a wistful expression on the young man's face.

They led him last to the kitchen and offered him coffee or tea to go with the chocolate chip cookies Mary had made the day before. Jack suppressed the impulse to suggest milk or cocoa. The GAL accepted coffee and put two cookies on his plate while the water was heating, devouring one before the coffee came. Mary, who could drink coffee before bed without it bothering her, poured herself a cup; Jack made do with a cookie and a glass of water.

The GAL sat back, ate the second cookie, and said, "Well, everything looks just fine here. I wish all my visits were as pleasant. If they're starting to send GALs out as a matter of routine, I suppose more of them will be." He wrinkled his forehead. "Are you sure you weren't told more than I about why I was appointed?"

Jack and Mary looked at each other, Jack trying to signal wordlessly that Mary should field this curve ball. After an awkward pause, during which Jack looked down as a further clue, Mary sighed and said, "There is something that happened. Has anyone told you about the test the Bureau has started making parents take?"

The furrows got deeper. "No. What sort of test?"

"Well, that's the problem. Most of the questions were about proper care of an infant or a toddler — safety things. But some of them were . . . I don't know what to call them except political. And our guess is that they didn't like our politics."

The GAL was sitting up very straight in his chair. "Is that what they told you?"

Jack started to nod and then caught himself. Sure as he was that their rejection had been political, he had almost forgotten what the administrator actually said. They had better be frank about something so easily checked. He kept his head high as he said, "What they told us is that we shouldn't have talked to each other about how the questions were political and what we should do about it. Even though they'd already told us it was all right to talk to each other."

The GAL tapped at his tablet, lips pursed. "When did you find out about the test?"

"That there was a test, a week or so beforehand," Mary answered. "That there would be questions with political content, only when we were in the middle of it."

"And that content? Do you have a copy of the exam?"

They both shook their heads. The GAL looked annoyed, which might be good news, since it could hardly be at them. Or could it? Jack hurried to add, "They didn't give us one. And the way the administrator treated us, I didn't think there was any use in asking."

The GAL shoved his chair back as if to get up. "Before I leave, is there anything else you want to show me or to tell me?"

Mary closed her eyes. When she opened them again, they had tears in them. "I've been writing a . . . a sort of letter to the baby, ever since we knew we were pregnant. It's awfully personal, but . . . I think maybe you should see it."

Jack held his breath. Mary had not shared the letter even with him, except to read him a few short pieces. It was an all-in move of desperation. And fury threatened to fill him again at the thought that she had had to make it.

The GAL settled back in the chair. "That might indeed be helpful. And — I won't include any of it in my report. Not verbatim."

Mary got up, fetched the notebook in which she had been writing the letter, and handed it to the GAL without a word. Her lip quivered, and she walked quickly out of the kitchen. Jack ached to follow her, but that would mean leaving the GAL on his own in their house. He stayed.

The GAL skimmed through the notebook, stopping every few pages to read more carefully. About halfway through, he stopped, read, and kept reading. He once again had the wistful expression Jack had noticed in the baby's room. The GAL finished reading a page and gently closed the notebook, placing it on the table. He finally stood up and looked Jack in the eye. "Please thank your wife for me. I'll be filing my report within the next couple of days."

Jack said nothing as he walked the GAL to the door. If

Mary had managed to cast some sort of spell, he would do nothing to break it.

As soon as he had closed the door, Jack went looking for Mary, finding her curled up on their bed, looking out the window. He sat on the bed and rubbed her back. "He's gone. And I think your letter did some good." He chuckled a little. "At least where you're concerned."

Mary rolled around to face him, cheeks damp, but smiling. "Maybe you too. I wrote a lot about what a wonderful father you're going to be."

He lay down beside her and pulled her close. "What was it the man at the deli used to say, years ago? 'From your mouth to God's ear.'"

Neja called almost exactly two days later. "What did you do to that GAL? I think he's in love."

"With Mary, maybe." It was hard for Jack to talk with his heart in his throat. "The report's good?"

"The report's very good. I was pretty sure he'd file something favorable, but I didn't expect *poetic*."

Mary ran in from the living room, dusting rag in hand. He gave her an emphatic thumbs up before asking Neja, "Was it the reasons you gave me before that made you optimistic?"

Neja got the smug expression that he would probably dislike if she wasn't, for now, thoroughly on their side. "Partly. But I also had some information I don't think the Bureau attorney knew about. That young man comes from a large, close family. And he's engaged to be married. Probably thinking about starting a family of his own. I don't suppose he fancied having some pencil-pusher decide whether he was good enough to be a parent."

* * * * *

Judge Rayner (Alex)

Alex scrolled through the GAL's report with her eyebrows raised and lowered and raised again. Either the man had some undisclosed connection to the petitioners, or the petitioners were gifted con artists who had prepared very quickly for the GAL's visit — or the Bureau's interference with this family was unjustified by any conventional measure.

The subjects' home was clean, comfortable, and appealing. The room intended for their child meets all safety requirements and current psychological recommendations. . . .

The mother allowed me to review a journal she has kept since early in her pregnancy, expressing sentiments and concerns I found unexceptional and in fact admirable. . . .

The father is an individual with strong passions and opinions, but does not appear intemperate or antisocial. . . .

In sum, both parents have prepared conscientiously for, and are well aware of, the responsibilities they will be undertaking in becoming parents. I see no reason why they should not assume that responsibility.

The man was young and had been certified as a guardian ad litem only within the last year. His inexperience should tend to make him hypercritical, for fear of missing any ominous signs. And yet here was this panegyric.

So much for the report rebutting the presumption in favor of these young parents. What would the Bureau try next?

Chapter 31

Valerie Greene (Toni's mother)

Valerie was overdue to touch base with Neja Patel, who was representing Jack and Mary Connor in their lawsuit against the Bureau. She settled down on the sofa and made the call. Neja greeted her with, "Heard the latest?"

Valerie refrained from pointing out that she could not, whatever she might have heard, be sure it was the latest news. "Which is?"

"The Bureau filed a motion to seal in Jack and Mary's case, and we have a hearing next Tuesday. I'm guessing the GAL report made some officials nervous about possible future publicity." She grinned wickedly. "So it's time for some publicity! I'll be having a press conference on the courthouse steps ahead of time. The judge refused to order me not to, which I take as a promising sign. I've cultivated relationships with a sufficient number of reporters that I'm likely to have decent attendance, even with a government entity as my opposition."

Valerie frowned. Neja was not usually naive. "Are you sure you're not trying to relive the bygone days when reporters valued a hot new story above political agendas?"

Neja narrowed her eyes in the familiar sign that she believed Valerie to be condescending to her. "I'm well aware of the difficulties. But I'll be contacting as many as possible who have children — young ones, so they can identify with various aspects of my clients' experience. And there are still a few independent, even obstreperous, broadcasters with an audience."

Valerie let Neja see her relaxation. "It's certainly worth a try."

Neja spun a pen in her fingers, a familiar "tell" revealing less than full confidence. "Might there be some advantage to any of your clients in your joining me?"

Valerie hid her smile at the possibility that her former protégée might still take comfort at having backup. "Well, I might be able to use some of the documents you're after as a basis for claiming fraud in some settlement negotiations. Or even setting the agreed judgment aside and getting a better result."

Neja made a barely audible humming noise. "After I talk about the vital public interest in maintaining public access to documents that lay out the Bureau's determination to go beyond its mandate, you could chime in with how the same material may be of crucial importance in other pending cases."

"It's a matter of definition whether, technically, we have a pending federal case – but that's a detail. Let me do some thinking. I'll get back to you soon."

She hung up and made herself an unusually elaborate lunch, then went for a walk to burn it off. The day was crisp, sunny, and cool enough to make a brisk pace easy to maintain. By the time she made the last turn for home, however, she was more than ready to ease off, stroll, and look about her.

The landscaping of the property she was passing caught her eye, a pleasantly disordered arrangement that included quite a few chunks of wood. One, in particular, a small one placed beneath a fir tree less than a yard from the sidewalk, reminded her of driftwood, even to the bluish-gray color,. She could easily imagine Toni sculpting it, though she couldn't predict what form it would take. And she wanted to see.

There was no one visible on the street, but anyone could have been looking out the windows. She picked up the piece of wood and stood holding it for close to a minute. No curtain stirred; no door opened; no voice called out. She dropped it into the deepest pocket of her oversized sweater and headed for home.

Talking to Neja had triggered something of an epiphany. She thought back to her first meeting with Neja, and the excitement she had felt at the young woman's acuity and her relentless drive. Now for the first time, she recognized what had so attracted her. Neja had been like an incarnation of what Valerie once expected any child of hers to be, before she had learned what so many parents learn: that children don't turn out according to plan, and instead force you to confront your assumptions of what qualities matter.

Valerie patted the pocket in which the piece of wood now made a soft bulge. She would give it to Toni when she next saw her, and hope Toni would take it for what it was: an affirmation, overdue, that what Toni did had worth, and mattered as much as any words written on a page, or spoken to judge or jury. And that Toni was the daughter of her heart as well as her flesh.

When she got home, she sat herself down to go through the pros and cons of joining forces with Neja so visibly. She had already mentioned some advantages in their phone call. Time to look at the other side of the scales. It was only worth adding to the ire the Bureau felt toward her client if she could have enough of an impact to permanently reduce their power. "When you strike at a king, you must kill him." But at least kings, unlike most bureaucracies, were mortal. And not all kings had as many powerful allies as the Bureau had, including DCS.

A decision with such serious potential consequences could not be made simply by the lawyer — or the mother. She called Toni. "Are Adam and Grace handy?"

"Adam's feeding Jessie, and Grace is working. Do you need to talk to all of us at once? We can call you back in just a few minutes."

Valerie had barely started making notes of how to ask her question when they called back. It was Grace who spoke first. "What do you need from us?"

"Instructions. We have a choice to make, but really, it's one for the three of you."

Toni surprised her by giggling, if only for a couple of seconds. Valerie guessed the explanation even as Toni said, "If only you'd told me when I was thirteen that I'd have the power to instruct my mother!" The smile dropped away quickly. "What's this about? Has something gone wrong?"

Perhaps she should have had this talk in person, so she could reach out and stroke her daughter's cheek. Too late now. "No, nothing's gone wrong. The issue is whether we should take a chance of making some sort of trouble more likely — a risk difficult to quantify — in the hope of turning the existing stalemate into something more like victory."

They talked it through, every detail, every guess, every threat, every blow already struck. And when any more discussion would only go in circles, three parents decided on the bolder, more hazardous course. Toni had the last word. "Go for it! Take them down, if you can. For the three of us, and for Mary and Jack, and for all the other parents who don't have you to fight their battle. Take that battle to them." She paused and made a sound like a chuckle, but less cheerful, before calling out, self-mocking: "Charge!"

Valerie said her farewells, hung up, and found that her hands were shaking. She curled up in blessed privacy on the sofa until they stopped, then called Neja to say, "I'm in. Let's work on our plan of attack as soon as you have time."

* * * * *

Jack

It was strange enough for Jack, and for Mary — though bright as Mary was, it shouldn't have been — to talk to a high-priced, highly respected lawyer on what he had to call an equal basis. But then there were two of them, Neja Patel and Valerie Greene; and Valerie's daughter Toni, who fought the Bureau before Jack had dreamed he would ever have a reason; and Adam Brown and Grace Allen, older than Jack or Mary or Toni, so self-possessed (Grace especially) and competent, but all now fighting together.

The lawyers already knew their clients' stories, everything they could think of to tell and everything the lawyers had seen happen. But what Jack and Mary and the others could still do was to brainstorm about how to spread the word. How to turn a legal case and, even more, a press conference, that almost forgotten relic, into something people would talk about, tell their friends about, get excited about. There were more ideas, more ways, than he would have guessed – not just the older and newer and brand-new types of social media, but church groups, book groups, support groups for artists, support groups for parents . . . .

Energized by this brainstorming session, they went forth and planted seeds. They overcame shyness, and they coaxed the uninterested, and they explained to the confused, and they shrugged off the few who were cruel. They worked, with phones and tablets and in person, until their fingers ached or their voices went hoarse. They tried to turn the planned press conference into something closer to a rally.

And they counted on the lawyers to make sure all their work would not be in vain.

* * * * *

Judge Rayner (Alex)

Alex let the last reluctant drop of coffee drain out of her mug, inspected the mug for more, put it down, and pulled up the Bureau's motion to put all documents obtained from its files under seal. There were judges who would routinely grant such motions, though Alex had never understood what moved them to do so. After all, the requirements for sealing documents in court proceedings were supposed to be substantial. Not only did the requested secrecy have to be in the (poorly defined) public interest and based upon a compelling need, but disclosure would have to create a serious danger to that interest that could not be avoided by any less restrictive means.

The Bureau was claiming "deliberative process privilege," protecting preliminary discussions of governmental policies. She would need to dig into the cited cases and the alleged facts to know whether the Bureau had met its initial burden of establishing the privilege and, if so, whether the petitioners could overcome it — if that privilege even applied when the documents had already gotten out and the issue was whether the public, as well as the court and the parties, should get a gander at them.

The real motives behind the Bureau's motion no doubt included the desire to avoid public and political embarrassment — which much case law had indicated was not an appropriate reason to deny public access. Alex suspected another, even more pragmatic intention. The services of Neja Patel did not come cheap. She had almost certainly taken the Connor case on a pro bono basis, with her compensation including the publicity the revelation of these documents would provoke. The Bureau might well be hoping that if deprived of that benefit, Ms. Patel would leave her clients in the lurch, or at least hand off responsibility for the case to some junior associate.

Alex had set the motion for a hearing. A hearing open to the public, at that, and public notice of it must be given ahead of time. If Ms. Patel could not make substantial hay out of that notice and the hearing itself, Alex would undertake to eat, or at least nibble on, one of the wigs that jurists like herself had formerly worn.

* * * * *

Poloma

Poloma watched Neja's press conference from the confines of her home. Neja had advised her to act almost as if she were under house arrest. "You can go out to buy groceries if you can't get them delivered, and if someone in your family goes to the hospital, you can visit. But lie as low as you can, so that if any trouble comes to you, it'll be clear who's the troublemaker."

Standing a little ways in front of several clusters of

energetic people waving handmade signs, Neja fairly glowed with righteous energy, moving her keen eyes from one member of the press corps — or rather, one camera — to the next, speaking with precision and intensity. "In advance of the upcoming hearing, I will not read verbatim from any of the shocking documents we have obtained from the files of the Bureau for Reproductive and — per their recent dubious name change — Infant Safety. But I ask those of you watching, and especially those members of Congress and of the executive branch charged with oversight over the Bureau, whether it is consistent with your intentions and with the public good to have unelected bureaucrats promise to nurture fetuses and then withhold the newborn infants from their families. I ask whether you intended to authorize consigning these infants indefinitely to government-run institutions, based not on the parents' failure to meet any previously established standards of parental fitness nor on any observed misbehavior, but on undisclosed algorithms applied to the results of newly written and suddenly required tests — tests, moreover, with a political dimension. I ask, in addition, whether a government agency should be allowed to obtain custody of such infants by concealing the existence of these tests, and presenting the parents with deliberately obscure boilerplate hidden in consent forms for the necessary surgical procedure. And I ask how it can be in the public interest for files documenting such machinations to be concealed from the public."

Poloma had planned to watch the press conference, take notes, and calmly assess her counsel's performance. So she was somewhat surprised to find herself bouncing up and down in her chair, pumping her fist, shouting affirmation, and grinning from ear to ear.

* * * * *

Alex

Alex did not make a habit of watching lawyer showboating, particularly when one of her cases was involved. She had no trouble separating their media pitches from the arguments and evidence in her courtroom, but there was some small chance she would be either amused enough or annoyed enough that she would have to resist the temptation to tweak her ruling in response.

She made an exception this time. She wanted to assess the likelihood that Neja Patel's and Valerie Greene's press conference would upset some bureaucratic apple cart. If the people in charge of the challenged policies were about to lose their jobs, or be shunted to new ones in some other department, the case could be rendered moot. There was little point in working late researching comparable precedents and crafting an order if the case was about to evaporate.

She watched the recording in her chambers, door closed. The room had good soundproofing: she could exclaim or guffaw without arousing comment. She did not end up doing either, but she did allow herself several snickers, and even a few whistles of surprise. The lawyers had apparently decided subtlety was overrated. Ms. Greene was perhaps the less fiery of the two, but still concluded their joint statement by saying, "With any bureaucracy, there is a potential danger of mission creep, where those in charge lose sight of their original purpose and seek ever greater power for the bureaucracy's sake. The Bureau of Reproductive Safety has become the Bureau of Reproductive and Infant Safety. If this expansion, undertaken without permission of our elected officials, goes unchecked – and those responsible remain in their positions of authority – we can expect more changes to that title, and ever more impositions on the fundamental rights of our citizens."

Once the press conference wrapped up, Alex checked what several savvy commentators had to say and sampled social media. Then she called her husband.

"You can go ahead and make those dinner reservations. I'll be home by six."

Interlude – The Aftermath

The infancy and preschool socialization facilitator frowned at the message she had just received. It should have been a short message with an attachment, her employment contract for the Bureau of Reproductive and Infant Safety's upcoming second boarding facility, but there was no attachment— just three paragraphs of dense prose. She was experienced enough at deciphering such stuff that it only took a few minutes to get the gist of it. Some sort of infighting or pushback or other obstacle was causing a delay in the schedule, and all hiring had been suspended until the unspecified issue was resolved.

She closed the message and sat back, considering her options. Working for the federal government had offered better pay and benefits — and job security — than the most conveniently located public school positions. She might have to relocate. Well, that was hardly a major obstacle. Her social life was superficial at best. Somewhere, she should be able to find a school with forward-thinking administrators who would value her training as it deserved.

* * * * *

A Bureau official

The Director of Information Dissemination Planning at the Bureau of Reproductive and Infant Safety (would they have to revert to the old name?) went through his old sent messages, finger hovering over the crucial keys on his keyboard. There were only a few about which he need be concerned. He congratulated himself on having invested in the software that reached out and wiped the messages from recipients' files, at least if they had taken no special measures to prevent such cleanup.

Unfortunately, he could not, practically speaking, engage in similar editing of emails for which he was one of multiple recipients. The software lacked that capability. But he could always plead inattention. He would no doubt have plenty of company in that assertion.

It was a shame, but the licensing scheme and related arrangements had simply become too hot a potato. Later, a few years from now, the idea could be revisited and probably revived. The public memory was short. And while there would always be archived news stories and social media to be found by those digging deep enough, a more cautious implementation might prevent anyone from searching for it, at least until the public had been better prepared to see the advantages of the plan.

As for the contractors and lower-level functionaries who had been directly involved, the latter could be moved to other positions. And the former . . . well, any attempt at innovation had its chance of failure, and its possible casualties. So long as he managed to insulate himself from the political fallout, any claims such people made, any details they shared, would only make their own situations worse without touching him at all.

And of course, he still had plenty of programs requiring his ongoing attention. Even if the Bureau itself were disbanded, as some of his coworkers feared, those programs would surely find a home, under the auspices of some division of some other agency. Nothing was so close to immortal as an administrative agenda.

* * * * *

A couple

The parents-to-be had not known what to make of the email about an exam. Neither had taken an exam since they dropped out of school at the age of sixteen, found a state where they could marry, and got whatever jobs would pay the rent on their tiny apartment. They had been so proud of working their way up — she within a company, he by several job changes — to where they could afford an actual one-bedroom with room for a baby. But the woman would have had trouble working through a normal pregnancy, with all the carrying of heavy boxes and time on her feet that filled her workdays. The clinic and its shiny, pretty incubators had seemed like a godsend. Had they been naive? Been taken in?

When they showed up, clutching each other's hands tight, the girl at Reception gave them a tight smile and said, "There are no more examinations scheduled for the foreseeable future."

The man stepped forward and a little in front of the woman as if to protect her. "What does that mean? Can we still pick up our baby on her delivery date?"

The receptionist looked down her nose at him and replied blandly, "Of course. You entrusted your baby to us for a fixed term, after which we have no further role except to reunite your little family and see you on your way. If you have no more questions, I believe there are other clients waiting."

The woman turned around and saw another couple, also holding hands, looking as anxious as she had felt when she walked in. It was suddenly easy to smile as she said to them, "It's going to be okay."

Chapter 32

Toni

Toni could see her phone screen when Poloma called, but she had her hands quite literally full, a spoon in one hand and wet wipe in the other, giving Jessie her supper. In fact, Jessie chose that moment to spray Toni with creamed broccoli; by the time she had used the wipe on her face, given up on the broccoli, switched to rice cereal, and finally gotten Jessie fed, Adam was the one getting a call. When he finished talking, she asked, "Was that Poloma?"

"Yes. She's been in court. In front of Judge Rayner, for sentencing."

Toni, still holding the spoon, almost dropped it. "Sentencing? What about a trial?"

"I gather they entered into some sort of plea bargain. She's on probation — no jail time. But I think the judge chewed her out pretty thoroughly. She sounded shaken."

Toni hurried to the sink, washed off her hands, dried them quickly on her overalls, and called Poloma back. Poloma took the call with vision off. Had she been crying? Her voice sounded thick enough that she might have been. "Toni? That was fast."

"I'm sorry I couldn't take your call. Are you free to come over? We'd love to see you and, well, catch up on things."

Poloma's laugh had an edge to it. "Yes, I'm free, in both

senses of the word. Though the judge made it sound like a narrow escape."

"Do come. We can have tea, or maybe a glass of wine — no, wait, you like beer, don't you? Andy brought over some craft beer yesterday. And you can finally meet Jessie Kyra."

The pause lasted about twenty seconds. Toni was about to double-check that Poloma was still there when Poloma finally said, "I'd like that very, very much."

* * * * *

Poloma

Poloma, walking up the path, could hear some sort of commotion going on inside, and felt rather as if she were eavesdropping. As she reached the door, she was able to separate out the sounds somewhat better: a high-pitched squeal, a man's deep voice repeating something she couldn't quite decipher, and someone clapping hands. As she rang the doorbell, she realized that like the observer in a physics hypothetical, her intervention would disturb whatever was going on before she could absorb it.

Adam answered the door holding a squirming, excited baby in one arm. He gave Poloma a warm and welcoming smile and nodded her inside, just as the little girl reached out her arms in Poloma's direction. Poloma stopped inside the door and held her breath. Adam looked in her eyes, smiled again, and asked, "Jessie-Ky likes her introductions up close and personal. How would you feel about holding her?"

Poloma held out her arms and Adam settled Jessie carefully in them. It had been years since the last time she held a child, a cousin's little boy. Relieved that she still remembered the feel of it, she pulled Jessie against her shoulder, noting the swirls of reddish-blonde hair. As if prompted by the thought, Jessie pulled on a strand of Poloma's hair and brought it toward her mouth; Adam intercepted it and extracted it from the plump little fist. "No, honey, that's not for chewing on."

Grace joined them and gestured toward a nearby couch, saying in a tone Poloma would have to call cheerful, "Won't you sit down?" Poloma carried Jessie to the couch and sat, settling the baby on her lap. She heard the clinking of glass before she saw Toni emerge from the kitchen, carrying two bottles of beer in each hand. Poloma looked from the beer bottles to Jessie; Toni laughed and swooped in to pick the baby up and hand Poloma a beer. "I'm an old hand at handling a drink without letting her get hold of it."

Poloma would rather have held Jessie for longer, beer or no beer, but she yielded her up with good grace. She took a swig and looked up in surprise. "That's really very good. Your brother knows his beer."

And because the beer tasted good, she could drink it without feeling that she was drinking solely to smooth the day's rough edges.

Adam sat down next to her, close enough to be companionable but not so close as to intrude on her personal space. "Do you want to talk about what happened in court?"

Did she? Would it be more or less painful to share the details? She may as well give it a try. "The judge pointed out what I could have done instead of violating my employment agreement and the law — like file a lawsuit myself. She said that breaking the law for some perceived public interest put the public interest at the mercy of everyone and anyone with an agenda and a belief in their own rectitude."

Toni's eyes went wide. "Sounds like you remember

what she said word for word."

Poloma bit her lip. "Pretty much." *Precisely. I'll probably hear it in my dreams.*

Grace snorted. "It's easy to say someone should go to court. How long would that have taken? And who says you would have won? The odds would have been against you. As it is, you did a great deal of good, quickly enough to make a difference for who knows how many people."

Poloma managed to muster a smile. The beer helped.

Toni sat on the other side of her, Jessie on her lap. Jessie reached for Poloma's beer; Toni captured the little hand and redirected it to push on Toni's nose, producing an apparently gratifying "beep!" sound. Jessie beamed. Poloma had the impression that Toni had wanted to say something, but had sabotaged herself by starting such an engrossing game. It took, by Poloma's count, seven more beeps before Jessie yawned and snuggled down into Toni's arms, leaving Toni free to ask, "What do you plan to do now?"

Poloma grimaced. "Well, as you must have guessed, I no longer work for the Bureau, or for the federal government. It's not so easy to fire a civil servant, but quitting was one of the conditions of my probation. I'd managed to save a little money —" She allowed herself a short and bitter laugh. "—by not doing much of anything other than working. I suppose I'll make a list of my skills and brainstorm about who might pay me to use any of them, in some field where it won't matter that I've pled guilty to a federal crime. At least Mr. Alister was able to keep it to a misdemeanor."

She would be good at proofreading, or technical writing, or some sort of personnel training. But she had never been good at finding a job. At least, she hadn't been good at it nine years ago, when she left social work and struggled for months before she at last found what she had thought would be stable employment. As it would have been, had she not decided to become quixotic for the second time in her life.

Though because she had, Mary and Jack were probably at home with their baby right now. And she might have indirectly helped her hosts as well. "Has DCS stopped harassing you?"

Grace looked around at her domain with obvious satisfaction. "So it seems. So Toni's mother tells us."

Poloma could cherish those victories, and might as well, given what they had cost her. In fact, she could even presume on them so far as to make a request. "Might I have another beer?"

* * * * *

Jack

Jack had grown up going to church every Sunday and on holidays, though he hadn't done it in years. He couldn't count all the paintings and sculptures and stained glass windows he'd seen of the Blessed Mother and baby Jesus. It was probably a sin to think his own Mary holding their baby boy made a prettier picture.

He might confess that sin, if he sooner or later went to confession, but he wouldn't repent of it.

And it didn't matter that Mary had circles under her eyes, and her hair was a mess, and she hadn't had a shower. She was still beautiful. And little Jack had finally finished his bottle and fallen asleep.

Jack could maybe do something about the shower, at least. "Hon, do you think I could take him without waking him? You could go clean up."

Mary looked up, obviously torn. "He might wake up. And I love holding him." Her eyes filled. "Nothing's ever felt righter."

He kissed the top of her head. "I know. But he isn't going anywhere, and neither are you."

She still hesitated. He leaned closer and said in her ear, "Hot water. Hot . . . water . . . ."

She laughed, then looked down all in a hurry to make sure it hadn't waked the baby. When he let out a tiny snore and barely stirred, she said, "I guess it's all right. Sit down next to me."

He did, snuggling up close and making a cradle of his arms. Slowly, gently, Mary moved the baby over. Slowly, carefully, she got up, stepped away from the couch, and stretched. "Oh, that feels good." She blew Jack a kiss and staggered off to the bathroom. A few minutes later, he heard the shower running, and a moan that reminded him of the last time they'd made love.

Which had been the night before they brought home the baby. But that was all right. There'd be time.

And Mary wasn't the only one who loved holding Jack Junior.

He bent his head low enough to smell the top of the baby's head. That was a smell like no other, sweet and milky and just a little like fresh-baked bread.

And here they were, the three of them, after all the panic and anger and worry. Here, together, home.

* * * * *

Paloma

The woman at the temp agency scrolled through her listings again as if to demonstrate her diligence. "I'm sorry, Ms. Clark, but there isn't anything new in the areas you've listed. We do have a night shift opening at a factory, lasting two weeks. There isn't a great deal of strength involved."

"Just a moment, please." Poloma checked her bank balance. She should probably have gotten a cheaper apartment as soon as she lost her job, but the effort of moving and the likelihood that she would need to find storage space had deterred her. Now, a week since her last low-paying assignment had ended, she was almost out of choices.

Almost, because her family would always let her come home. *"Home is the place where, when you have to go there, they have to take you in."* She would be stretching their already stretched resources, but she could make herself useful somehow.

Not yet. "I'll take it. When do I start?"

Five days later, stumbling in two hours after dawn, she almost missed the message light on the phone she had left at home as per factory regulations. She could check it after she slept, but not knowing what it said would niggle at her when she was trying to get to sleep, difficult enough on this unnatural schedule. She left the phone on the kitchen table as she pulled the leftover half of a roast beef and apple wrap out of the refrigerator, then sat at the kitchen table and took a giant bite as she opened the video.

The man looked a little younger than she, and more energetic than she could currently imagine being. Something about his clothes, or the way he wore them, suggested that someone older or more interested might have picked them out. "Ms. Clark, I'm Mitchell Banes, deputy director of Future Dawn, Incorporated. We are opening a private incubation facility in your area in a few months, and we would like to talk to you about possibly becoming our chief administrator. Please call back for an appointment if you're interested, as I certainly hope you will be. Goodbye."

Poloma set the phone gently down on the table, took another bite of the wrap, put it down next to the phone, put her head in her arms, and cried. After about three minutes, she wiped her face, finished the wrap, and called the number, giving her name to the pleasantly polished receptionist.

"This is Poloma Clark, returning Mr. Banes's call. I have business occupying me for the next week and a half, but would be happy to come in any time after that."

After all, she had agreed to a two week assignment. She would not renege. A great deal had changed — changed her — in the last months, but not that.

five months later

Poloma

Poloma Clark stood at the entrance to the Safe Cradle clinic and welcomed the first of its clients. The small crowd that had gathered included mature women and mere teenagers, expectant mothers alone and those accompanied by future fathers or supportive friends or their own mothers. She offered her hand to shake, or her hands to clasp, though not all took advantage of it.

When 8 a.m. came, she cleared her throat and said, "Your attention, please! A word before you enter." When the louder and softer mutters and murmurs of conversation died down, she stood up tall and said, "Welcome, all of you.

We're here to help you and your baby. If you're here to donate, we'll find loving adoptive parents — but before we notify them, we will get in touch with you, in case you've changed your mind. If you're here to avoid known or potential risks of continuing your pregnancy, we will take care of your baby, and you may visit as often as you like. We are a nonprofit organization, and though we must charge fees in order to meet our operating expenses, we have grants available for those who can't pay them. We are here for you and your child, and for no other purpose.

"This we promise. This we pledge."

Poloma tapped on the glass, and the receptionist opened the door.

Epilogue

five years later

Toni

Jessie danced from foot to foot. "We're going to the baby place!" She probably thought all babies lived in incubators until they were ready to be born. Toni had managed to keep from her daughter the soul-searching and doubts and late-night qualms that had, finally, led to her and David's decision to entrust their baby to a clinic's care. A very different clinic, and for very different reasons, than before — to keep her unborn son safe from the potentially harmful byproducts of the materials she was using. And this time, in spite of the greater difficulty of the procedure, she had waited to feel the baby quickening . . . .

Enough reliving the past — her daughter was waiting. "Hurry up and pick a book, Jessie. Mommy Grace has your coat all ready to put on." Toni shrugged into the oversized sweater Grace had knitted for her and picked up the scarf she had managed to knit for herself.

Jessie ran over, holding a book a good deal bigger than her head and sporting a huge grin. "*This* one!"

Grace, holding the coat, smiled at Toni and said, "I certainly can't argue with that choice! And Daddy will be flattered too. He's meeting us at the clinic, you know. Will you let Mommy Toni carry the book while you bundle up warm? After all, it's about the art she makes, so it's only fair."

Jessie studied Toni as if she were applying for a very important job before handing her the book. "All right." Toni tucked the book into her bag; Jessie moved closer to Grace and squirmed into the coat. Grace completed the ensemble with the hat which had been Toni's second completed knitting project and looked a little less ragged than her first.

Adam had taken the subway to his last appointment and would catch a bus to the clinic, so they had the car at their disposal. It was Grace's turn to ride in back with Jessie. Toni buckled Jessie into the car seat and then climbed in up front, but Jessie reached out and wailed, "My book!"

Toni and Grace exchanged glances. Grace said, "Honey, last time you tried reading in the car, you felt sick, remember?" She tactfully omitted that Jessie had actually *got* sick, which had done nothing good to the book she'd been holding.

Jessie stuck out her lower lip. "I was only five then! I'm six now!"

True, as of last week. Toni floated a compromise. "How about you let Mommy Grace read it to you, this time? She hasn't got to read it out loud for ages, since you got so good at reading it yourself."

Grace, on cue, turned big eyes on Jessie and said, "Oh, please! It's been so long!"

Jessie pursed her lips, considering, and then said solemnly, "You may." Toni turned away to hide the fact that she was struggling with a laugh, then back to hand Grace the book. Grace opened it and began, "Have you ever made something out of clay? Was it fun to do? Well, there are people who make shapes out of wood — all kinds of shapes, animals and people, and even shapes where you have to use your imagination to decide what they are. Would you like to see some pictures, and learn how it's done? . . . ."

Rather than risk carsickness of her own by riding facing backward, Toni relaxed in her seat and watched the houses and storefronts go by, many already decorated in holiday lights that would not be properly visible until early evening. Maybe she and David could go for a ride after dark to look at the lights, giving Adam and Grace some just-us-three time with Jessie.

The car pulled up and parked itself in the small lot and they all tumbled out, Jessie now clutching the book again. The receptionist, a woman who looked like and might well be a grandmother, beamed at them as they rode around twice in the revolving door and finally came in. Leaning forward to look Jessie in the eye, she said, "Here to visit your little brother? Oh, you have a book! Will you read it to him?"

Jessie held the book toward the receptionist for inspection. "I will! It's my daddy's book, and it's about what Mommy Toni does! Do you think the baby'll like it?"

"I'm sure he will, pumpkin. You can go right up." She gestured toward the colorful spiral escalator in the middle of the lobby, a favorite of child visitors and some supposedly past childhood. Grace took Jessie's hand and led the way while Toni followed, looking around for any new wall art. She found a few seasonal scenes along with the familiar landscapes near the bottom of the escalator, and both old and new portraits of babies and families near the top. The escalator arrived at the wide, well-lit hallway, its walls painted in light colors that avoided those used in the now-shuttered Bureau facility. Grace assisted Jessie with her dismount and let her scamper toward the room where her half-brother's incubator waited, along with three others. The parents of the four babies had agreed that any of them could visit in that room rather than in the separate visiting areas, unless they planned to bring a big enough crowd to make things too chaotic. Today, only Adam sat inside, looking at his phone with the absorbed expression that said "work." He looked up as they entered, stood, and held out his arms for Jessie to run into them. Jessie managed not to hit him in the face with the book as she jumped toward him to be swung in the air. As soon as he put her down, she showed him the book and said, "See what I brought to read to Christopher?"

Adam laid an open hand over his heart and said, "Sweetheart, I'm honored. Here, let me move the chair right up next to him." As he did so, Toni leaned over the sea-green incubator, made sure the microphone was on, and stroked the warm surface, murmuring, "Hello, boo bear. Big Sis is here, to read you a book that Uncle Adam wrote." (Though Grace had contributed here and there to the final text, and both of them had observed Toni at work to get the details right.) "When you come out, you'll get to see the things he wrote about."

Jessie plopped herself in the chair and declared, "It's my turn!" Toni assessed her tone, decided it was just the right side of acceptable, and made way, standing behind the chair where she could admire the watercolor illustrations. The thrill of seeing wooden sculpture, some of it her own, rendered in such a different medium and rendered so well had yet to wear off.

Jessie began, with what might have seemed like surprisingly fluent reading to anyone who didn't know how many times she had heard the text and how much of it she had memorized. "Have you ever made something out of clay? Was it fun to do? . . . ."

The door opened a crack, quietly, as Jessie was finishing, but not until she had finished did it swing open all the way. Jessie caught the motion, swiveled toward the door, and jumped out of the chair, shouting, "Auntie Poloma!" She dropped the book on the chair and ran over for a hug, Poloma squatting down to deliver it. When she stood back up, she looked around at the adults, smiled a little awkwardly, and said, "Reception told me you were all here, so I came to say hello."

"Auntie Poloma, I read to Christopher! Should I read it again so you can listen?"

Poloma hesitated before replying, "Why not? But then I'll need to get back to work."

As Jessie sat back down, Poloma managed a quick query to Toni. "Working on anything new?"

"Yes, two big pieces. I feel as though I should take advantage of being able to spend hours on my feet hauling wood around and mixing vats of resin. I'll show you some photos before we go." Toni was particularly proud of the larger piece, loosely inspired by the idea of an infant leaving an incubator behind like a chrysalis. Would Poloma recognize it? She might — she was learning more about art these days.

Jessie opened the book and said, "Now listen, little brother and Auntie Poloma! Have you ever made something out of clay? . . . ." This time, Toni stepped back and waved Adam forward, leaning against the wall next to Grace. She would have liked to thank Grace one more time for her work on the book, but Jessie would be rightly offended if she spoke during the reading. She contented herself with a smile that she hoped managed to show her gratitude. Grace smiled back and then looked at the incubator, pain and longing in her face. Toni hoped it wouldn't be long before Adam could persuade her to use the newest methods to start a baby of their own. The odds were very good that everything would go well. Though they might want to wait until Christopher was out of diapers.

Jessie had finished the book again while Toni was woolgathering. It was time to go. Grace needed to go with Adam to the office, and Toni had work to do in the studio. David would meet them in the little playground outside and take Jessie to the art museum, where she would no doubt tell him which paintings and sculptures she liked best.

Jessie made the rounds of the other adults, giving a hug to each, and then kissed the incubator. "Bye, Christopher. You be good, now." Over her head, Toni and Poloma exchanged amused smiles.

Poloma left first, her low heels clicking down the hall. The rest of them put their outerwear back on, Grace assisting Jessie before she and Adam left, Grace in front, Adam close behind.

Toni put out her hand to Jessie, and mother and daughter headed out, hands clasped together tight.

THE END

Author's Note

Looking at the teasers for my near-future science fiction novels, one could easily conclude that I distrust new technologies. That isn't the case. I'm actually something of a technophile. I just have this but-what-if quirk, which, combined with a distrust of bureaucracies and centralized government control, yields cautionary tales of the sort you've just read.

In particular, I am not opposed to the development of prenatal incubators. In fact, one of my favorite authors, Lois McMaster Bujold, features such incubators (called uterine replicators) in her Vorkosigan Saga, always in a favorable light. I have no quarrel with her prediction of how useful this equipment can be. But I hope that when it becomes available (which may be sooner than I expected when I started this story), the concerns I've raised will be part of the discussion about how to deploy it.

Acknowledgments

A comment from Gwynne Powell, fellow member of the Lois McMaster Bujold email list, in a discussion I no longer recall gave me the idea of regulators wanting to make incubator use mandatory for mothers who would expose a fetus to tobacco byproducts or alcohol.

My fervent thanks to my beta readers for this book: Jennifer Bourgeois, Margaret DeVere, Jill Franclemont, Steven Karel, Katrina Knight, Samantha L. Strong, Wendy Teller, Kay Timbreza, Dedaimia Whitney, and Elisabeth Zguta. Readers may assume that the book's deficiencies are due in part to my not taking even more of these helpers' suggestions.

About the Author

Karen A. Wyle was born a Connecticut Yankee, but eventually settled in Bloomington, Indiana, home of Indiana University. She now considers herself a Hoosier. She and her husband have two wildly creative daughters. (Return readers may notice that I no longer claim to have a sweet though neurotic dog. She left us in June 2019. We miss her.)

In addition to writing novels (science fiction, afterlife fantasy, and historical romance) and picture books, Wyle is an appellate attorney (though quasi-retired) and photographer. Her voice is the product of almost five decades of reading both literary and genre fiction. It is no doubt also influenced, although she hopes not fatally tainted, by her years of law practice. Her personal history has led her to focus on often-intertwined themes of family, communication, personal identity, the impossibility of controlling events, and the persistence of unfinished business.

Connect With the Author

Learn more about Karen A. Wyle by looking her up on her author website (http://www.KarenAWyle.com), Twitter (where she is, prosaically, @KarenAWyle), Facebook (similarly, https://www.facebook.com/KarenAWyle), Goodreads, or her sadly neglected blog, Looking Around.

Like the book? Please tell readers! Online book reviews are enormously helpful — and old-fashioned word of mouth is terrific as well! (I particularly appreciate Amazon reviews, if you're able to leave such.)

You can sign up for Wyle's monthly newsletter, including news of upcoming releases as well as looks at her writing process and frequent extras like excerpts and cover reveals, at Wyle's newsletter signup link (to be found in the lower righthand corner of her website's landing page).